supersymmetry

supersymmetry

S. R. Schulz

Ooligan Press | Portland, Oregon

Supersymmetry: A Novel

ISBN13: 978-19-47845-53-4

Ooligan Press
Portland State University
Post Office Box 751, Portland, Oregon 97207
503.725.9748
ooligan@ooliganpress.pdx.edu
www.ooliganpress.com

Library of Congress Cataloging-in-Publication Data
Names: Schulz, S. R., author.
Title: Supersymmetry : a novel / by S.R. Schulz.

Identifiers: LCCN 2024009099 | ISBN 9781947845534 (paperback) | ISBN 9781947845541 (epub)
Subjects: LCGFT: Novels.
Classification: LCC PS3619.C4788 S87 2025 | DDC 813/.6--dc23/eng/20240610
LC record available at https://lccn.loc.gov/2024009099

Cover design by Kaitlyne Bozzone
Interior design by Ariana Espinoza

Printed in the United States of America

Ooligan PRESS
Portland State UNIVERSITY

Content Warning

This book contains mentions of abortion, scenes depicting child neglect, drug use and addiction, suicidal thoughts and depression, and mentions of war and violence.

To my Croatian family

croatia: one

Bass radiated off the dance floor and shook Lisa's skull. Her hair was heavy with sweat, and her clothes stuck to her skin. The world was a swirl of dim lights and wet faces—a party trapped in a hurricane blowing colors and words, laughter and music. Lisa floated somewhere between death and dreams. Despite the turbulence of the night, she felt warm and happy and safe. Luka materialized from the haze and his smile came into focus.

"Another *rakija*?" Luka asked.

"Sure," she said. Her words slurred into a fit of laughter.

Luka spoke to the bartender in Croatian but was waved off. He tried again and was rebuffed. He shouted over the music, cussing in English and Croatian, loud enough to draw stares from the people around them. The bartender made no response.

"What's this guy's problem? He can't just ignore you like that," Lisa said.

"Oh, he's a real tough guy. A real hero!" Luka yelled at the bartender. "He says you've had too much. I say *odjebi*!"

The bartender shook his head and walked away.

Lisa closed her eyes and felt herself slipping toward the floor. "I don't need anymore. I'm fine. You're such a nice guy, Luka. You've always been so nice to me." She tipped forward, lifting herself onto her toes, and kissed Luka's cheek.

"You're a princess. An American princess here on holiday, and this asshole thinks he can tell you what to do." Luka took her hand. "I'll take you someplace nice. Someplace where we can get real rakija, not this watered-down European union shit."

For weeks, they'd been trading glances, simple touches, shared laughs, and yet Lisa had resisted Luka. She was scared of what they were becoming or could become. But she was tired of living like that. She was tired of building up walls and making excuses. She was tired of being bound to her past. Luka wasn't Bryan. He wasn't like anyone she'd ever met. More importantly, Lisa wasn't even Lisa anymore. She'd left that person back in Oregon and had become something impossible, free flowing, and non-adherent to the past or future. As the drinks kept coming, Lisa fell into an inebriated void, and at the bottom—right at the edge of darkness—she felt a warm embrace radiating its tendrils out toward her, and for a second, she thought maybe it was love.

Luka tried to lead Lisa away from the bar, but she lost her balance and drifted into it. She bounced off the wood, her hand knocking over a glass in the process. She heard it shatter on the ground. The pain—in her hip and hand—was strong enough to break through the haze.

"Miss, you must go. Please, get out of here," the bartender said. Luka shouted at him in Croatian, moving his hands as if kneading invisible dough. This made Lisa laugh, which quieted Luka's anger for a moment. Then her face flushed red, tears forming in the corners of her eyes. Her hand was bleeding, a trickle slowly turning into a pool of blood that dripped from her palm onto the floor. She held it up to show Luka and laughed again. He laughed too. The bartender threatened to call the police.

"You should call the paparazzi. We're going to be famous one day," Luka said. He picked Lisa up and carried her out of the bar. They stumbled out into the street, hysterical in their folly and coated in Lisa's blood.

Outside, the bouncer looked disgusted. Luka's white shirt was covered in blood.

"It's not my blood guys. Not to worry, it's not mine," Luka shouted to the crowd out front, smoking cigarettes and sipping Ožujsko beer. Sweat evaporated from Lisa's face as the cool night collided with her skin. Luka carried her down the street, away from the judgment of others, and let her feet touch the cobblestone again. Lisa was still laughing. Her hand continued to bleed, and she did little to stop it. She waved it back and forth, recanting the looks on the crowd's faces as he'd carried her out. Luka took his shirt off and wrapped it tightly around the wound.

"Oh, you're so sweet," Lisa mumbled.

"I'm a real man. I'm chivalrous. I'm chivalry?" Luka said.

"You're—" Lisa started to say but then vomited. The bilious food matter coursed through the cobblestones and coalesced near a drain.

"Oh, fuck. I'm sorry. Oh my God," Lisa said.

"It's not a party till someone goes too far," Luka said. He lifted her onto his shoulder. "Let's get you home."

Lisa started to cry as she wiped puke from her chin. She was a mess. Their night—it was their night—and it was all a mess.

"Don't cry. Let me sing you a song," Luka said. He began to sing loudly and dance with Lisa slung over his shoulder. Lisa laughed, Luka sang, and the two of them waltzed through the streets of Rijeka, Croatia. The streetlights pulsed as she bounced up and down on his naked back. Her heart was beating wild and erratic, like the flopping rainbow trout she pulled from Timothy Lake, but Lisa wasn't dying. She was living. Maybe for the first time ever. Certainly, the first time since leaving Oregon. She'd carried her guilt all the way across the Atlantic, and part of her believed she'd never shake it. But tonight, as she was tossed back and forth on Luka's back, she felt alive and free.

Lisa woke up as Luka threw her down onto her bed. The door to her bathroom was open a sliver, dimly lighting the small bedroom. The windows were open, letting the summer air waft in and out. The sound of Vespas and horns rose from the street. She could hear a couple arguing in Italian.

"Come back. Where'd you go?" she asked.

Luka glanced at her from the open door of the bathroom. He smiled a drunken smile: careless, sloppy—beautiful.

"I'm cleaning this blood off of me. Fuck, Lisa, make me look like a vampire or something. I bet the police are out there following this track of blood and people are wondering what the hell is goin—"

"Come to bed," Lisa said.

"Come to—you want me to come to bed now?"

"Yes."

"I'm literally covered in your blood, and I'm pretty sure your hand is still bleeding. Doesn't seem like the best—"

"I don't care about all of that."

"You don't care about all that," Luka mumbled and closed the door. "You should check your hand," he shouted from behind the door. "You know. Is it, like, gangrenous? Or salvageable? How are you going to be a famous concert pianist?"

Lisa unwrapped her hand. It was fine. A small cut in the webbing between her thumb and pointer finger. It had stopped bleeding.

"It's fine. If I keep my hand closed, like in a karate chop pose, it doesn't bleed. That should be fine then, don't you think?" Lisa said.

Luka didn't answer.

"Hello?"

Lisa opened the door to the bathroom. Luka had wiped off the blood from his chest. "That towel," he said, pointing to the red-stained towel on the floor, "is fucked."

"Are you avoiding me?" Lisa asked.

"You're drunk. You're sexy. No one's going to argue that, but you're drunk," he said.

Lisa steadied herself on the sink, grabbed her toothbrush, put too much toothpaste on it, and brushed her teeth aggressively. Luka left the bathroom and lay down on the bed. Lisa emerged from the bathroom and said, "I forgot I puked for a second there, but then I tasted it in my mouth and, yeah, that's gross."

Luka smiled with his eyes closed. "You're such a crazy girl. How did I get so lucky to have you come into my life?"

Lisa lay on him, their eyes level, hands intertwined. The smell of mint was abrasive.

"I'm not crazy. I'm a lot of fun," Lisa said.

"You probably need stitches on that hand. Or were you planning on sticking with the permanent Judo-chop hand posture for life?"

She kissed him. Their tongues met, pushing and sliding, mouths open, bodies pressing into each other. Luka began kissing her neck. Lisa pulled at his short, black hair as he kissed her earlobe. His stubble was rough and comforting against her cheek. Luka got on top of Lisa, and her legs circled around his waist as they moved against each other. He pulled her shirt off and kissed her bare chest. Lisa thrust her hips into his and bit his lower lip. Luka undid Lisa's jeans and slid them off. There was a rush of excitement mixed with dread, like the moment was so good that it couldn't be real, or if it was, it wouldn't last. Luka kissed her stomach, just below the navel and gently pulled her underwear off. Lisa closed her eyes and ran her hands through his hair and down her own body, gently rolling her hips into the bed and his kisses.

"What is that?" Luka asked suddenly.

"What?" Lisa asked, her eyes flashing open, the moment interrupted.

"This scar right here," Luka said and pointed to a scar just above her pubic bone.

"It's just a scar," Lisa said.

"Did you have surgery?"

Lisa laughed, "What the hell, Luka. Why are you so interested?"

Luka went back to kissing. Lisa ran her hands along her hips and through his hair. He stopped again.

"I'm just wondering what it was from?"

Lisa gave an annoyed laugh. "Why?"

Luka traced his finger across the scar.

"Sounds like you know what it is, Luka."

Luka looked up at her. "From a baby."

"Yeah. A C-section scar."

"You had a baby?"

Lisa pulled the sheet over her naked body and turned on her side. "Yeah, Luka."

"You never told me you had a kid. Why wouldn't you tell me something like that?"

Lisa pulled the sheet closer. "I didn't know I was supposed to just inject it into our conversations."

"Is this kid around? Is it still a baby, or is it grown up now?" He sat on the edge of the bed. Lisa's bare feet touched his bare thigh. She pulled her knees up into her chest.

"If I wanted to talk about it, don't you think I would've brought it up?" Lisa said.

"When will we talk about it then? I feel like I have a right to know."

Lisa sat up. "You have a right to know?"

"Maybe not a right, but I think if we are going to move forward with this, me and you, this thing we were about to have here, I want to know about any kids."

Lisa let her mouth drop open. These were her secrets. Her mistakes. They belonged to her.

"I barely know you, Luka."

"Oh, come on," Luka said. "I'm not trying to fight. Let's not discredit what we've got going. We know each other. We have a connection. We have something good."

"I don't know you, and you don't have a right to anything," Lisa said. Her features hardened and hands trembled.

"Listen," Luka said. He reached out to touch her, but she moved away. "I didn't mean it. I'm sorry. I'm sorry. You don't have to tell me. I shouldn't have asked. We're both drunk. Let's not fight. Right?"

"You're right, Luka. It's late. I'm drunk. I think you should go home."

Luka sat on the edge of the bed and stared at the floor. After a few seconds, he got dressed and kissed Lisa on the cheek. After he left, Lisa lay in the bed, feeling the world spin as she ran her fingers along her scar. It was the first time she'd really thought about it since coming to Croatia. It brought dread and a deep penetrating guilt, like someone standing on her heart. She put a foot on the floor to try and calm the spinning and eventually fell asleep.

oregon: one

Three years prior, when Lisa was nineteen and living in her mom's house in Milwaukie, Oregon, she peed on a plastic stick and her world changed. The room spun fast enough that she gripped the toilet seat as she imagined her future careening out of control and crashing against an insentient and immovable mass. She stared at the pink positive sign, willing it to turn back. She flipped it back and forth in her hand, looked at it upside down and sideways, checked the box for the fifth time but nothing changed, and everything changed. While she sat on the toilet, her head started to feel small, like her eyes were too big for her skull. The room began to shrink. Inside her chest, her heart shrank. Her lungs felt like they were wrapped in saran wrap like the sandwiches her mom used to pack her for school when her mom was sober. Lisa reached out to grab something, anything to keep from shrinking into nothing. Her palm met cool tile, and she was brought back to reality.

Jesus Christ, I can't be a mom, she thought. Lisa refused to continue the cycle. She knew how the universe worked. Things slowly got shittier until they couldn't get any worse. She'd join a legacy of unfit and inept parents if she had a baby, a genealogy slowly toiling away with each consummate offspring—every generation more unsuitable than that last. She could not be a mom. It was as simple as that. She didn't even need to tell her boyfriend, Bryan. She would get an abortion, and he'd never have to know. They'd continue their lives like it never happened. Maybe after a while, she'd forget it ever happened.

Lisa drove to work. It was March and the streets were flooded. It made Lisa happy when the first rain fell, sometime in October, because there was no arguing or bartering or begging—there was no going back—but now the rain was depressing. She was done with rain even if rain wasn't done with her. Her old VW Jetta, with a CD player from Car Toys and miles the odometer had stopped counting, pushed through the heavy downpour. She parked and ran across the parking lot to work. She got soaked regardless.

She worked in a seafood place in a nearby suburb named after a stupid nineties' movie about a simple man who liked to run from Alabama or Mississippi or some state like that. Lisa didn't know or care. All she knew was that the tips were okay, and Bryan was her manager, and that made up for all the bad parts of the job.

She went in through the back and was hit with the smell of fried shrimp, fried potatoes, and fried fish. She was used to the smell. She only smelled it when she walked through the doors on arrival and on her clothes after her shift. For the eight hours that her lungs consumed it, the smell was invisible, like carbon monoxide. The front smelled like cheap perfume and spilled Coors Light. Everyone was always drinking, like it was some special place you'd go to celebrate instead of a place you'd be damned to. Sometimes, Lisa felt like she was born in the wrong place. Wrong place, wrong era. She belonged in the future. Someplace where she could shine. There was either something wrong with her or everyone else, and she was betting on it being everyone else.

Bryan was in the back talking to one of the cooks, Chip, whose eyelids drooped, and he stuttered every time he talked to Lisa. Bryan lifted his chin as she walked in. His hair was full of pomade and spiked up in the front. She liked it better when it was flat and natural, the way it was when they woke up together in his twin-sized bed. The way it was when he read her his favorite song lyrics. Bryan finished his conversation with Chip and walked over.

"Blazers game tonight. Might be able to catch some of it on the TVs by the bar," Bryan said.

"Cool," Lisa said, opening her locker and grabbing her uniform.

"I forgot. You don't like basketball."

"It's not that I don't like it. I just don't care."

"Means more tips."

"Means more work. Not for you though. I'm not a manager. Just minimum wage slave labor," Lisa said and slammed her locker shut.

"Is this one of those times where I did something stupid like, a while ago, and now you're holding it against me?" he asked.

"Don't talk to me about basketball," she said and went to change her clothes.

When she came back, the room was empty except for Bryan. He was checking the dates on boxes, pretending to be busy.

"I'm sorry," she said. "Not sure what came over me. I almost crashed my car like three times on the way over here. I don't know if they are shipping in shitty drivers from out of state or what." She felt foolish and reactive. She'd gotten angry because he hadn't asked how she was doing. He just started talking about the Blazers. How was she supposed to tell him? Or not tell him? Both seemed equally impossible at this point.

"Don't worry about it. Have a good shift," Bryan said and walked out into the restaurant.

Lisa fought back tears. She hated how he would do that. How he seemed ready to throw her away at the slightest inconvenience. For a moment, she thought she felt the baby growing in her abdomen, and in every passing moment, it doubled in size exponentially, like it would swallow her up. She sat on the bench alone and willed her body to expel the baby before it killed her—killed them all. The thought made Lisa feel sadness and guilt. How could I feel sad? Or guilty? This baby isn't a baby. It was a speck, she thought. But somehow, she knew it was more than that. It was life, an invisible, impossible life, living an imagined existence somewhere in her hips. Its only beacon pulsated on the plastic stick with the pink plus sign.

Bryan walked back into the room. "I don't know what the

whole thing was about, but I just want to say that I'm sorry. Not sure for what. But you seem upset, and you know I only want to see you happy."

Lisa rushed into his arms and began to cry. He held her tight. He smelled like the cologne section at Macy's. He stroked her hair like he did when they were in bed and didn't say a word. She thought about Bryan comforting their crying baby—shushing and stroking, swinging the baby with love. If she hadn't already made her mind up, the moment might have convinced her to think about having the kid. He'd be a good dad. With him to lean on, maybe she'd be a good mom. Maybe this speck was an answer, not a problem. She wiped her tears off her face. Black mascara smeared across the side of her hand.

"Goddamn it," she said.

"It's fine. Don't worry about it. Just take some time in the bathroom. Whatever it is, I'm here for you," Bryan said.

Lisa almost started crying again but held it together long enough to kiss him on the cheek and escape to the bathroom. She looked in the bathroom mirror. The whites of her eyes were painted with lightning bolts of red. Thunderclouds of mascara blotted beneath her eyes. She looked old and tired. She practiced a tough face, making her eyes look determined, her mouth a tight rope. She'd take a pill, and this would all be over. She threw some water on her face to wash the mascara away and puked three times in the toilet. The bile and acid burned her tongue and left a gritty, sandy sensation between her teeth.

The Blazers game brought in a lot of people. Lisa tried to hide her disdain for them as she flashed fake smiles and pretended to be invested in the Blazers' win. It wasn't hard. Playing a part was a welcome escape from the thoughts swarming her brain. She got through the rest of the shift. Bryan sent all of the staff home early, and Lisa helped him close up. He'd been distant for most of the shift, but as the night wore on, he was nicer, flirtatious, even generous. She couldn't stand the thought of anyone touching her tonight though. Her body felt foreign, strange. When she brushed her own abdomen by accident, it emitted alien waves. Bryan came over and started wiping down the table next to the one she was cleaning.

"Great game tonight, right?"

Lisa gave him an annoyed look.

"Just fucking with you," he said. "So, what's a pretty girl like you doing in a dump like this?"

Lisa stopped cleaning. Half her mouth cocked into a smile. "I just love movies. Especially ones from the nineties."

Bryan laughed. "You say nineties like it's the fucking twenties or something. How old were you in the nineties?"

"I only stay because the manager's cute," Lisa said. She started wiping the table down again.

"You got some time to kill, or you gotta go home?" Bryan said. That was his line. He couldn't come straight out and say it.

Lisa puked on the table she had just cleaned.

"Shit!" Bryan said. "You okay?"

"I'm fine. I'm fine," Lisa said. She furiously scrubbed the table but only succeeded in knocking food bits onto the seats and floor. "This is so gross. Bryan, please. Just go home. Let me clean this up. I'm so embarrassed."

"It's cool," Bryan said. He bent down next to her and placed a gentle hand on her back. "My kid sister used to hurl all the time. Doesn't bother me. I just need to get some stuff to clean with from the back."

"Thanks," Lisa said. "But honestly, I'd rather just be alone."

"You didn't tell me you were sick," Bryan said.

"Sick?" Lisa wiped her mouth with the back of her hand. "That's one way to say it."

"What do you mean?"

Lisa exhaled forcefully, like she was blowing a pinwheel.

"I'm pregnant, Bryan."

Those first few hours held an anxious tension between the two of them, like they'd stumbled across the plans for the end of the world and had no one to tell—and no one to save them. Lisa cried and Bryan stared past her with dead eyes, like he saw something floating in the air. Lisa mentioned an abortion. Bryan suggested they not rush to any conclusions, yet Lisa felt he was just saying that. His response told her everything she needed to know.

They finally settled down days later, each on their own, and when they reconvened, Bryan said they should keep the baby. Lisa was surprised. The thought had never entered her mind since the day she'd found out. He smiled and took her hand. He said that maybe it'd be fun and easier than they thought, and maybe it was the best thing that had ever happened to them. Somehow in their bubble of a conversation, they'd floated away from some of the harsher realities, and the idea of an abortion faded into the background and disappeared.

"A little you or a little me," Bryan said. "What could be bad about that?"

Lisa wanted to get down to brass tacks and was more interested in getting out a notepad and writing down their exact finances. A stroller. Daycare. All the other baby things. And that was just when the baby was a baby. There was a whole lifetime after that.

"Just slow down. One step at a time. Everything happens for a reason. I'll take care of us," he said. He had that dead look in his eyes again like he'd seen something impossible. Lisa wanted to pull the embryo out of her uterus and show him that it was real because she had a feeling that this was all still a fantasy to him. He was playing house for a few weeks and soon they'd be at the event horizon. Still, she couldn't deny the allure of it. He was so convincing, and Lisa wanted to be convinced. She wanted to be told it would all work out. That it was all part of a plan—a destiny.

As they sat in the waiting room to meet the obstetrician for the first time, Bryan seemed bored. Lisa's heart was pounding, and the morning sickness made her regret the half a bagel she'd eaten an hour prior. She stared at the other women sitting in the waiting room. Some were nervous rookies and others were seasoned vets wrangling nearby toddlers. One thing united them though. They were all adults and made Lisa feel like a child. She put out her hand to hold onto Bryan's, hoping to find some comfort like the other women in the waiting room seemed to find, or have. They all sat in their Zen-like states despite having bellies like planets, or too many children already to keep control of. Bryan's hand lay limp in hers. He'd promised with such earnestness to love her and the baby and said one day they'd probably get married. In some ways, she felt the vigor was already fading. She squeezed his hand and he squeezed back. He gave a forced smile but stayed silent.

"Lisa?" the nurse said.

She took them back to a large room with a sterile looking bed and a large machine with a TV screen on it.

"Congratulations, you two," the nurse said.

"Thanks," Lisa said, trying to keep her voice from trembling.

Lisa lay down on the bed and the nurse explained that the plan was to do an ultrasound and check to make sure the baby was in the right place and quantify the heartbeat. Lisa wanted to ask, *What if it's not in the right place?* but kept silent.

"Let's just lift your shirt up, and we'll put down some ultrasound gel," the nurse said, squeezing blue, warm gel across her abdomen.

Lisa had the sudden vision that the ultrasound wouldn't show a beating heart but instead, an empty uterus, or something worse—a giant tumor, grossly shaped like a fetus but harboring something malignant and terrifying. There was no pause in the forward march of the ultrasound probe. Lisa closed her eyes as the nurse pressed the probe down on her abdomen and made Lisa feel like she had to pee. When Lisa opened her eyes, the screen was a blur of gray and black. At first, she thought she could make out what she was looking at, but then the image would shift and transform into something nebulous and indistinct. Lisa tried to read the nurse's face, something that would tell her it was right or wrong, a tumor or nothing. Maybe there was nothing. Maybe Lisa had been hysterical and the whole thing was a delusion. Bryan studied the blurry, greyscale images with the same look of puzzlement and confusion as Lisa, except he didn't look troubled, just bored.

"So?" Lisa said, her voice almost cracking. She wasn't sure if she wanted there to be a baby or not. As much as she wanted this to all be over, she couldn't handle the thought of it not being real.

"Everything looks good, just trying to get a good view of the heart. And there it is. There's the heart," the nurse said, pointing to the screen.

A grey oval sat in a sea of black, and within the oval, something flickered. Lisa put a hand instinctively on her neck and felt her pulse thundering through the artery. It felt fast, uncontrolled, and feral, but it couldn't match the speed in which her fetus's heart beat. It was already shoveling blood through its tiny oval body. Bryan studied the tiny heart, smiling, squeezing her hand tighter. Lisa felt dizzy. The stench of hospital cleaners flooded her senses, and she felt vomit sneak up her chest.

"It's beautiful," Bryan said. "Isn't it?"

"It's. . ." Lisa said.

She thought it was beautiful like a tiny flame in a sea of ink. But the longer she stared at it, she saw something more ominous—a bat beating its wings in the depths of a cavern.

"It's beautiful," she agreed.

"Congratulations again," the nurse said. "The doctor will be in soon."

She put the ultrasound away and left Lisa and Bryan alone. They both stared at the screen of the ultrasound machine, the images playing on the blank black screen inside of Lisa's head. She thought about her own heart beating and filling channels with blood to feed this little heart, churning in the dark. Having something living inside her was alarming and beautiful. She turned to Bryan, hoping to share the thrill of the moment—the fear and happiness coinciding—but the smile was already gone from his face. He looked detached and somber.

The doctor came in and laid out the game plan going forward. Regular appointments. Healthy eating. No alcohol. No drugs. No smoking. No medications except Tylenol. Bryan had come to life again in front of the doctor. He nodded and pretended to take notes. Lisa felt lost and alone. This journey had only just started, and yet she felt like she'd already lost Bryan. Afterward in the car on the drive home, Lisa turned to him and said, "There's no going back now."

Bryan stared ahead toward the horizon, sounding defeated and tired, said, "I know."

croatia: two

Lisa woke up naked in her bed. Her hand ached and so did her head. Last night's memories played back in a short, jolting nightmare loop. She got out of bed, wrapped herself in the bed sheet, and looked around her apartment. Luka was gone. Pale sunlight drifted through the window. It was early. The street below was silent. She sat on the bed, letting the hangover filaments creep from the back of her skull. Dull pressure seeped through her eyes, and bile bubbled up in her chest.

Her scar had to screw it all up. No. That wasn't right. Luka had to screw it all up. He could've glanced at the scar and moved on. He could've saved it for this morning when they weren't both drunk and naked, and maybe, just maybe, she would've told him the truth. He was disarming in that way, and she trusted him too much. It made her feel weak.

She didn't move from her bed for a long time. She felt warm under the sheets while the cool morning air moved invisibly around her face and ears. Her head pounded, and deep inside her mind, something sparked. Memories flooded back. The world felt supersaturated. Too busy. Too full of mistakes and worries and bad vibes and regret. She pulled the sheets closer, suffocating herself—barricading herself. She kept her eyes open long enough for them to sting and the world to go blurry. When she shut them, she left them closed for a long time.

Her phone buzzed on the wood dresser and her eyes flashed open. She'd fallen asleep. The street was louder now, still the subdued sounds of a Sunday morning, but alive. She jumped out of the sheets and grabbed the phone—it was Luka.

"*Dobar dan*," he said. He was cheerful. She thought he'd be angry, but for the time that she'd known him, he'd never been angry or upset with anyone, except the bartender who'd cut them off last night, but that guy was an exception. He stood in polar opposition to Lisa in many ways. He was determined to never let the world drag him down.

"Dobro dan," she said.

"You know, young lady, you need to work on your Croatian. *Dobar, dobar.* Not *dobro.* It's okay, I know you Americans have enough trouble with English. It's hard to learn more," he said.

"Luka—"

"I'm not giving you shit. I would never give you shit. Not to Lisa, the American princess."

"I don't know if we have the same definition of shit giving."

Luka laughed and an awkward silence settled in.

"Are we going to talk about last night?" Lisa asked.

"We can talk about anything you like."

"I think we need to talk about it."

"Let's talk about it. By all means. Of course. Just follow your trail of blood on the street and come meet me for a coffee."

Lisa agreed and hung up. She didn't feel as comfortable as Luka with the whole situation. She was half angry and half embarrassed. Maybe embarrassed about being angry? Or angry about being embarrassed? A little of both, and it wasn't helped by the hangover crowding her skull.

The hot shower felt good on her skin and made her brain stop throbbing. She washed the dried blood off her hand and the stench of spilled alcohol and cigarettes from the club. The cut was still there. It probably needed stitches, but Lisa had no idea where to get stitches and was pretty averse to the idea of needles, especially needles that passed in and out of your skin with a thread, so she figured she'd have to just see how it all worked out. As the water ran down her body, she followed it to her abdomen and ran her fingers along the scar. Of course Luka would comment on it. She'd been a fool to think he wouldn't notice. To think no one would ask. She knew she had to tell Luka something. She dried off and put some clothes on.

Outside, the weather was warm. She walked down to the café. Luka was sitting by himself, sipping an espresso. He stood to greet her as she walked up.

"You're walking much better than last night. I believe the street is not crooked for you any longer," he said, smiling.

"Har har," Lisa said.

She sat down across from him. The sun moved from behind the clouds for seconds at a time, causing bursts of light and long shadows. The waitress took Lisa's order. She resisted the urge for alcohol and instead ordered an espresso and small roll of bread with strawberry jam.

"About last night," Lisa said when the waitress left.

"I've been meaning to talk to you about it. No more rakija for you. I don't think you can handle it. You might need to go back to Jell-O shots or whatever you drank at your college."

"I never went to college."

"Rakija is a man's drink. Maybe some *medena rakija* for you, you know, honey or *borovička*. Have you had borovička? It's the one with berries in it. It's sweet—"

Lisa closed her eyes and waved her hand at Luka. "You're making me sick. Stop talking about liquor or I'm going to puke."

Luka laughed. "Sorry, sorry."

"And how are you not hung over?"

"Hangovers do not exist in Croatian culture. You either jump back in the saddle or you sober up forever."

"That sounds like alcoholism."

"Alcoholism does not exist in Croatia."

"Gotcha," Lisa said.

"So, the fix for your—"

"We need to talk about it, Luka," Lisa said. "I feel like you're avoiding it. It's going to just be in the background of everything we do or say. I'd love to just forget about it, but the scar isn't going anywhere. I don't want to feel awkward about it, so it's better we just get it out. For better or worse."

"Okay," Luka said, exhaling. Lisa realized he had been holding his breath. "I'm sorry then. Sorry about the way I acted."

"It's okay. You didn't know. I should've just told you."

Luka sat back in his chair and stared at Lisa.

Lisa rubbed her temple. "I guess that some part of me felt like it wasn't real anymore. Like it was a bad dream. But it was real. It's hard for me to talk about. I haven't talked to anyone about it." Lisa sipped her espresso the waitress had brought and stared at the cup.

"You don't owe me anything. I wasn't trying to pry. I was drunk and it surprised me. I mean," Luka leaned forward and talked quieter, "you're so goddamn sexy and we were really in the heat of the moment and it hit me, like wham, and all the sudden I'm thinking about kids and babies, and it's not that I didn't want you—I want you. All kidding aside, you drive me crazy. . . in a good way. When I'm drunk, I don't know what I'm doing. Really, it's probably better this way. It's not good to hook up when we're drunk like that anyway. At least not for me. I want to be my best. More importantly, I don't want you to puke on me."

Lisa let out an embarrassed laugh.

"No, I'm just messing with you. I'm serious about the sober hook up thing though. I want to be present. I want to remember. I want to do it right."

"I agree."

"It's settled then."

Lisa felt the urge to tell him everything. "Do you want to know the story?"

"The story about the scar?"

"Yeah."

"Oh, okay. I didn't think we were—sure, sure tell me. Just don't feel like you have to."

Lisa took another long sip of her espresso and then began to talk.

"It was a few years ago. I got pregnant by accident. I lost the baby. For whatever reason, it feels important for you to know. I don't have much more to say about it. It's done and over and the scar lives on. And really, I'm okay with that. It's who I am now. At least it's some part of me, somewhere. . ." Lisa trailed off. She stared into the black swirls of espresso, letting the words flow out. She hadn't told him the truth. She hadn't lied either though. She had lost Wyatt.

"Thank you for telling me," Luka said and kissed her hand with the cut.

"Let's not fight anymore. It sucks."

The clouds began to dissipate and the sun shone vibrantly

onto the square. People walked between coffee shops and restaurants. A family with young children walked by. The children tried not to trip while eating pink gelato out of paper cups. Lisa loved Rijeka. At first, it hadn't been love. She hated feeling like a foreigner every time she walked into the Konzum supermarket to buy produce and bread, but once the imposter syndrome receded, the city opened itself up to her, revealing some familiar elements along with the unexpected. When she'd picked Rijeka randomly, she'd pictured a quaint, quiet city, but Rijeka was a full-blown busy city—complete with office buildings, mass transit, bars, clubs, and a shopping district. It was also beautiful, sitting on the edge of the Adriatic Sea, with ferries and boats coming in and out of the port every day. And it was old. She loved walking from the newer parts of the city to the older. The center square of the city—the Corso—was lined with shops and beautiful old buildings, and then a few miles away, up on the hillside, there were brutalist cement apartments. The two stood in contrast to one another, each marking a period in its history and beautiful in its own way.

Lisa loved the secret squares full of café tables and chairs that the sun sat perfectly above, warming her face and arms while she drank espresso or beer in the early afternoons. Those few minutes when no one was walking through and a car couldn't be heard, and it was so quiet that Lisa forgot where she was. Hideaways like that didn't exist in the US. At least not that she knew about. Then again, as far as cities go, she hadn't seen much. Portland, Seattle, San Francisco, Boise, and the part of LA where Disneyland was. As perfect as Rijeka was, she longed to see more, experience more. She felt like she'd already missed out on so much.

"What was the city you promised to take me to?" Lisa asked.

Luka sipped his espresso. "You might have to be more specific than that."

"You said it's nearby. A day trip or less."

"We could take a ferry to Venice and back in a day if we wanted. You're at the center of the universe now," Luka said then waved down the waitress, ordered a lemon Karlovačko and kept talking. "We should go to Opatija. Have you been?"

"Are you having a beer?"

"A lemon beer."

"I'll have one too."

Luka called the waitress over and ordered another lemon beer and two shots of *medena rakija*. The waitress brought the beers and dropped the two shots of honey liquor in front of them.

"This is more your speed," Luka said.

They raised their glasses and clinked them together.

oregon: two

Lisa's mom Cathy pulled up twenty minutes late. Lisa had been standing in the rain and her windbreaker was soaked and stuck to her skin. Lisa got in Cathy's purple Ford Ranger pickup and slammed the door.

"Sorry I'm late, hon," Cathy said. Her speech didn't imply that she was actually sorry. There was coolness to it like her tongue had gotten lazy and fallen half asleep in her mouth. Cathy pulled forward and jumped the truck up on the curb.

"Are you kidding me right now?" Lisa asked.

"Oh stop," Cathy said and corrected the wheel with some effort. "The power steering must've given out." Either that or her mom had taken some tranquilizers and her arms weren't working Lisa thought.

"Mom, are you going to be able to get us there?" Lisa asked. She took her wet windbreaker off and cranked up the heat. She turned all the vents blowing warm air toward her.

"Am I going to be able to get us there. Now, there is a question," Cathy said. She squinted to see through the rain and furiously swiping wiper blades.

"Last time I ask you to drive me."

"You didn't ask. I offered and you accepted. No reason for you to be taking the bus to your appointments. The germs on those buses. We can't have the baby getting sick."

"I'm not sure that the germs on the buses are any more dangerous than you driving under the influence," Lisa said.

"Excuse me?" Cathy asked, looking at Lisa sideways.

"Just watch the road, Mom."

"I took my meds just like I was supposed to. My medications are prescribed by a doctor, someone much smarter than you, and I don't think you should be questioning his expertise."

Lisa threw her hands up and covered her face in frustration. "Great. Tell that to the coroner when you flip the truck and the baby and I are dead because you're high."

Cathy laughed an irrepressible type of laugh, fueled by angry surprise. "You've always been such a drama queen. Even when you were only three years old and liked to put on those shows for me and your dad. You thought you were Britney Spears or Shakira. Thought you were destined to be a star. And all I could think was what a handful you were going to be."

"Whatever you say," Lisa said.

"Maybe the doctor can recommend some medicine for you too. Might do you some good."

Lisa had seen the good it did her mom. She'd seen her without her anxiety pills, her wake up pills, her calm down pills, her take the edge of pills, her it's-three-PM-and-I'm-bored pills. Her mom could start her own pharmacy with the bottles behind her bathroom mirror. But when it came to which version Lisa would rather have driving her and her unborn child around, the sober mom was preferable, if only for the driving acumen it entailed. As far as reliability and stability, that was a toss-up.

Lisa would've driven herself, except her Jetta had broken down and she didn't have the cash to fix it. Not since she'd quit her job after Bryan started getting worried that human resources might find out about their kid and freak out. We could both get fired, he'd said. Lisa had been happy to quit. She thought she could find something easily but had honestly felt too fatigued to even look. Bryan had offered to drive her to the appointments. He'd even offered to fix her car. Lisa had declined. She didn't want to owe him. Even though it was a forty-five-minute bus ride to her appointments, she didn't want to be in debt to someone who was increasingly distancing himself.

Bryan had become increasingly despondent and reclusive since the OB appointment. Lisa tried to be empathetic, but it was easier to be angry. She told him that maybe it was best if they didn't pretend that this was going to be something it was not, namely, a happily ever after perfect family. Lisa was nineteen, and they weren't in love. She half wondered about an abortion, but now that she'd lived with the idea of something living inside her, she could not get rid of it. It all felt like a mistake. Something slowly becoming permanent and could not be undone. But there was a small part of Lisa that believed it wasn't a mistake. Maybe having a baby was what she was meant to do. She could've given Bryan more time to adjust, she could've cooled off and tried to work on it, but he jumped at the opportunity to step away and Lisa let him go. They'd left it at that. There was no plan to reconnect. No plan to stay in touch. It had been a few weeks now and Lisa felt increasingly alone.

"It's here, Mom. Jesus," Lisa said and covered her eyes. Cathy barely made the turn and almost popped the truck's front wheel over the curb in front of the OB clinic. Lisa stepped out of the truck into the monsoon rain. Cathy swore under her breath and went to park the truck. Lisa walked toward the main door, moving quickly to avoid being completely soaked. She checked in and sat down in the waiting room. Her stomach was starting to show. She was normally very thin—something she'd admired about herself and grown accustomed to—but now her abdomen protruded like she'd swallowed a cantaloupe. Today, she would find out the sex. She couldn't deny the excitement she felt about finding out if it was a boy or a girl. In some ways, it felt trivial, and in others, it seemed integral to her future.

"Lisa?" the nurse called.

Lisa raised her hand and started walking back toward the exam room. She glanced back at the door to see if Cathy was coming. She wasn't. Lisa didn't know if she was intentionally dragging her feet after she'd been rude in the truck, or perhaps she had more pills to pop before she was ready to be in public. Either way, Lisa wished her mom would come in already. She was all Lisa had now.

"My mom is coming. She's parking the car," Lisa said.

"We'll bring her right back as soon as she's here," the nurse said.

The nurse emphasized that the point of the ultrasound was to evaluate if the baby was developing normally, and the added benefit was finding out the sex. Lisa half listened because she already knew the baby was growing normally. She could feel it. She also had a strong sense that it was a girl. She'd felt it since the day she'd stared at the pink plus sign in the bathroom. Nothing against boys, but Lisa needed it to be a girl. It was selfish and Lisa knew it, but having a little boy would be like a reward to Bryan. She didn't want to be raising a little him while Bryan gallivanted about, living life like nothing changed. She pictured raising a son that would idolize Bryan, and as soon as he was able, he would bolt from Lisa just like Bryan had. She couldn't imagine a worse nightmare than having lived a life of service to two men who could care less about her own joy and satisfaction. But a girl, a girl could grow up and love Lisa like no one else could.

The thought of raising a boy all on her own felt suddenly overwhelming to Lisa, and while there was no going back, she experienced a brief second where she thought about not going forward. Not having an abortion but maybe giving the baby up for adoption. There was no denying that when Bryan began to withdraw it had crossed her mind. She had pushed the thought aside quickly, but now it came sneaking back in. As convenient as it may seem to her at times, she knew it was an impossibility. How could she break something before it had a chance to bloom? The fantasy of a family in the suburbs, desperate for a child and in excess of cash and love was just that, a fantasy. That wasn't how love worked—not in Lisa's mind. She couldn't imagine living a life of regret thinking *what if?* Not just for her, but for her kid. *What if my mom kept me? What if my mom loved me? Who would I have been if I hadn't been given up?* She felt like they'd both end up spending their lives searching for something that could never be found—trying to fill a void that was boundless. She was in this for better or worse. Plus, she wasn't alone. She had her mom.

Lisa asked the nurse to hold off on the ultrasound until Cathy came back. She left Lisa alone in the room. Lisa ran her hands over her belly, feeling the taut skin shielding life beneath. Cathy burst through the door and sat down on a chair.

"I'm sorry, Mom," Lisa said.

"That's okay, sweetie. We'll get through this together," Cathy said.

"Are you ready for the ultrasound now?" the nurse asked.

"Yes," Lisa said.

The black and gray images fluttered to life on the screen again as the nurse slid the probe along the gel. Lisa exhaled sharply and squeezed Cathy's hand. The images moved around, and the nurse would point out something and say, "That's the appendix," or "That's the pancreas," or something like that. Lisa nodded approvingly. She didn't want to appear like she didn't know what they were looking at, or worse, like she didn't care. She waited in quiet anticipation to find out it was a girl and that everything would be okay. Bryan would slowly become an afterthought.

"So, do you have any names picked out?" the nurse asked.

"I like Matilda or Maddy. I'm on the fence about Lily and Piper," Lisa said.

The nurse smiled at Lisa. "Those are cute. What about boy names?" she asked.

"Matilda?" Cathy asked.

"Yeah. I told you I liked that one," Lisa said.

"And boy names?" the nurse asked.

Lisa looked at the screen, trying to decipher the images. "Why do you keep asking that?" Lisa asked, panicked.

"Is it a boy?" Cathy asked. "I always wanted a boy in the family."

"Oh my God," Lisa said, slamming her head back into the bed and hiding her face in her hands.

"I don't have to tell you anything if you don't want to know," the nurse said. She removed the ultrasound probe from Lisa's belly.

"Is it a boy?" Cathy asked, again.

"I think you've said enough," Lisa said, her face buried beneath her palms.

"It is?" Cathy asked.

"Yes, Mom. Jesus Christ. Yes," Lisa said.

The nurse nodded.

"It can be hard to find out something when you're not expecting it," the nurse said.

"Oh stop," Cathy said. She kissed Lisa's hand and giggled. "How exciting, Lisa! A boy!"

Cathy looked legitimately happy for the first time in a decade and her joy filled Lisa with her own. Lisa found herself smiling despite the baby being a boy. Her mom's hope gave her hope.

As the months went on, Lisa became like a globe, the ones she used to spin and run her finger along until it stopped over some country she couldn't pronounce and she'd tell herself that she'd live there one day. She found herself holding her belly up when she walked. It didn't help really. It was some sort of maternal instinct she didn't try to fight. Her legs, too, were swollen like those overinflated party balloons that clowns twisted into swords and dinosaurs. She preferred to wear sweatpants and hooded sweatshirts. She had no one and nothing to dress up for. She watched a lot of daytime television, at least she did until she found herself crying over a soap opera and decided enough is enough. She thought about applying to college. She'd planned on going to Mt. Hood Community College before she'd gotten pregnant. Maybe study French or Communications. Lisa didn't really know then and didn't know now. She had no plans, no ambition. She was just going to get through this pregnancy thing and then try to figure it out. Cathy had agreed to support her, at least for now.

Summer was in full swing in Oregon. Lisa spent most nights in her upstairs bedroom half asleep with two fans on either side of her naked body. Cathy had been doing her part to try to make Lisa's existence less lonely. Last weekend, she decided to take Lisa to the Willamette River and rent a stand-up paddleboard. They made it about twenty yards from the dock before Mom fell in and was unable to get back up on her board. Lisa laughed so hard she thought she might go into labor. That was the last time she'd left the house. Her friends didn't call or text. No one really even knew she was pregnant. She was embarrassed, ashamed even. Most of the time, she sat around with closed shades, ordered pizza, and wasted time reading pregnancy blogs. Her doctor had suggested a birthing class seeing as how Lisa was a first-time mom and quite young. She hadn't said the young part, but Lisa had picked up on it. That last thing Lisa felt like doing was being in a room with a bunch of other pregnant women all breathing heavy and visualizing their *birth plans* while doting spouses looked on. Lisa was not worried about giving birth; it was the after she tried not to worry about.

Bryan had started sending a text every once in a while after he heard it was a boy, and Lisa mostly ignored them or tried to. They made her feel weak. She wanted to shut him out completely. She wanted to be immune to his absence, but in the end, she knew Bryan would always mean something, and that hurt more than his ambivalence about being a part of her life.

One night when Lisa was feeling especially overwhelmed with the idea of being a single mom, as well as feeling tired and lonely, Bryan texted her: *Hope our little dude is growing strong!* The text made her happy and somehow forget about the truth that Bryan wasn't all that interested in being a dad. She started to think that maybe Bryan wasn't such a bad guy, and maybe he'd be a good dad. Maybe this whole thing would be a story they'd tell their kid one day. She texted back, *Doing my best,* and fought the urge to cry. *I know you are,* he wrote. Then, a few minutes later, *What are you doing later? Want to grab a bite?* Lisa stared at her cellphone screen, rereading the message, picturing his face, her mind a swirl of anger and longing. Anger at her longing. Anger at what she longed for. She'd tried to ignore it—its ultimate inconvenience and impossibility—but there it was. She'd finally let it sneak into her mind. Her mind was eager to cast Bryan aside, but her heart could not. Some things couldn't be explained, only understood. With a baby between them, he was not so easily shed.

They met the next night at Shari's. Lisa had cleaned up. She wore makeup and a cute top. She'd somehow squeezed into a pair of jeans, but her swollen feet only fit into a pair of boots. Bryan didn't seem to notice. He kissed her politely on the cheek when she arrived and sat down in the booth. They forced small talk—Bryan asking about the pregnancy, Lisa asking about work. It felt like they were reading off a script in some made for TV movie. The waitress saved them from their forced niceties.

"I'll just have a salad and a Diet Coke," Lisa said.

"Are you sure? Don't you want a cheeseburger or at least some fries? The baby and all," Bryan said.

"Sure, I'll have a side of fries," Lisa said.

Bryan ordered a cheeseburger, and after the waitress left, he reached out and held her hand across the table.

"I'm so sorry," he said.

Lisa pulled her hand back and sunk against the red pleather of the booth. They sat there motionless, Bryan's hand still outstretched on the table, Lisa's gaze affixed to the floor, in the background, the gentle white noise of people talking.

"I'm glad you agreed to meet me," Bryan said after a moment.

Lisa didn't move. She was petrified with indecision. She feared being with Bryan as much as she feared being alone.

"You aren't going to talk to me?" Bryan asked.

Lisa turned to look at him. His hair was wavy, the way she liked it, and his expression was soft and earnest. His eyes were stretched wide like a small child, innocent and inquisitive. The fear loosened for a moment.

"I'm talking," she said.

"I was stupid. I don't know what came over me. I was scared and—"

A surge of emotion bubbled up, half hormones and half anger. Not just anger but a desire to hurt Bryan for the way he'd hurt her. She wanted to tell him to go fuck himself. She didn't want to let him come back into her life, telling his sob story while she'd spent the last few months alone.

"You were scared?" Lisa said. "*You* were? I have a baby growing inside of me and I'm nineteen and have no job and no future and—I have nothing. Nothing. I'm completely alone."

"You're not alone," Bryan said.

"I'm not—you know what? Screw this. Screw you." Lisa got up from the table.

"Wait." Bryan grabbed her hand. "Just sit down. Please, just sit. You don't even have to talk. It just feels good to be around you. I feel alone too. I know you don't believe me. That's okay. You don't have to believe me, but I miss you."

Lisa paused. His hand holding hers seemed to trigger tears somehow, like he was pulling a lever. It felt good to be touched. She knew she should leave. Someone who ran away so easily could never be trusted to stay. She was better than this. Somehow though, she didn't leave. She stood there for a long time, trapped at a crossroad. Bryan didn't say anything. He just held on. She sat back down. They didn't talk until the food came out, and even then, the only thing Lisa said was, "Actually, I want a cheeseburger." Bryan didn't try and hold her hand again, but his eyes never left her. She wondered if he loved her. She'd never been in love before this, so she wasn't too keen on just jumping right out there and asking about it. Maybe this was all love was, sharing a meal in silence and not feeling lonely. Before, she might've hoped for so much more, but for now, it was enough.

Lisa came home to find Cathy asleep on the couch. Some sitcom with a laugh track played in the background. Lisa sat down next to her. The room was mostly dark, the only light radiating from the television screen. Lisa lifted the cover off Cathy's feet and wrapped herself in it.

"Now my feet are cold," Cathy said.

"Sorry," said Lisa. She used a small corner of the blanket to wrap Cathy's feet.

"So, how was it?" Cathy asked.

Cathy's eyes didn't leave the television screen. She'd taken the right-before-bed pill and was half there.

"It was fine. He's the same but nicer. We didn't talk much."

"Sounds nice."

"It was."

Some good-looking people made food in a large New York apartment. Lisa pulled the blanket tighter. She could smell Bryan's cologne on her.

"Do you trust him?" Cathy asked.

Lisa spoke while staring toward the light in a trance. "I don't know."

"Be careful."

Lisa tried to think of the times prior when her mom had given her ominous advice like this but couldn't think of one. She had to believe that Cathy wanted to say more but was holding back. Lisa had to believe that Cathy respected the instant maturity that came when the pink plus sign changed her life. Changed both their lives. Cathy must feel a bit of déjà vu at how things were unfolding. Cathy had been a teenage mom. Alone. Dad had only stuck around until Lisa was five. She remembered him playing Barbies and having tea parties. He was quiet but always laughing. She remembered his stubble scratching her face when he kissed her good night. She remembered his gravelly voice, the voice of a smoker, and how his clothes always stunk like cigarettes. She had no memory of him actually smoking though. She'd found out later that he'd smoked Marlboro reds—the ones Lisa identified with cowboys. She started to tell herself that her dad was somewhere out on the trail. *He's out on the trail alright.* That was what her mom would've said if Lisa had ever talked to her about it. Lisa felt bad that she remembered so little because now he really was gone. Killed by liver cancer two weeks after finding out. He never even got to come home. Just stayed in the hospital in Fresno and turned yellow and delirious. It was hard to not think of the cancer as evil. Even if it wasn't sentient or purposeful. Lisa couldn't help but think it had its own agenda of ending lives that weren't ready to end. If her dad was a cowboy, then the bad guy shouldn't have won. That wasn't how it all was supposed to work.

Lisa felt her eyes closing. It had only been the two of them, Cathy and her, for so long. If things worked out with Bryan, her mom would be alone. Lisa didn't want to think about that. She sometimes saw too much of her own future in her mom's present.

"I'm doing my best, Mom. That's all I can do," Lisa said.

"I know, honey. I know."

croatia: three

Lisa and Luka didn't have a car, so they rented a Vespa for their drive to Opatija. Luka let Lisa pick, and she picked, much to his dismay, a vintage, canary yellow scooter that lacked in power but compensated with style. Happy in their mildly inebriated state from their breakfast drinks, they zipped along the seaside road. Lisa sat on the back, her arms wrapped around Luka's waist, the wind whipping her blonde hair around her face and making her eyes water. They'd tried to talk, but between the wind and the motorbike, they couldn't hear. So, they gave up and rode in silence. Luka drove fast. Lisa felt like he was trying to show off as he accelerated into corners and out of them. She was happy when the traffic picked up and he had to slow down. In the mountains heading down from Rijeka, Luka passed cars recklessly, unbridled, losing himself in the rush of adrenaline. Lisa felt the adrenaline too and squeezed him tight, half out of fear and half excitement. Lisa liked it more when they drove slowly and she got to admire the Adriatic, sparkling in the sun hundreds of feet below the green mountains. It was more than a marvel. She tried to think of something to compare it to, but everything came up short. The closest was probably the Pacific off Neahkahnie Mountain. She remembered driving down the mountain's twisting roads on her first long drive after she'd gotten her license. How the ocean stretched and sparkled in the warm summer sun. But the Pacific in Oregon was a dull, sober blue, and the Adriatic was luminous, effervescent—almost visceral in its beauty.

When they pulled into Opatija, Luka parked the Vespa in the middle of town. Beautiful, ornate old buildings lined the streets. It was different from Rijeka, small but not quaint.

There was something grand about it.

"This is where royalty used to vacation," Luka said as they walked toward the sea.

"What do you mean?" Lisa asked, staring at the rooftops, trying to think of a way to describe the architecture.

"When Croatia was part of the Austrian-Hungarian Empire, the royal family used to vacation here."

Lisa looked around. "Why here?"

"How should I know?"

"You don't know? I just figured you would."

He smiled. "I'm more of a superficial-facts tour guide. I'm not writing my thesis on it."

"Either way. Keep going, I'm enjoying it."

"Really, I don't know why they came here. I mean, it's nice. I think they came for the water. The streams start there at the top of Učka," Luka said and pointed to the massive, green mountain rising behind the city, the tallest in the range, "and travels down to meet the ocean. It makes the water cold but special. Unique, I guess."

"Magic?" Lisa asked.

"Magic? Right. Of course. They came for the magic water. Youth, beauty, healing properties."

Lisa looked up at the mountain. It reminded her of a green volcano. She thought of Mt. Hood back home in Oregon. Its jagged peak piercing blue-white glaciers. She wondered what Luka would think of it.

"Does it snow up there?" she asked.

Luka laughed, "We will go up there. I'll make a snowman with you."

Lisa pushed him playfully. "There's no snow."

"There's no snow. Not right now. But in the winter? Who knows? The truth is that I've never been up there. Could be fun. Maybe Rudolph is there."

Luka put his arm around her, and they kissed. She liked the way he kissed. When their tongues met, she could tell he was smiling.

"Are you hungry?" Luka asked.

"I want to swim," Lisa said, grabbing his hand and making him hold her tighter.

"The American princess wants to swim. Did you bring a swimsuit?"

"No."

"You can go naked and no one will care. This is Europe. In fact, people will be joyous. They will call the newspapers and photographers will be down on the beach ready to document the foreigner as you bravely try out our Slavic ways."

"I think I'll just wade in," she said.

"Okay, your choice. Not ready to be a Slav yet, I understand. Not sure how much the magic can affect you if you only wade in, but it's worth a try."

"Knee-deep magic."

"That's about as magic as I like to get, honestly."

They continued walking through the town. Lisa loved the buildings, grand and decadent—meant for royalty and people of importance. And us, Lisa thought.

They reached the beach. It was small and lined on both sides by concrete boardwalks. The beach was covered in white, round rocks and mostly empty. Lisa hobbled over the rocks. They were hard and warm on her feet. The water was perfectly clear, with a green-blue hue farther out. Nearby was a marina with yachts and sailboats belonging to people more important than them. The people Opatija was built for.

"Come on," she said. Luka was sitting on the edge of the cement boardwalk, his bare feet hanging over the sea but not touching.

"You go, girl. Isn't that what they say?" he said and gave her a thumbs up.

Lisa turned back toward the water and slowly waded in. She felt the mix of the cold mountain stream and the warm Adriatic along her legs. It chilled and exhilarated her. She kept walking until the water was up to her thighs, and the small waves threatened to soak her shorts. Out in the distance, boats motored or sailed along, and beyond that, nothing but empty horizon. She closed her eyes. The sun warmed her face, and the water temperature vacillated between cold mountain stream and warm open sea. With the water lapping her legs and the sun beaming down, she thought that maybe there was magic in the water, because in that moment, she felt so far away from Oregon and her prior life that it seemed unimaginable.

"Nice, huh?" Luka said.

She nodded and waded a little deeper. Suddenly, she caught a jet of mountain stream, giving her the sensation of liquid spilling down her legs, and she flashed back to the day her water had broken and Wyatt was born, and every single memory threatened to spill out. She bolted out of the sea.

"Whoa, easy there. There are no sharks in the Mediterranean. Did you think you saw Jaws out there or something?" Luka asked.

Lisa didn't say anything. She walked right past him and away from the water, violently wiping the water from her legs.

"Where are you going?" Luka asked, chasing after her. "Did the little fishes bite you or something?"

"I needed out of there," Lisa said when Luka caught up to her. She sat down at a round table shaded by a green umbrella.

"It's true. Nothing makes me want a drink like a dip in the sea. Maybe you're Croatian and you don't even know it."

Lisa was silent. She felt her heart racing and worked hard to keep her mind closed.

"Where is the waitress?" she said impatiently.

Luka looked at her concerned. "I'll find her. I'm on it."

Luka walked over to the bar and came back with two large beers. Drops of condensation dribbled down the sides of the green glass. Lisa lifted the bottle to her lips and didn't let go until a third of it was gone. Luka watched her in puzzlement, his perpetual smile becoming flat and forced.

"Listen, if you don't want to be here, we can head back to Rijeka. I took you here because I thought you'd enjoy it," Luka said.

Lisa closed her eyes and exhaled deeply. "This has nothing to do with you."

Luka thumbed the drops on the side of the bottle. "I'm here with you. It feels like it has something to do with me."

Lisa leaned forward. "It doesn't. Trust me." She kissed Luka on the cheek.

Luka's face remained unchanged. His eyes were focused on hers. Questioning. Worrying. Lisa smiled. It was a gentle, poignant smile, like she'd just delivered bad news but wanted everything to be all right.

"My life is pretty complicated right now. That's the best way I can put it," Lisa said.

"I'm all for complicated. Complicated is good, boring is bad," Luka said.

"You're the only good thing I've got going, Luka. I know I seem like a mess. It feels like there is a lot of bad, but it's not. I think I'm just being real, and I worry you're going to hate who I really am."

"How could I hate you? Is this about the scar? I feel really bad that I brought it up."

"Don't feel bad. It was inevitable."

They both broke eye contact and stared at the water.

"Please, let's not dwell. We have to go back to work tomorrow, and we should enjoy ourselves. No more of this shit. We can have fun," Lisa said, clinking her glass against his.

"Forced fun. I've never tried it."

"It's not forced. It's a conscious decision. I want to be happy. I'm going to be happy. Drink with me. We'll drink to the royals."

"The royals are dead."

"Let's drink to the politicians then."

Luka laughed and almost spit out his beer. "You obviously don't know the politicians here. Let's drink to lovers."

Lisa crinkled her nose. "That's cheesy."

"No it's not. This isn't just a city for royals, and it's definitely not a city for politicians. It's a city for love."

"Love then," she said, and they clinked their glasses.

Luka put his bottle down and looked at Lisa sideways. "You don't believe me about the love thing, but there is a statue very close to here. It's a woman and she is waiting for her lover. But the story goes that his boat sank and he drowned so he's never coming back."

"That's messed up," Lisa said.

"What? It's true. It may be morbid but it's a good morbid. It's love. Her love is so strong not even death could break it."

Lisa felt a tear run down her face.

"Oh, Lisa. I'm sorry. It's just a story," Luka said, wiping the tear away.

"It's sweet. Morbid but sweet."

Lisa knew the tear wasn't because of the story. Not in the way Luka thought anyway. It was because she couldn't imagine loving someone that much. Enough to wait for an eternity. She knew it was just a story, but it made her feel less human in way. Like she was an invader, or maybe someone or something had invaded her, taken over her mind and body so that she looked like everyone else but inside she was hollowed out.

"I'll show you the statue after our drinks and you'll see. This city is about love."

They drank more until the day wore on and they were good and drunk. They stumbled down the path and found the statue Luka had told her about. It was a woman, green and holding a bird, staring out at the sapphire water. Her face was obscured. She was facing the horizon forever, or at least for as long as statues lasted. Whoever had sculpted her took great care to create a lifelike face only to have no one see it. Lisa felt like the woman. Even now, with a new life in Croatia, and Luka by her side, she felt like she was still staring across the ocean, unable to move forward. She was stuck in a time that didn't exist, somewhere between the past and the present, a purgatory of her own creation. But it wasn't love that kept Lisa looking back—at least she didn't think so. It was regret and guilt about her inability to change what had passed. It had all busted her into the same mold as the statue.

Lisa stared out at the sea until the sun began to set and the world glowed in a grapefruit light. Luka sat beside her, unmoving and silent. He wasn't trying to fix her, and she was comforted by his silence. When the sun finally set, he kissed her on the top of her head and said, "I'll take you home."

oregon: three

Lisa sat alone on the aluminum bleachers behind an assortment of drunken observers. It was Sunday, which meant she was at Delta Park watching Bryan play softball with his friends. It was mostly people from the restaurant with a few friends of friends of acquaintances. That was how Sunday softball teams were—a random assortment of dudes that drank too much beer and grasped at perpetually fading glory days. Everyone was trying really hard but pretending they weren't trying at all. They were following the Sunday softball protocol: drink beer, act casual, and throw your back out trying to hit one over the fence. Bryan used to be an ace pitcher on his high school team, somewhere near Coos Bay where he grew up. He took it seriously. He pretended it was all for fun, but Lisa could tell that he was trying to prove something to someone. Anything to anyone. Last week he pulled a hamstring while rounding first, trying to stretch a single into a double. The week prior, he plowed into the catcher—a balding dad whose kids came to watch—and gave him a concussion.

She and Bryan had been together for a few months now. She'd even moved into his place in Southeast Portland. With that closeness, she'd been able to see other sides of him. She watched him pluck his eyebrows for forty-five minutes, try on six different T-shirts before picking the right one, and watch reality TV with a deep-seated desire to star in the next reincarnation of The Real World. Sure, he was classless in a lot of ways. Then again, Lisa wasn't anything to write home about. She had her own boring vices. She binge-watched Dr. Who and hadn't read a book since graduating high school. Still, she wanted more. She wanted more for her child. Bryan wanted more but in different ways. His dream was climbing the corporate chain and buying a big house in deep suburbia. It left Lisa feeling ambivalent. She liked it when he was sweet and funny and caring. She liked it when they stayed in and ate popcorn in bed and talked about what kind of person their kid would turn out to be. She disliked him the rest of the time. He was the guy with the loud truck with tinted windows and huge subwoofers. The guy who cried when he got a bad haircut. The guy that made poetry out of thinly veiled pop lyrics. The whole thing made her feel dirty and stupid. How did she end up with someone like him—get pregnant by someone like him? She tried not to think like that. It was pointless. It may have been a mistake to have it with Bryan, but the baby was a blessing—she hoped.

Bryan walked off the field and brushed dust off the front of his pants. "Game's almost over. Are you holding up okay?" He sipped his Rainier. He'd been drinking more since Lisa hadn't been able to. He hadn't put on any sympathy weight but had more than his fair share of sympathy beers.

"I'm holding up fine. You wanna get me a drink?" Lisa asked.

"Sure. I was going to get myself something. You want a LaCroix or something else?" Bryan bent down and sifted through the cooler.

"You sure you need another?" Lisa asked.

"What? This again?"

Lisa shrugged. "I'm just checking in. You don't have to get so up in arms about it."

"I know you aren't drinking so maybe your radar is a little off, but I'm fine. I'm totally good. I don't even have to finish this one, okay?" he said and poured his beer on the concrete.

"Make a scene why don't you?" Lisa said, rolling her eyes.

"You brought it up."

"I just want to make sure you're good to drive if we need to head towards the hospital."

"This pregnancy has really turned you into a worrier."

Lisa stood up and walked down the bleachers.

"Just forget about it."

Bryan followed her, speaking louder. People were starting to stare. "You really know how to make me feel bad, Lisa."

Lisa didn't turn around. "Just have fun, Bryan. I'll call my mom. It's not a big deal."

"You're going to call your mom? You throw that out like it's some sort of threat. Like I'm so bad, Lisa. I brought you out here. Try and make sure you're included, like you're part of my life. I pay our rent—"

"Bryan, stop. Please," Lisa said and then whispered, "People are watching us. I don't want to do this here."

Bryan tried to whisper but failed. "I'm not doing anything. You're doing this."

He jabbed his finger violently toward Lisa as he spoke. She thought about tackling him to the ground and stuffing sod down his throat.

Bryan walked back to the dugout. Everything went back to normal. No one talked to Lisa. No one told her, Don't worry he's a good guy. No one cared. She was an outsider here. She closed her eyes and took a deep breath. Her thoughts were rolling in faster than she could process them. No one was looking. No one cared because no one had to.

A rush of fluid went down her leg. She froze, petrified in embarrassment and fear. No one had noticed—yet. She sat down in the grass and instinctively put her hand between her legs, as if her hand might be able to move the fluid back into her bladder and she wouldn't ever have to tell anyone she'd peed herself. The fluid felt thick and warm. She pulled it to her face in horror thinking, somehow, she'd shit herself but saw that the fluid was clear. Her water had just broken.

She made her way to the bathroom and locked the door. Her brain buzzed and flipped. She was not prepared for this. She needed a few more weeks, a few more days, anything to get more experience, more knowledge, more love. Did she love the baby? Not yet. That would come. It would have to come. A contraction squeezed her insides. She needed to get to Emanuel hospital. She needed to go now. She got out her cell phone and dialed her mom.

"Yello," Cathy said as she picked up.

"Mom. It's happening," Lisa said.

"What is happening?"

"My water broke."

Cathy's voice perked up. "Oh my God. Baby, it's happening!"

"I know. I know. Can you come get me?"

Cathy paused. "Where's Bryan?"

"He's here."

Cathy hesitated again. "Listen, Lisa. He's the father. He should be there. He should take you. I don't want to get in the middle of whatever you have going on this week. Go tell Bryan. Get going to the hospital. I can meet you there when you two decide you want me to come."

Lisa stayed silent. Cathy did too. Lisa wiped the fluid from her legs with some paper towels, threw them in the trash, and then looked at herself in the scratched metal mirror. Her face was blurred by knife scratches and graffiti. Her green eyes were dull, her hair flat, her skin flushed. It didn't look like her. She wasn't all scratched and dirty nor tired and depressed. Not the real her. This baby would save her.

"Okay," Lisa said and hung up. She went out to get Bryan and a contraction hit her hard, like she was standing on the deck of a boat in rough seas. The pain was intense and jolting. Then, as quickly as it came, it went away.

"Bryan!" she yelled and then realized just how melodramatic she must appear.

Bryan saw her stumbling in pain and ran over. No one else did. They probably assumed more drama and were reluctant to get involved.

"What's wrong? What is it?" Bryan said, his eyes painted with fear.

"My water broke," Lisa said.

"Fuck. Really? Oh man. Okay, no problem. No problem," he said and helped her toward the truck.

"I can walk. I can walk. Just go get the truck ready. You remember where to go?"

Bryan nodded. "I'll put it in my phone. I'll put it in my phone right now." He fumbled with his phone and ran to the truck. Lisa knew she had to be calm for the sake of everyone. They left the parking lot, everyone wishing them well and patting Bryan on the shoulder, sending them off with, Good luck! and, Your life is about to change, brother! Bryan wore a petrified smile that faded once they hit the highway. He was pushing eighty in a fifty-five. Lisa reached out a hand to calm him.

"We've got time," she said. "Just get us there safe."

"What do you think I'm trying to do?" he snapped.

Lisa grimaced as another contraction hit, the same as the last but lower in her pelvis. It took its time petering out. Bryan's face contorted into a grimace.

"You okay?" he asked.

"Fine. It's gone. Just drive slow. Everything will be fine," Lisa said, her eyes closed.

Her body remembered the pain but was trying to relax. Bryan slowed down. The sky turned pink as the sun surrendered to the horizon. Lisa kept a hand on her stomach—so she could feel the baby move—and the other on the door handle ready to bail. It was some sort of maternal protective instinct. Like she'd jump out of the truck before they'd collide with another car. She'd tuck and roll along the highway, her arms wrapped tight around her stomach as she rag dolled along the pavement. Her heart fluttered as she pictured her fractured and broken body strewn along the road, and a perfect, healthy baby lying on the asphalt. She looked over at Bryan. He gritted his teeth. His eyes squinted to try and see the road in the blinding coral sunset. She felt like she could read his mind for a moment.

How could this possibly work, Lisa? We're living a fantasy. We can't even get along for more than a day and we're going to be parents together? We couldn't even decide on a restaurant without you thinking that I'm a fraud and me thinking that you're a drag. This is impossible. This isn't the way I wanted to bring a baby into this world. I'm not sure either of us are good people. How could we expect that our son will be any different?

"You're right," Lisa said.

"Huh?"

"Nothing," Lisa said. She closed her eyes and readied herself for the next contraction.

Even at the hospital, Bryan continued to freak out. He panicked and pushed her in a wheelchair, shouting down the hallway like he was Paul Revere, The baby is coming! The baby is coming! But between contractions, when Lisa could actually think for a second, she realized it was all for him. He wasn't scared for Lisa, or the baby, only for himself. A nurse caught them as they veered right and told them they were on the wrong side of the hospital and Bryan shot Lisa a glance like maybe he needed a turn in the wheelchair.

During the birth he wasn't much better. Whatever she thought she'd seen in him before was gone now. To her, he was a shell of a man, or at least the man she needed—the person that her and the baby deserved. Bryan was interested in being a kid. He wanted to go out drinking, have sex, play video games, sleep in, eat shitty food, spend money, and feed his ego. None of the qualities she needed in a potential husband or dad.

The monitors started to wail, and the room filled with nurses and doctors and people with surgical masks. Lisa looked to Bryan for comfort. His eyes darted around the room like he was looking for an exit. She watched him wilt into the corner, scared of the blood and confusion. The baby wasn't doing well and needed to come out, now. Lisa could keep trying to push and risk the baby's life and her own, or they could take her back for a C-section. The doctor acted like it was a choice, but it wasn't.

Lisa was wheeled away into the operating room, and all she could think was that if she died, at least she died for something. They put a needle into her back and draped a blue cloth over her like a tent. Beneath the blue, with an oxygen mask hissing in her face, she felt the tug and pull of her baby being cut out. Tears flowed down her face. She was happy she'd been paralyzed because otherwise she would've rolled off the table in fear. There was a lot of tugging and then suddenly, nothing. A loud, warbling scream filled the operating room that filled Lisa with a mix of overabundant love and intense sadness. While the doctors stitched her up, the nurses brought her baby underneath the blue tent so his face could be pressed against hers, and she could smell his breath, and kiss his skin, and see he was real. Wyatt. She would call him Wyatt. It made her forget about the bleeding, the pain. She was filled with a joy that she never knew possible, and the sureness that she would never be alone again.

A month later, Lisa heard Wyatt's wails from the back room of her mom's house. It still made her heart skip. She reacted the same every time. The same mix of emotions she'd felt since he'd been born. She'd pictured the crying as an annoyance, a sound to drown out with whistling or singing, but instead it had become an affliction. She'd learned to stop running. Stop checking Wyatt's body for injury or to make sure he hadn't fallen apart. She was learning about his inherent resiliency, despite his fragile appearance. He kept growing and living. Sometimes she felt like he was invincible—that he'd live forever—and other days she thought his heart would stop in his sleep. A genetic defect. Faulty ticker. She would wake up in a violent panic. Her mind searching for the last time she'd heard him cry or take a deep breath, and for that second after waking, before she turned to check on him, she'd picture his perfect skin turned blue and cold and dead. She'd bite her lower lip and think to herself how it had been her fault that it all ended in heartache, just like she knew it would—like it had to. Happy endings were for movies and massage parlors. Cathy quote. Maybe bleak life outlooks were transmissible, Lisa thought. Sometimes she felt like life was an inherent tragedy playing out in a rapid cycle of slow motion and fast-forward.

Eventually, she'd come to her senses and realize that Wyatt was only asleep, not dead. His pink, little lips would part and life-filled breath would spill out. Cathy kept reminding Lisa that it was his only way to communicate, but Lisa couldn't help but feel like he was screaming from pain or fear when it was always a wet diaper, or a feculent one, or because he'd woken up, or because he was hungry, or because he wanted to, or didn't want to, or because who knew why.

Lisa lifted him out of the crib, careful to support his neck, and placed a bottle in his mouth. She'd tried to breastfeed but couldn't get over the feeling. Too primal—animalistic. It grossed her out in ways she couldn't really explain. The nurses at the hospital kept telling her it was natural, but for Lisa it felt anything but. She shushed him while wiggling the bottle in his mouth. He stopped crying and began to eat. She carried him over to the living room. It was small. The whole house was small. It was cramped. Especially with all of Wyatt's stuff in her room now. There was barely room to walk between her bed and the crib.

Outside, the trees were turning. A handful of leaves continued to hold on to the branches. Their vibrant gold juxtaposed against a dull gray sky. The weatherman seemed to throw out arbitrary temperatures for the high and lows of the day. Lisa wondered when it would turn gray and rain nonstop for months. It was inescapable. When it wasn't raining you thought about the rain, and when it was raining, you thought about the rain. Lisa wondered what people living in Arizona thought about. Maybe about when the cacti needles would fall out. Maybe about pool parties. Maybe about the vastness of the desert.

Wyatt stopped crying. He was almost finished with the bottle and his eyes were wide open. His gaze locked onto Lisa's and made her feel unworthy. His ash gray eyes couldn't focus completely yet. He could see her. She was sure of it. But he also seemed to see everything all at once. His pupils stretched as he tried to absorb it all. His tiny brain couldn't comprehend the world she'd brought him into. All he knew was her. Lisa didn't feel like she was good enough to be someone's whole world. How could anyone? She wished she had someone to turn to in her moments of terror. Someone besides her mom, who had become a master at invalidating Lisa's feelings by brushing them off and telling her she'd get used to it all. She'd only seen Bryan once in the last month. It was all very lonely despite never being alone.

Bryan never came into the operating room. He told her later that they'd told him he couldn't, that it was an emergency, and he could see her after, but Lisa knew it was a lie. He'd been too scared. He was almost too scared to hold Wyatt when they first met. If Lisa felt inadequate now, Bryan looked like he felt ten times that. After the nurses left and the adrenaline petered out of the room like a balloon losing air, he had sat calmly in the rocking chair, holding a sleeping baby, looking like the man she might have fallen in love with. But it didn't last. It wasn't long before he was listing things he had to do, tasks to complete, work he couldn't miss. So Lisa did them both a favor and told him to leave. There wasn't a long, knock-out, drag on fight. She'd simply said, I'm going to my mom's and Bryan said he'd drop her stuff off. Over the last month, they'd exchanged texts and pictures of Wyatt. Lisa would mix in a He's doing great with an I don't want to have to hire a lawyer and eventually, Can I count on you to support our, son?. Bryan swore he would, and for him, that must've given him pride. He'd only come to see Wyatt once in the last month, but he was quick to post the pictures Lisa sent him on social media, praising his newborn and taking credit for his good looks. Sometimes when Lisa was up in the middle of the night feeding Wyatt or swaying him back and forth, barely awake, she wanted to write on his posts that he was a fraud, that he had abandoned his family—that he was a coward. She wanted the world to know how pathetic she thought he was. She wasn't mad, not anymore, more disappointed and dumbfounded that he was who he was. Now that she was connected to him through a life—the most important life possible—she only hoped that whatever made him the way he was, wasn't hereditary, and that Wyatt would grow up to be a better man.

croatia: four

They never made it to the top of Učka. Luka raced back to Rijeka on the Vespa, and the summer's night air chilled Lisa's bare legs and arms. He pulled up to her apartment and asked if he should come in for a nightcap. Lisa hugged him and kissed him on the lips and thanked him for the day.

"There's something about you. Something really good, like magic," Lisa said.

"Now you're being cheesy," Luka said.

"I mean it. You know how black holes work?"

Luka stared at her blankly. "I majored in physics."

"Okay, right. So, you probably know way more than me."

Luka smiled. "You think black holes are magic?"

"No. They're this place where everything gets pulled into. Super dense and powerful. Anything that gets close enough gets sucked up and absorbed. That's how I feel around you. All of my chaos falls into you, and then it's gone, like nothing happened."

"I'm a black hole?"

"No, you're like the opposite. You're like the sun."

Luka laughed. "I have no idea what you're talking about, but I like it."

"How do you do that?"

"Do what?"

"That. Take all the bullshit and keep rolling with it."

Luka's smile lost its color. "Honestly, that's a conversation for another time. Another adventure."

They agreed to see each other again later in the week. Lisa figured she'd stop by his work and surprise him, but it was good to let a little time pass and let the weirdness from the scar and the trip to Opatija wear off.

Lisa went up to her room and lay in bed but was too restless to sleep. Deep inside, she felt a longing, a tug. Somewhere in her brain a little blinking light turned on and would not turn off. It was a reminder that things never really ended. They would never heal.

Still, Luka and his unwavering optimism stirred something else in her. She was hesitant to give too much to him but felt herself falling headfirst regardless. She needed to be careful. Nothing good could come from trying to resist life too hard. She might end up breaking something that wasn't meant to be broken. She'd come to Croatia to move on with her life. To enjoy it, not wallow and push everyone away. She looked at her hand. The wound was healing. She'd come here to heal. She deserved love and happiness and fun and youth. There was nothing standing in her way but herself.

She woke up in the early afternoon. She hadn't fallen asleep till four or five in the morning. She'd finally succumbed when the sound of commuters spilled into the street. Luka was already at work. In fact, he was probably halfway through his day of renting cars to tourists as they came off the ferries. He had a degree in physics from a college in Zagreb, but work was hard to come by here, unless you planned to work in tourism. If you wanted a job that paid well, chances were that your best bet was to live abroad—Germany, South Africa, Iraq, Saudi Arabia. Luka had friends working in Ireland too, but he was satisfied with his job at the car rental. Lisa couldn't care less about what his job actually was. Jobs told you nothing about who people truly were. They were a mask. A conversation starter. Hey what do you do? I do this, blah, blah. Lisa worked at a bar selling drinks and dressing skimpy for tips. She had to believe that her job wasn't a commentary on who she was deep down. It was just what she had to do to survive. Plus, Luka's job had perks. After all, that was how they had met.

She'd rented a car in Zagreb with no idea how to make her way toward the coast but hoped it would be similar to driving in Oregon. It was and it wasn't. There were roads. There were signs. There were painted lines between the lanes. That was where the similarities stopped. She had almost been run off the highway a dozen times, clearly not understanding the unstated rules, and arrived clueless and crying at almost every highway toll she hit. When she arrived in Rijeka, exhausted, frustrated, and alone, Luka made her feel safe and even managed to make her laugh. Something like Did you fall from heaven? only worse, and cuter, however impossible that seemed.

She walked down the street to the local café and bakery and bought a pastry, called a burek, a flaky pastry filled with meat and cheese and, according to Luka, hard to find in this part of Croatia. It was something that he ate regularly growing up in the eastern part of the country, on the border of Bosnia, but here in the west, the food was different.

The western part of the country was called Istria, an arrow-head shaped peninsula jutting out into the Adriatic. Luka loved to talk about the history of his country, and though he was fairly new to the area too—he'd moved to Rijeka about five years prior—he knew a great deal about its history. Istria had started out as a Roman territory, then onto the Venetians, Napoleon, Italy, then Austria, then Italy again at some point, eventually falling into the hands of Yugoslavia and then finally Croatia. But out of all its suitors besides the obvious Croatian natives, the Italian influence was unmistakable, even to Lisa who hadn't really traveled anywhere. The ferries coming into port were full of Italians, the shops catered to Italians, and when Luka had shown her pictures of the other coastal cities in Istria, they looked the way she thought Italy would—bright, pastel-colored buildings lining the sea.

Lisa turned the corner and followed the road down to the water. Luka was sitting behind a desk at a small storefront for a car rental. He beamed when he saw her approaching. Lisa leaned on the counter and offered some burek to him.

"Breakfast?" he asked.

"Yep," she said.

"Lisa, it is like two in the afternoon. What kind of trouble did you get into after I left you last night?"

"It's jet lag."

"You still have jet lag?"

"Mm-hmm."

"Wow, this is amazing. Jet lag this far out from your arrival from America. My God. Someone call a scientist. We need to conduct some studies."

"How is work?"

Luka shrugged. "Work is work. At least I get to wear this cool uniform. I look like a traffic cone." Luka pulled the orange polo toward his face and let it go with a snap.

"It's not bad," Lisa examined the polo and gave a thumbs-up. "You look official."

They chatted a bit more. A customer came up and Lisa got to watch Luka go into work mode. He was less gregarious—quieter, his hands rarely moved—and he came across like he was pissed off at something or someone.

When the customer, left Lisa asked, "Why are you so mean to the customers?"

"Mean?" Luka asked. "I'm not mean. I just try to set a precedent. Like, they aren't doing me any favors coming in and renting a car. I got better things to do."

"How would you make any money then?"

"You capitalists," Luka said. "Money is ever flowing. You shouldn't have to work for it. It's like karma. What goes around comes around."

"You majored in physics not economics, right?"

"Same thing."

"Right. I gotta go." She blew him a kiss.

She walked along the water toward work. The air smelled fresh. A large sailboat floated past. A man and a woman stood at the wheel. She leaned on him, and they both stared out at the horizon. On the surface, they looked like a J. Crew advertisement which made Lisa want to puke. But their faces seemed happy. They looked like everything in life had turned out the way they had planned. Lisa couldn't even decide if that was something she wished she had. What did she want her life to be? How far would she rewind time? Birth? Grade school? When Dad left? The boat sailed off and she kept walking. She got to work and found her boss, Tomislav, cleaning and stocking the fridge with beer.

He greeted her with his deep gruff voice and thick Slavic accent.

"Hey cutie," Lisa said and gave him a hug. He was cute, in a dad sort of way. He was short and large—mostly around the middle but also in the neck and hands—and had kind, brown eyes and a warm smile wrapped in an unruly beard. He blushed when she called him cutie.

"Ah, cutie. You know how much I love this word," Tomislav said.

Lisa went to the back and found Angela eating a salami sandwich and swiping her thumb across her phone.

"Oh my God, I'm glad to see you," Angela said without looking up from her phone. "I thought I'd have to suffer through this shift with Mark or just Tomi."

She greeted Lisa with similar statements every time they worked together. Tomislav liked to hire pretty women, girls as he called them, preferably not Croatian. He thought it added some sort of exotic energy to the bar, which in turn would increase tips, but it just created a strange milieu of expats, local teenagers, and tourists. No one tipped well. Not unless they thought they were taking Angela or Lisa home, which only happened when they were about to be eighty-sixed, so it didn't work out well for anyone.

Angela was beautiful, even as she squinted at her phone and stuffed a sandwich in her face. She kept her thick hair in tight braids. The Croatians thought of her as exotic, with her light brown skin and heavy English accent. She was an anomaly, and for some patrons, her voice and appearance were an aphrodisiac in itself. For others, she was something to be obtained, something to be conquered. At their worst, Angela embodied all their racist, stereotyped preconceptions, and they openly let her know who and what they thought she was.

"I hate working Fridays," Angela said. She put her phone down and looked at Lisa for the first time.

"It's not so bad," Lisa said. "Saves me money. Everyone bumps their prices up on the weekend when the ferries come in."

"There are no cute guys or girls who go out on the weekdays. It's impossible to meet anyone in this city. I should be down in Split. I could be making twice as much in tips and have my choice of consenting adults nightly." Angela threw her phone on the couch. "Fuck dating apps by the way. The people that post themselves in a group picture, like, am I supposed to guess which one is you? I pass every time."

"I've never really spent much time on them."

"Well, who needs to when you have green eyes, freckles, and blonde hair? The men come to you, right? At least Luka did, and he's quite the catch. He looks like a young Liam Neeson. Less broody. Or maybe more broody. I feel like I've seen both. What is going on with you two these days?"

Lisa smiled, "I'm not sure what is going on, but I think it's good."

"Oh, well then, I want every juicy detail."

"There are no details. Just something I feel inside, and I think he feels too."

Angela walked over and put her hands on Lisa's shoulders. "Lisa, don't fall in love."

Lisa put a shirt on. "I didn't say I was falling in love."

Angela followed her as Lisa tried to walk away. "When we met, you said you'd come here to have fun, live life, and do anything but fall for a guy, and now you're feeling something inside?"

"We have a good time together, that's all. When we're together I feel happy."

"Happy is good. Love is bad." Angela spoke like a caveman. "Take it from someone who's been there."

Lisa ignored her. She wasn't in the mood for Angela's life lessons.

"Girls, time to open up," Tomislav shouted from the bar into the back.

"Oh, fuck. Let the night go quickly," Angela groaned. "In fact." Angela rummaged in her purse and then brought out a small glass vial with white powder in it.

"Come on, miss, have a bit," she said, offering the glass vial out to Lisa.

"Coke? I've never done it before," Lisa said, feeling excited and scared.

"Never? Well then, it's about to be the best work night you've ever had." Angela snorted some of the cocaine out of the vial.

Lisa felt her heart race in anticipation, and before she could talk herself out of it, she grabbed the vial and snorted.

"Atta girl," Angela said and kissed Lisa on the cheek. "Let's go get 'em."

oregon: four

Downtown Portland was bustling with young people wandering the freezing, dry streets. The sky threatened snow flurries as Lisa pulled her parka closer to her chest. Her legs were bare and her feet were frozen as she hobbled along in black heels. Up ahead, in the dim glow of roving headlights, she saw Jessica and Holly waving as they stepped out of a red BMW and into the night, looking equally cold in bundled top halves and bare shins and toes.

"Lisa!" they shouted simultaneously.

Lisa smiled and felt more excited than she had in a long time. She hobbled a little quicker down the street to greet them. They hugged, and smiled, and held Lisa at arm's length so they could look her up and down, showering her in It's been too long and You look amazing! and How did you drop that baby fat so quick? It's only been three months, right? to which Lisa thought, It's been so long because you basically abandoned me when I started dating Bryan and then got pregnant, but the smile stayed and the words never came and they moved together in a hugging, happy group inside the restaurant.

They sat at a giant booth on the bar side of the steakhouse. It was a mix of business professionals and college kids back on winter break. They took off their coats and traded more compliments on their dresses and jewelry. Lisa almost never dressed up, but when she heard they were going to Manhattan Blue, she knew what she had to wear. It was one of the nicest restaurants in Downtown. A place where they cared less about your age and more about putting good looking women on the bar side. Lisa glanced at the menu in front of her, saw the prices, and panicked.

"How are you ladies doing tonight?" a short waiter with a gap between his front teeth said.

"Fine," Holly said. Her black hair cascaded around her shoulders as she flipped it from one side to the other. The waiter took notice and Jessica followed suit, less obvious, but it attracted the same attention. Lisa cracked a sideways, toothless smile and dug around in her purse. The waiter raised an eyebrow as Lisa handed him her ID. It was fake. She'd had it since she was seventeen and only used it once. It had worked, despite the picture being of someone at least thirty years old and twenty pounds heavier. Her hand shook as she handed it to the waiter. She was a mom but still couldn't drink. Sometimes she wanted to escape somewhere that seemed more civilized. A place that had its priorities straight, like Norway or the little country that made the peace agreement. Geneva. Lisa wasn't sure that was a country, but it was a place that probably understood things a lot better than Oregon. A place where if you were a mom and you were out, they grabbed you a barstool and poured you a drink without a second thought.

The waiter glanced at the picture, braced his face against the smile sneaking up, and nodded. "Just fine, miss. The rest of you are twenty-one I presume?" he asked. Holly and Jessica rolled their eyes and nodded. They were the same age as Lisa, only twenty, and the only place they drank at besides here was Pogo's, a dive bar in Milwaukie. The bartender at Pogo's wasn't more than a few years older than they were. He'd laughed at their fake ID's but still served them wine coolers and pink, fruity shots that Jessica later vomited all over Lisa's driveway when they snuck home at 3 a.m. There was a time when Lisa thought they would all head off to college together and get drunk every weekend. But Lisa didn't have the grades for college, nor the drive. By the time she'd realized, it was too late. Jessica didn't either and Holly had never planned on it. College just sounded like a waste of time. Most of the people they knew who'd graduated college had ended up moving back in with their parents anyway.

They ordered their drinks. Lisa ordered a cosmopolitan because she recognized it from Sex and the City episodes. It wasn't the cheapest option but once she realized no one planned on eating she relaxed and stopped eyeing the cheap beer specials. She'd only drank beer while standing out on a damp, freezing golf course, drinking expired Henry Weinhard's from someone's dad's garage. Lisa didn't remember what her dad drank or if he drank. She'd never had the opportunity to steal his beer.

When the drinks arrived, they all toasted and sipped. Jessica had a vodka cranberry and Holly had a whiskey sour.

"So, how is your little one, Lisa?" Holly asked, her eyes scrunching up.

Lisa took another sip. The cosmo was good. She felt like it was hitting her even before she swallowed.

"He's great, you guys. Honestly, he's like my everything now," Lisa said.

"It's gotta be so much work, right? I just don't know how you do it," Jessica said. "It's like one minute we're in school and the next you're a mom. It's hard to wrap my head around it."

Lisa nodded. Her lips pressed tightly together. "It's a lot of work but I've got my mom."

Holly laughed and then abruptly covered her mouth. "Sorry. Sorry. I just—you know. We grew up together. I know how your mom is."

Lisa gave a polite smile and said, "Yeah. She is who she is."

Holly gave a knowing nod and sipped her drink.

"How's Bryan?" Jessica asked.

Lisa sighed. "A dick? I don't know. I don't know how to answer that. We haven't seen each other much in the last few months since Wyatt was born. He's so uncomfortable with babies I'm not really interested in leaving him alone with Wyatt. And since I can't really stand to be in the same room as him, he's not around much."

"That's too bad," Jessica said. The booth brimmed with silence. Lisa knew why. They'd both warned her about Bryan. They met him one time and afterwards warned Lisa that he was a creep. Lisa had figured they were just jealous, but she'd been a fool. They'd seen right through him. Lisa hadn't seen Holly or Jessica since then. Three girls who'd grown up together since elementary school. Swimming at the community center. Riding the tube behind Holly's dad's boat. Muddy fall soccer at the park. Slumber parties and secrets. A friendship bound more by proximity than compatibility, but still, they'd shared their lives with each other. The good and bad. Holly was loud mouthed, callous, and funny. Jessica, sweet and thoughtful. And Lisa. Whoever Lisa was in all of this.

"I just want to say something to you both," Lisa started, and took a deep breath to calm herself. "You were right about Bryan from the beginning. I should've listened to you." And in her head Lisa thought, Maybe everything would be different, but that was something she wasn't ready to say out loud, because wishing for things to be different was basically wishing for Wyatt to disappear, and that was not something moms were allowed to think. Wyatt was here and she was thankful for him. She felt responsible for him. She not only felt compelled to take care of him, but she also needed to. Had to. His birth had carved out a section of her soul that was only filled momentarily when she was caring for him. How could she wish for things to be different? How could she wish for him to not exist? Mostly she wished that she loved him more. She tried. She wanted that love, desperately. Maybe with that love she'd feel complete. Maybe then she wouldn't wish her life was different. Maybe it would fix everything.

"That's okay," Jessica said and smiled. Lisa could tell this was the confirmation Jessica needed. She could only imagine what they had been saying behind Lisa's back.

Lisa asked them how their lives were going and as the liquor disappeared and subsequently refilled, they recounted their post-high school lives, the one Lisa had known so well up until almost a year ago. The more they talked, the more Lisa felt like decades had passed instead of just over a year. Jessica and Holly were trapped in a life full of dating drama and weekend parties, like perpetual high schoolers, but with no school and the same perceived and formulated hierarchy. They'd changed but only superficially. Time had lashed a few pounds across their thighs and hit the dimmer in their eyes.

The biggest difference wasn't the content of their conversation but the obvious stagnation of their life trajectories. Lisa supposed she was the same way, except her life seemed to have jumped to a new level of meaningfulness—one devoid of a need for a specific location, or goal, or love interest in it to derive meaning. It was a higher calling being a mom—a life of servitude—and with that thought Lisa pictured herself old, boring, and addicted to pills like her mom. For Holly and Jess, neither of them had left the suburbs. Holly worked the front desk at a salon and Jessica was a cashier at Trader Joes. Their lives revolved around who stayed in town and who was home on break, who was getting married, and who had gone to rehab. Lisa's stories were solitary ones. Moments she could recall but with intricacies only she fully understood or appreciated. Her life was filled with bottled formula, diapers, exhaustion, and a happy, smiling baby. It was also filled with moments where she held Wyatt tight and felt so lonely that she told herself she couldn't do this. Lisa didn't feel more mature, just different. Like their lives were alternative realities, side by side—the life she could've had versus the life she did have. She wasn't sure they were different.

Jessica suggested they move down to the actual bar, out of the secluded booth, now that the after-work drinkers were filing out, and the bar was filling with twenty somethings and a few thirty somethings that looked out of place. The two cosmopolitans had done a number on Lisa's empty stomach, but she felt it less in the gut and more in the head. She was floating somewhere between drunken contentment and absolute panic. She kept checking her phone thinking Cathy was going to call at any minute and Lisa would have to go rushing home. Her phone stayed silent though, and Lisa tried to keep from tripping in her heels as she walked. Two young guys in Ralph Lauren polo sweaters and too much pomade walked over to the three of them, drinks in hand.

"Can I get you ladies a drink?" the taller, and better looking of the two asked. His green eyes trained on Lisa's.

"Sure," Lisa said a little louder than she meant to. The excitement overwhelmed her ability to mimic sobriety and she embraced the inebriation with open arms. She hadn't had a moment where she could feel irresponsible in over a year—between the pregnancy and Wyatt's birth. This was her chance to let loose and live. She thought about the constant vigilance she'd shown during pregnancy—making sure she was getting exercise, making sure the baby was moving, making it to every appointment—and then the total responsibility to Wyatt at every moment of every day. It was beyond exhausting. It was superhuman to maintain. A break was long overdue. I'm fucking drunk and it feels so good, Lisa thought. The other guy—older, shorter, and with a beard—asked Holly if she'd like a drink too, and she nodded but added, "Only if you get one for my friend," motioning to Jessica who blushed and gave an awkward nod. They returned with their drinks. Holly and Jessica toasted with one man while the other chatted up Lisa.

"I'm Bryan," he said.

Lisa laughed uncontrollably. The irony of the moment was too much.

"What's so funny?" he asked.

"Nothing. Nothing. My dad's name is Bryan," she lied. "I'm Lisa."

They talked some more. Lisa was careful not to drink her cocktail too fast. She still had to drive home at some point, but that point was some point in the future and could possibly never exist or never happen, and she needed to live for right now. After all, maybe me and this guy might go somewhere, she thought. Impossible, but in the moment it seemed plausible. Anything did. Wyatt seemed worlds away.

Bryan was droning on about sports, and Lisa politely nodded and threw in a, "Well, isn't that something?" every once in a while.

"People say the Timbers will never be much. They think that because—"

"Hi," Jessica said.

They both politely nodded, and then eager to continue their personal conversation, turned away. Jessica didn't move. Lisa turned and locked arms with her. "Jess, this is Bryan. He's studying to get his law degree from Lewis and Clark."

Jessica laughed. "Oh my God. Did you tell him that your ex-boyfriend's name is Bryan?"

Now it was Lisa's turn to blush. She didn't try to cover up her lie. Bryan asked if her ex-boyfriend and her dad were both named Bryan, and Jessica cocked her head sideways. The conversation halted. Lisa tried to salvage the flirty, preteen feelings of attraction she'd felt minutes earlier.

"So, do you live around here?" Lisa asked.

"Not really. I'm over in southwest. I'm actually here with that guy tonight," he pointed to his friend still talking to Holly. "Well, not here with him. That's Colton. High school buddy. We both went to Lincoln. I mean he's more than that. I hate to just say he's a high school—"

"Don't you need to go home and check on your baby soon?" Jessica asked.

Lisa turned to look at her, the world feeling simultaneously supersonic and glacial. Jessica wasn't looking at her, only Bryan.

"Your baby?" Bryan asked, looking confused.

Lisa wanted to smile but couldn't. She felt betrayed, devastated, drunk and alone. All the calm suddenly disappeared and was replaced by a whirling uneasiness, like an airliner that had lost power and floated in ominous silence before its plunge. She felt a bit melodramatic. Of course she needed to get home soon. Of course she wasn't going to hook up with a stranger. That was a fantasy. But Jessica wasn't her friend. Not anymore. Maybe she never was. She was a young single mom. When people her age were getting married, she'd have a teenager. Being here at the bar tonight was a mistake. A cruel illusion. It was midnight and her dress had turned to tattered rags right in front of everyone.

Lisa reached into her purse and pulled out her phone. It was eleven-thirty. "Yeah. Yeah, I need to go." She left without saying goodbye. Holly and Jessica didn't seem to mind. Bryan quickly settled into a conversation with Jessica before Lisa was even out the door.

The cold struck Lisa in the face. The pain was almost welcome until the wind wiped her eyes dry and the cold leaked through everything. She walked quickly to Cathy's truck, unlocked the door, and sat in the frozen cab while the engine sputtered and tried to come to life. She started to cry, felt stupid, and then punched the steering wheel. Some people on the street looked up as the horn went off.

"Sorry," Lisa said, mostly to herself.

Get ahold of yourself. Fuck them, she thought. Sadness quickly shifted to anger and resentment. She started driving before the heat could come on. She embraced the cold. She was stronger than this. The only reality that mattered was the cocoon she'd created back home. Just her room. Just Wyatt.

It was the fourth time she drove onto the bumpy stripe marking the edge of the road that Lisa realized she was drunk—very drunk—and should definitely not be driving. She slapped her cheeks a few times to wake up. That just made her face hurt so she turned the radio up and cracked the window. It woke her up, but the song was all wrong. She fiddled with the radio and when she looked back up at the road—the road that had been empty only seconds before—there was now a semi-truck at an almost complete stop. Red brake lights beamed, and warning lights flashed amber like an airstrip to eternity. Lisa pressed down hard on the brake pedal and the world froze. She thought about Wyatt.

I can't die. He needs me.

She thought about her life and how much she had left to do. And then somehow, an impossible amount of time passed inside her head as the world crawled by. She realized she'd spent her whole life leading up to Wyatt's birth in anticipation. She was a chrysalis ready to burst from childhood and spread her wings, but instead, the world had played a cruel joke. It had thrown her down into the dirt and now she scraped her knees down with the slugs and spiders while trying to raise a child she never wanted.

She'd kept some maternal instinct and thought of Wyatt first, but in the end, as she swerved, nearly hitting another car and narrowly missing the stalled semi, she was left with the guilt of knowing that as hard as she'd tried to convince herself that the cards she'd been dealt were the cards she'd chosen. She knew she was living a lie.

When she arrived home, the lights were out and the TV was on. The sound blared loudly. Mom was slumped on the couch, her face lit by the pale electric glow of the television. She paused for a second, catching a sound beneath the TV noise. She moved back toward the hallway and could hear it more clearly. Wyatt was screaming. His voice was hoarse and raspy. He sounded desperate. Lisa sobbed when she heard the noise, feeling lost and out of control. She rushed into the room and turned on the light. Wyatt lay on his back, wrapped in a blanket with his red footie pajamas poking out the top and bottom. Lisa swept him up and tried to console him. His face was flushed red. He screamed louder as she swung and shushed him. He was sweaty and urine soaked his pajamas. Lisa sobbed.

"It's okay, baby. It's okay, Wyatt. Mommy's home. Mommy's here," Lisa whispered. But Wyatt didn't stop crying and screamed louder. Lisa swung him faster, harder, her shushing a step below shouting.

"What's going on?" Cathy said. She stood in the doorway, face still groggy as a yawn crept across her face. "Why are you getting him all riled up for, Lisa?"

Lisa gritted her teeth and glared at Cathy.

"You need to calm down. You're—" Cathy said, grabbing Wyatt out of Lisa's hands. "You're swinging him too hard! What are you trying to do? Shake him to death?"

Lisa's tears felt cool against her hot face.

"Give him to me!" Lisa yelled and pointed at Cathy. "You fucking druggie! You fall asleep? The one night I ask you to take care of him, you fall asleep?"

Cathy's lips pressed together and eyes narrowed. She slapped Lisa's finger away from her chest and held Wyatt away with the other. "You better get control of yourself. We had everything under control. You're drunk and acting irrational." Cathy's tone was one Lisa hadn't heard since she was a child.

Lisa sat down and buried her face in her hands, crying. Cathy swung Wyatt gently and hummed. Within a few minutes, he was calm. Cathy changed his diaper and pajamas while she continued to hum. Once he was dry, she put him down in his crib, waved Lisa out of the room, and turned out the light. Out in the hallway, Cathy stopped Lisa as she headed toward the bathroom.

"Stop," Cathy said, putting her hands on Lisa's shoulders. "Listen."

But before saying anything else, Cathy hugged Lisa and Lisa's knees buckled. The world swayed. She floated in her mother's embrace—the two of them lost at sea.

"It's okay, honey. I know it's a lot for you," Cathy said. Lisa shrunk a decade in her mom's arms, small enough to be swung like a baby. But then Lisa remembered Wyatt. She remembered she was a mom now. She remembered the way her friends had treated her at the bar. She remembered Cathy passing out on the couch. Lisa lifted her head from Cathy's shoulder. Cathy had been crying. Tears swelled at the sides of her eyes.

"Don't ever fall asleep like that again," Lisa said.

"Don't drink that much. You're a mom now," Cathy said. Lisa knew she couldn't leave Wyatt alone with her. She knew she would never go out again. She wished she could disappear and start over. With Wyatt. Maybe without.

They both went their separate ways. Lisa lay in the dark listening to Wyatt breathe—feeling trapped and free, content and restless, her life over and just beginning.

Months later, Wyatt wailed from the bedroom. It had been going on for almost ten minutes. Lisa poured milk into a bowl. It was two in the afternoon, and she was just getting up. She reached into the cupboard and pulled down a box of Cinnamon Toast Crunch, opened the top and poured it into the bowl. A few squares of crystal strewn grain fell into the milk and with a second shake, cinnamon dust cascaded out into her bowl and across the table.

"Shit! Shit!" Lisa yelled and hit the bowl with her hand, sending it crashing down, leaving jagged pieces of ceramic strewn across the floor. Wyatt's screams amplified. The whole world went quiet except his cries. It crushed Lisa's chest and made her want to pull her hair out. It made her simultaneously want to run out the door and never come back and run to his side and never leave. She couldn't leave him even if she wanted to. He was something beyond clingy. Sometimes beyond dependent. A parasite. At times, he fed off her. She'd come out for one minute to pour a bowl of cereal and he'd lost it. She slumped down to the floor of the kitchen, letting the puddle of milk soak into her sweatpants and her old T-shirt from a middle school talent show. She couldn't decide whether to run or stay. Instead, she did nothing. Went catatonic. The world froze while Wyatt's cries continued indefinitely.

It was hard to know how long it took before Wyatt stopped. It could've been instantaneous—like her collapse to the ground had appeased some God and he'd blessed Lisa with a moment of peace—but more likely it was much longer than that. Somewhere less than hours and more than minutes. That was what she told Cathy when she pulled her up from off the floor. The milk was cold. It had always been cold. It hadn't warmed. "Was that a measure of time?" Lisa asked.

"Oh, honey. Let me go get the thermometer," Cathy said, holding Lisa's arm in one hand and Wyatt, like a football, in the other.

Wyatt was six months old now and life was changing for Lisa in unexpected ways. After the night out with Jess and Holly, she'd stayed in and recommitted herself to being a mom. But the more she stayed in, the more Lisa felt depressed in a way that was previously unimaginable and currently indescribable. She was madly in love with Wyatt but also physically sickened by his presence. Sometimes, just staring at him made her nauseous. It wasn't just nerves from all the responsibility either. It was disgust, for herself, for her feelings toward her baby, but mostly, unexplainably, for Wyatt. The fact that the feeling was inconsistent was even more confusing. At times, Lisa worried she'd been possessed or had contracted a brain tumor. Something to explain the intrusive thoughts that told her she hated her baby.

Hate my baby? Lisa thought one day, trying to assess the insanity of the statement. She felt the urge to vomit. When she looked at Wyatt, she didn't feel hate. Really, she didn't feel much of anything at all—a great empty pit in her heart where she was supposed to feel love. Later that night, while she lay with Wyatt in bed—which she knew she wasn't supposed to but didn't care—he pursed his little lips and made a sweet half smile, which made Lisa smile too. She kissed him on the forehead. *How could I hate something that makes me smile?* Lisa thought.

Weeks went on and the smiles were rare while the impossible feelings of disgust, resentment and at times, hatred, became common. Lisa couldn't see a way out.

The first time Lisa froze was in the shower. Wyatt had been laying on a blanket on the floor. She'd slept maybe three hours the night prior and now, with Wyatt finally asleep, she thought she had her moment of relaxation, but not five minutes into the shower—the time when it had gotten steamy, her muscles had started to relax, and she had just closed her eyes and let her head rest against the cool tile wall—Wyatt had begun to cry again. Her heart twisted like a wet rag in her chest. Then it hit her. The terror of it froze her in place. She didn't come out of it until the water had long since turned cold and her naked body was shivering, and Wyatt had screamed himself hoarse. She hated Wyatt. She felt like he'd stolen her last bit of whatever she had left that was hers, only hers, and when their two lives couldn't possibly become more intertwined, he conquered her final refuge, and with it, her sanity. Wyatt wasn't a baby she held in her arms. He was a monster that had crawled back inside of her. He was a cancer, a seething malignancy sucking the life out of her. But that wasn't what made her seize up. Her hatred flashed so hot in her mind that horrible, disturbing thoughts cascaded across her brain like the shower was dropping napalm on her head. She wanted to hurt Wyatt. She wanted to—but she would never. She didn't think so at least.

And she hadn't. But she had confided in her mom. An innocent question at first. *Did you ever, get like, stressed out and feel a little crazy?* Lisa had asked. *Sure,* Cathy replied. Then Lisa blurted out what had happened. That day in the shower and once more after that. Cathy's face was serene. It was kind but sad. She hadn't known what to say, only that it didn't seem normal and that maybe she needed to get some more sleep. Cathy had taken shifts of watching Wyatt so Lisa could sleep, but sleep didn't help. When Lisa slept more, all she wanted to do was sleep. Or not really sleep but lay in bed and think about all the things she should be doing but didn't want to or couldn't—it was the same thing now.

Lisa stood up from the floor of the kitchen. Cathy held Wyatt as she looked at Lisa's clothes soaked in milk. Cathy put her body between Lisa and Wyatt. Subconscious, surely, but blatant.

"I'm starting to get really worried about you, honey," Cathy said and rubbed Lisa's back.

"I'm fine, Mom. It's called stress.

I'm not sleeping."

"I think you should see a doctor." She bent down to pick up pieces of the broken ceramic bowl.

"Don't do that. You'll cut yourself," Lisa said and began picking up the pieces herself. She cut her finger on a small, sharp piece and it pumped crimson, spilling into the pool of milk on the floor.

"Of course. Of course," Lisa said. She squeezed her finger, trying to stop the bleeding.

"Let me see," said Cathy, looking carefully at the laceration. "Now you have to see a doctor. You need stitches."

Lisa sucked the blood away and pried the flayed edges apart on her finger. It filled with blood before she could see how deep the cut was. Cathy handed her a paper towel and Lisa wrapped it up tightly. The towel turned red within seconds.

"I'll drive you," Cathy said.

"Where are you going to take me?" Lisa asked.

"There's an urgent care very close. They'll fix your finger and maybe recommend someone to see for your other stuff."

"I'm not going. My finger will be fine. I'm not going to talk to anyone about my *other stuff*," Lisa said, her heart pounding. She regretted telling mom what she felt. It was hard enough to mask her feelings when Wyatt's pediatrician asked her how she was doing. She always deflected during the check-ups, trying to keep the focus on Wyatt who by some miracle was growing and developing properly.

"I think—" Cathy tried to say.

"I'm not going!" Lisa shouted and took Wyatt away from her.

Lisa slammed the door to her room. She laid Wyatt in his crib and changed out of her milk-soaked clothes. She slid a new shirt over her head and realized she'd just stained it red with blood. The paper towel was dripping.

"Fuck," Lisa said.

Wyatt started crying as Lisa tried to change her clothes. Her exhaustion and pain gave way to anger. She tried to calm him, but he only screamed louder. His face turned red with effort. Lisa focused on the bleeding. It blocked any thoughts that threatened to bubble up. Any doubts. Her body went catatonic, like it had in the pool of milk, like in the shower. It was a defense mechanism. She felt her mind spinning just before she collapsed. It was trying to solve a puzzle, and as the pieces tried to fit together, it threw out solutions she'd heard before. Throw it away. Smother it. Leave it to rot. But the gears of her mind froze up long before it could solve something so unsolvable. In a way this was the solution. She got stressed out and froze up. No harm done. A broken bowl. A baby crying to exhaustion. She didn't want to hurt Wyatt. She loved Wyatt, and if she didn't, she wanted to. Cathy walked into the room, picked Wyatt up, and calmed him.

"Lisa, are you alright?" Cathy asked.

"Yeah," Lisa said. "Got lightheaded from the bleeding. You know, seeing your own blood and stuff. Almost passed out."

"Jesus, Lisa. Can you not be so goddamn stubborn? At least let me take you to the doctor for the finger." Cathy was surprisingly lucid. For the first time in her life, Lisa felt more unstable than her mom.

"That's fine," Lisa said. "I need to go."

croatia: five

It was around one in the morning when the crowd started to swell like an incoming tide. The speakers pounded out classic rock—Credence Clearwater Revival—music Lisa always associated with movies about Vietnam or hippies marching on the Washington monument, never with a drunken night in Europe, that was until now. Tomislav played the same twenty classic rock songs every night. It annoyed Angela and Lisa, but the patrons didn't notice. Even if they did, it didn't stop them singing off key, usually with the wrong words or noises that sounded like words that probably were before the whiskey and rakija spilled over their tongues.

"*Ej mačko, hoćeš provest jedan od devet života samnom?*" a man said to Lisa at the bar.

Lisa leaned over and shouted, "I don't speak Croatian."

"Sorry, sorry. You look so beautiful. I thought you must be Croatian. Only Croatian women are as beautiful as you."

"What did you say to me?"

"What?"

"In Croatian. What did it mean?"

The man paused and thought hard. "I called you kitty and asked if you wanted to spend one of your nine lives with me."

"Huh," Lisa said, "never heard that one."

The man was tall with a bald, bullet-shaped head and a shaved face. He was coated in a thick sheen of sweat. Lisa forced a smile and turned away. She felt great on cocaine. It was one of her favorite shifts ever. The drug made her brain spin, but in a good way, basically the exact opposite of alcohol. Instead of stuporous, heavy, and emotional, she felt productive, dialed in, and luminescent. She hadn't even thought about being tired until now, six hours into her shift. Between the deafening rock music and the men constantly hitting on her, she was fading.

"Did you want a drink?" Lisa asked.

"I've just been standing over there looking at all of these women and saw you, like an angel back there. I knew I had to talk to you." The man's eyes steadied on Lisa while his body swayed slightly, offbeat to the music, moving in response to some invisible wind.

"Thanks, but if you don't want a drink I've got work to do."

"What are you doing after?"

Lisa walked away. Sometimes, she didn't mind the attention. Sometimes, she liked it. She still felt guilty even though her and Luka weren't technically a couple. They'd never talked anything out or made a deal for exclusive rights. Still, she usually backed out if it came to exchanging numbers or the talk moved past the initial pickup line.

The only thing she did enjoy was when friendly and hopelessly drunks tried to start a conversation but couldn't remember what they'd asked. Too drunk to follow along, Lisa took the story wherever she wanted. Her uncle was Croatian. She was born in Fiji and loved to snorkel. She'd chartered a submarine to Antarctica. She'd hiked rain forests in Canada. She'd never left Nova Scotia till this summer. It was exciting to create a new narrative. Plus, it was practice for when she found a backstory she liked and would make it permanent. But for now, it was better for it to be fluid, ever-changing. At least for the boys at the bar. Even with the fake stories, she never hinted she was from Oregon. She worried she might run into someone who knew someone who knew someone who knew her, and that wasn't a risk Lisa was willing to take. For Luka, she'd given something closer to the truth. She'd grown up in the Pacific Northwest, lost her kid, wanted away from her mom, and came to Croatia looking for fun and adventure. But they rarely talked about the past. Luka seemed as disinterested in it as Lisa. They only brought it up to recall funny stories or interesting details to add to the current moment.

"How's it going?" Angela asked. Her eyes looked dull, hair frizzy, and sweat beaded down her nose.

"I've pretty much had it with men telling me I look like an angel. A fucking angel? Is that a good thing? Like genocidal, demon fighting angel or like Hallmark movie angel?" Lisa said.

"Need a pick-me-up?"

Lisa shook her head.

"How about a take-me-down?" Angela poured two shots of Jose Cuervo.

Lisa laughed. "You know me so well." They both toasted and downed the shots.

"Girls, please, I need you to work. We have customers wanting drinks. More party for them, less party for you," Tomislav said and then disappeared into the back again.

"Fuck that guy. Fucking creep," Angela said, and poured another shot.

"Tomislav?"

"Yeah. Takes a share of our tips and sits in the back so he can smell my change of clothes I keep in the locker."

"Oh my God, what?" Lisa tipped back the shot. "That's a terrible thing to say about him. He's always been nice to me."

"I saw him do it." Angela took her shot and slammed the glass down. "Fuck all men."

"Not me though, right?" The sweaty bullet-headed man was back at the bar and flanked by two of his friends. One was short and had a half smile leaning off the side of his crooked face. The other was a muscle bound twenty-year-old with a thick black beard and eyes that rolled around unfocused.

"Of course not. What will you fine gents have?" Angela said. She threw her accent on heavy in front of the customers—it added to the exoticism.

"So, you're saying you wouldn't sleep with us?" the short man said.

"Hey, guys, take it easy," Lisa said. She could feel anger throbbing up the back of her neck and tightening around her chest.

"What makes you think we'd fuck you, crnčuga?" the blacked-out man slurred, reeling from invisible wind and trying to stay awake.

Lisa recoiled at the word. She didn't know exactly what it meant but it was some derogatory slang for black people. Angela smiled. It was a scared smile. The type of smile Lisa had been forced to use a few times in her life. It was her way of trying to prevent violence from men who seemed ready to be violent. A smile to appease them when she wanted to bash a bottle over their heads. But she was smart enough to know that she had no edge. No advantage if things got violent. Angela knew too. Lisa looked toward the back to see if Tomislav was in sight, but he wasn't there. They were on their own.

"Gents, I think there's some late-night confusion. No disrespect here. Just—"

"Please, pay no attention to these guys." The bullet head man leaned forward. "They can't handle their rakija. They aren't real men. I know how to spot true beauty. Just because you skin is that color does not mean—"

"I think you better shut the fuck up right now," Lisa said.

"Whoa, we pay you both compliments and this is how you treat us?" the bullet-headed man said, throwing his arms up in confusion.

"You guys are cut off. Get out of here," Lisa shouted.

"It's alright," Angela said.

"No, it's not alright," Lisa said to Angela.

"You're lucky I don't slap both of you for being so arrogant," the blacked-out man said. Spit flew from his mouth as he spoke. Lisa grabbed a glass full of beer from someone sitting at the bar and threw it in his face.

"Get the message yet?" Lisa asked, anger surging around her like blinders. She could only see the man. The rest of the world was black fire.

"*Možeš odjebat!*" the man shouted. He tried to grab Lisa but slipped on the beer and fell to the floor. Lisa spit on him and tried to pour more beer on his head but was lifted and carried away by Tomislav. The world started to come back to life. Two of the Croatian men were trying to control their angry friend. Angela had her hands up shouting for calm. Jimi Hendrix's "All Along the Watchtower" blasted over the speakers, unperturbed by the chaos below.

Lisa stayed in the back. Tomislav didn't say a word. He had put her down on the couch and ran back out to the bar. He didn't look scared or worried. If anything, he looked how a fireman does when they get the call to run out and do their job. He was ready for his moment. Lisa supposed it was only a matter of time before someone got out of line.

The cocaine had worn off and the alcohol left her sleepy and introspective. Had she been wrong? She didn't think so. Those guys had been way over the line. First the racist comment to Angela, then they talked to Lisa like she was less than human. A piece of meat. Disposable. And Angela, even less. She wouldn't stand for it. Tomislav shouldn't either. She was sure Tomislav would return, showering her in gratitude for doing what was right, but the longer it took for him to return from the front, the more she doubted herself.

Well, if that was the case, she didn't want to work in this place anymore. If this was normal, or accepted, or supported, then she was going to get out of the whole fucking country and move to Norway or Alberta, someplace where women were treated fairly, revered even.

Lisa started spinning herself into a stubborn, angry loop until she cemented herself in the opinion that Tomislav was a chauvinistic pig, and the whole male culture here was toxic in general, and maybe, as sweet and caring as he seemed, Luka deep down was the same as those drunk guys at the bar tonight, and he didn't give a shit about her either. He was just like Bryan, and her dad, and every other man. To them, Lisa wasn't an equal. She wasn't a person. Men didn't want Lisa. They wanted a caricature. A body to touch. Eye candy. They were all the same. Kindness was all just a smoke screen. Tomislav was just some fat prick with a small dick and a testosterone-poisoned brain.

Tomislav opened the door from the front. No music followed him through. The bar was closed and silent except the sound of Angela gathering glasses. Lisa looked at her watch. It was almost four in the morning.

"Are you okay, Lisa? You are crying. Why are you crying?" Tomislav asked.

Angela stood in the doorway holding a bucket of glasses, her face tired but resilient. She slumped against the doorframe, obviously ready for the night to be over.

Lisa wiped away the tears. She felt the angry thoughts returning. "Tomislav, what did you do with those men?"

"I kicked them out. Why? What did you think I did? Offered them my niece's hand in marriage?" Tomislav laughed. Angela did too, nervously. The room filled with silence. Lisa stared warily at Tomislav.

"Why did you have me stay back here? If they left, I could've worked," Lisa said.

"Me and Angela took care of it. Don't worry about it. I won't dock your pay."

"It's fine, Lisa," Angela said. "Seriously, after the drama, most of the people left and there wasn't much to do."

"I was standing up for you," Lisa said to Angela.

"I know. I appreciate that. Believe me. It's happened so many times since I've been here that I don't even get angry anymore. But I should," Angela said.

They all sat in silence for a minute. Lisa thought about forgetting about the whole thing and going home, but part of her had to know.

"Do you go through our things in the locker when we're out front?" Lisa asked.

Tomislav scrunched his face up and cocked his head. "I don't really know what you are saying."

"Lisa, don't," Angela said.

"You know exactly what I'm saying," Lisa said.

"No, actually I don't. And I don't like what you are hinting at."

"You smell our clothes while we are working out front. Just admit it. Fucking admit it. You could at least have the decency to do that."

Angela shook her head.

"Lisa, where do you get this stuff?" Tomislav said.

"Just admit it you pig."

"I've had enough."

"You've had enough?"

"You're fired. Please go. I will not tolerate this," Tomislav said. He pointed his finger at Lisa and then at the door. He looked like he might cry or yell or throw up.

"I don't need this fucking job," Lisa said. She wiped tears away from her face and grabbed her things from the locker.

Tomislav put a stack of Kuna on the table. "Here's your tips from tonight. I don't have to give them to you, but I am trying to be a good man. I don't want to see you around here again."

Lisa grabbed the money. "The world is the same everywhere."

"Maybe for you," Tomislav said, and walked out of the room.

oregon: five

Lisa clocked out Friday feeling good. She'd started work as a cashier at Fred Meyer and was finishing her first week. She loved it, surprisingly. If someone had asked her year ago if she'd be happy working as a cashier at Fred Meyer, she would've thought it was impossible, but a lot had changed since then. Most notably—besides Wyatt's birth—her mood was better.

The day she cut her finger and went to the doctor ended up being positive. Even though she thought he'd scorn her, call the police or at the very least, Child Protective Services, he'd listened, slowly nodding as she relayed her darkest thoughts and worries. He'd even handed her a tissue when she talked about wanting to hurt Wyatt and began to cry. She couldn't believe it once it came out. She hadn't planned on telling him. The thought was so disturbing that she had trouble admitting it to herself. But she'd said it, and then it was out in the world, out in the open, like a summer cold, or a feral dog, something no one wanted and yet was there all the same. But the doctor hadn't been disgusted with her. She'd felt disfigured, ugly, maybe even downright evil, and the doctor had looked her right in the eye like she was anyone else. He started her on Zoloft, an antidepressant. It was a long way from a magic happy pill, but it made her life livable. She was able to find joy in little boring things—like working at Fred Meyer.

"Have a good weekend, Lisa!" her manager said as Lisa walked out of the store. It was summer again and the late afternoon heat slammed up against her perpetually air-conditioned body. She had a sudden flash back to last summer, still pregnant and living with Bryan, sitting in the baseball stands with her stomach the size of the moon. It seemed like a long time ago. Lisa headed out of the parking lot, turned left onto the road, and drove another ten minutes to a small gray house. Before she even got out of her car, she could hear laughing children.

Janet—an older, robust woman in a simple dress and heavy red glasses—held open the door. Her silver-streaked hair was pulled back in a thick braid.

"Hello, dear. How was work? Everything go, okay?" Janet asked. "Jameel, don't touch that. Please don't touch that. We talked about that. Thank you."

A young boy, four maybe five, backed away from whatever he was touching that he wasn't supposed to. There were about five kids in the house, all different ages and races, yet somehow everyone got along like a family. Wyatt had only started daycare this week, but Lisa stopped worrying after the first day after she'd heard how much he'd laughed and giggled, and she saw how Janet held him lovingly in the backyard. In fact, Lisa heard about all the things Janet was working on with Wyatt and had a somewhat guilty feeling that maybe Wyatt was better off at daycare than he was at home. Janet knew what she was doing. She'd been doing it a long time and she was good at it.

The Zoloft had helped with a lot of things, but Lisa still got pangs to escape. More for Wyatt's sake than her own. Watching someone like Janet effortlessly take care of him and make him happy made her feel like maybe she should leave. But not today. Today she felt successful and content and thankful for the weather, the weekend, and Wyatt.

Lisa walked into the house. There were toys strewn about. Wyatt sat on the carpet with Maggie, Janet's daughter, who was ten or eleven, a skinny girl, timid, with her black hair pulled back into a braid like her mother. She was holding some plastic keys out for Wyatt, and he was reaching for them, letting them brush his fingertips, and laughing each time Maggie pulled them away. Lisa kneeled down next to Wyatt, planting a kiss on his forehead. She scooped him up, and he began to cry.

"Oh, it's okay," Maggic said and then started singing a Taylor Swift song, which made Wyatt laugh.

"He is such a joy," Janet said. "He lights up this whole place."

"Yeah, he's a real party starter," Lisa said and hugged Wyatt closer.

"So, did the schedule work out?" Janet asked. She grabbed Lisa's bag and walked toward the door.

"Worked out perfect," Lisa said. "I was promised a similar schedule next month. Can I pay at the end of the month?"

"Of course you can," Janet said, waving Lisa off. "I know you're good for it and I know you won't get your first check for a while."

"Okay, thanks. I'm really glad he's happy here. Makes going to work a lot easier," Lisa said.

Janet rubbed Wyatt's back and soon they were loaded up, and back on the road. Lisa looked at Wyatt through the rearview mirror. He was zoning out, staring back into his own reflection or marveling at the sunbeams bouncing through the window. For a moment, everything was perfect.

Lisa pulled up to her new place, a basement in a nice house, on the edge of Lake Oswego. The lake and city were bustling in the summer. People walked the main street in search of a cold beer from the local brewery or a scoop of ice cream, and the lake was full of speed boats pulling wakeboards and tubes. It was far too expensive for Lisa to ever hope to rent or buy here on her own, but the basement she rented was Bryan's family friend's house, and they were letting her stay for cheap.

She pulled into the driveway and went around to the passenger side to pull Wyatt out when she noticed Bryan's truck pulling in behind her. The humidity coming off the lake and mixing with the heat from her car made standing next to the open rear door impossible. She grabbed Wyatt from his car seat and carried him toward the house.

"Hey, wait a second," Bryan said, stepping out of his truck. "I know you saw me. Why do you have to be like this? You're running away like you don't even see me?"

"It's hot, Bryan," Lisa said, opening the garage door into the basement and placing Wyatt on the carpet inside the air-conditioned room. He was asleep.

"Listen, I only have a minute," Bryan said and then glanced over his shoulder. His girlfriend was in the car. The one that might still be in high school. They'd met at the restaurant. Lisa wanted to yell, *Make him wear a condom or you'll be in deep shit*, but thought better of it. Meanwhile, here Lisa was with her piece of crap car, Fred Meyer employee shirt, and a basement rental that Bryan had set up. Everything good suddenly felt depressing.

"You only have a minute?" Lisa asked.

"I just have to be somewhere in a minute, but I wanted to stop by," Bryan said.

"How kind."

"Please don't be like this. I don't want there to be drama every time we get together."

"We don't get together that often."

"I'd like to see Wyatt more often. I really would."

"Okay, Bryan," Lisa said. "What can I help you with?"

"What can I say? I'm doing my best," Bryan said.

Lisa scoffed. "Your best. How many times have you even seen Wyatt in the past year? Five? Six times?"

A mild look of surprise came over his face as he realized that over the span of Wyatt's life, he'd only spent a week's worth of time with him. "We can't all be you, Lisa. I'm glad he's got you."

Lisa almost laughed and cried simultaneously. *If only you knew what it was like to be me*, she thought.

"You're enjoying the place, aren't you?" he asked.

"The basement. You're talking about the basement."

Bryan leaned on the car but quickly removed his hand from the hot metal. "You're making this impossible."

"Thanks for the basement rental, where your son lives." Her words were all spikes and poison. Her tongue felt like a sea urchin.

"I'm trying to do the right thing."

"Is that a tattoo?" Lisa asked and pulled down the neck of his polo shirt.

Beneath was italic lettering across his chest—Wyatt. He was so proud of his accomplishment, Lisa thought. That was what Wyatt was. A finished product that he would take credit for. Lisa would end up killing herself to raise him right and Bryan would always be his dad, regardless of whether he put the work in.

"I thought you'd like it," Bryan said, looking down at his chest.

"I'd like it better if you just helped take care of him instead of getting tattoos of his name."

"That's what I'm here to talk about." Bryan looked back at the truck. His girlfriend was scrolling on her phone. He wiped sweat from his brow. Lisa peaked inside at Wyatt. Still asleep.

"I'm moving," Bryan said. He made a 'there-there' face as if he expected Lisa to collapse into his arms and beg him not to go.

"What, to Vancouver?" Lisa asked.

"Wyoming."

Lisa nodded like she'd always known but had only now allowed herself to accept it.

"I would ask you what is in Wyoming, but I imagine people there would probably ask you what the hell is in Oregon. The difference though, is that your son is here. So, Bryan, what the fuck is in Wyoming, and if you tell me it has anything to do with this junior prom bitch over there, I'm going to lose my shit." Lisa felt a quiet rage pulsing in her chest. If he was really going to leave, then she was really going to let him have it.

"A job," Bryan said. "With real money this time. Life changing money, for you, for Wyatt. They want me to open up another restaurant in Cheyenne and if that goes well, then, who knows. But I want you to know, it's all for Wyatt. I'm doing this so he can have a better life. You too, Lisa. I want you to be happy."

Lisa put a hand over her eyes. "You think the way to give your son a better life is to move away?"

"You guys can come visit on weekends."

"You think I'm going to come visit you? Stay at your house? Sleep in your bed?" Lisa's face contorted and her upper lip curled.

"Let's try and be adults here, okay?"

Lisa got within inches of Bryan's face. "I'm the only adult here."

"Sure, whatever. You don't need to come. I meant as a courtesy. Wyatt can come visit. Weekends. Summertime. When he's a little older. He won't need you then."

"You're living in a fantasy, Bryan. Good luck in wherever the hell Cheyenne is."

Bryan began walking back to his truck. "I bet you'll still cash the checks, though. You can act all tough, but you'll still take handouts."

She glared so hard the world went blurry. She had an overwhelming urge to slap him across the face. To grab his head and slam it into the windshield and then drag it across the hot cement. She wanted to scream, *It's not a handout you stupid piece of shit, you're his dad!* but she stayed calm. Maybe it was the Zoloft, maybe it was just that she was too tired to really care anymore.

Lisa walked inside and closed the door behind her. Bryan's tires screeched as he drove off. Wyatt was still asleep, unperturbed by the raised voices and squealing tires. She took a moment and once everything had registered, felt happy. Now she was really wondering if the Zoloft was messing with her mind. Bryan being gone meant she didn't have to worry about recruiting him to help or talk him into spending time with Wyatt. It also meant, if Bryan was to be believed, that there would be more money in those measly child support checks. The downside, obviously, was that Wyatt would see Bryan very little—if at all. As much as that might have broken her heart before, she felt nothing now.

That evening, while Lisa flipped through cable network channels and Wyatt played on the floor, an urge overcame her. She hadn't felt it in a long time. It was part restlessness, part indulgence. The way she explained it to herself was that she deserved to be rewarded. More than that, she deserved a break. She hadn't let the thought pass since she'd been out with Jessica and Holly and had the subsequent breakdowns. She hadn't allowed herself to believe that she needed a break, or she needed a reward, because all she really thought about was how she was a horrible parent, and sometimes, a terrible person. But her brain didn't work like that now. She had things to be proud of. She was doing a good job with Wyatt. She was making money. They had a place of their own. She was doing her best.

Lisa pulled out her phone and skimmed through the numbers. She realized she had Amber's number. Amber was a coworker from Fred Meyer. They'd been in the same training group at corporate and had exchanged numbers during orientation. Amber was a mom, too. Double mom. She had a three- and a seven-year-old. Lisa barely knew Amber, but she'd given Lisa her number and said, Call me sometime. Us moms got to let loose too, right?

Before Lisa knew what she was doing, she had pressed the dial button and the phone was ringing.

"Yo," Amber said.

"Uh, hi," Lisa said.

"Who is this?"

"It's, uh, Lisa from Fred Meyer."

"Lisa from—oh okay. Hey, Lisa. How you doin' girl?"

Lisa relaxed when Amber started sounding like she did in person. At first, she was worried she'd dialed the wrong number.

"I'm doing pretty good. I just, you know, you can totally say no, but I was wondering if—"

"You wanna go grab a drink or something?"

"Yes!" Lisa almost shouted and then felt the hot flush of embarrassment. "Yes. I thought, you know, if you can get someone to watch your—"

"Oh please. He's watching them right now. It won't be any different if I take off for a while. You thinking tonight?"

Lisa looked at Wyatt playing quietly on the floor and then at the clock. It was seven.

"Let me call you right back."

Cathy had been more than accommodating, and surprisingly sober when Lisa placed the call. *I'm glad you're going out. Wyatt will be fine. Don't drink so much and you'll have a great time.*

Lisa said *Thanks*, rather than responding with *Don't pass out on the couch and ignore my baby and you got a deal.* She owed Cathy. Cathy had been consistently coming through for her—from watching Wyatt to paying to get her Jetta fixed so she could drive to work. Tonight, her mom seemed happier than Lisa was about her going out. On the drive out to meet Amber, Lisa wondered if Cathy saw too much of herself in Lisa. The shutting in. The silent, withdrawing depression or whatever it was. Catatonic, nauseating, overwhelming angst. Lisa remembered some of it. They were her earliest memories besides those of her dad. Her mom losing it in the kitchen with the stove on fire. Lisa screaming from the smoke and her mom staring at the black plumes with a placid acquiescence, like she was welcoming the flames but was also scared of the pain. Cathy pressing herself against the wall like a smashed spider, her hands spastic and tremulous while her trunk contorted into a sickly, paralytic posture as the flames danced along the popcorn ceiling. Lisa just screamed. Screamed until Cathy snapped out of it and doused the flames with water.

Lisa pulled up to a bowling alley. *Hollywood Bowl,* the neon light exclaimed. Inside, the walls were a dirty beige with shiny red velvet booths strewn above the gleaming wood alleys. Lisa walked right past the scattering of teenagers, *old professionals,* and drunk college kids from Portland State University and headed for the bar in the back corner. It smelled like shoe cleaner and popcorn, but Lisa didn't mind. There at the bar, hunched over a yellow, bubbly beer, was Amber.

Amber was dressed in grey Jordan sweats. Her black hair accented her dark eyes and round face. She wore no makeup. She looked tired but also pretty. Lisa wondered if she looked tired too. Amber didn't have the bags under her eyes of a laborer or an addict but instead bore a wisdom—like she might sprout grey hairs any minute. It was the fatigue that came from carrying the burden of multiple lives dependent upon you. It wore people thin. Lisa put her hand up to her cheek and could feel herself ageing. When Amber stood up to greet her, it was almost comical how short she was. They hugged, briefly, because they were still strangers to some extent. Lisa sat down at the bar and immediately became self-conscious, feeling the nagging urge to leave and the suspicion that Amber never wanted her to come in the first place. Amber must have noticed, because she took a drink from her beer and said, "I'm glad you came out. I know we don't know each other, really. But what better way to fix that than by having a few drinks. Away from the kids. Shit, it's not just for men, you know?"

Lisa couldn't help but smile. She was one of those "though she be but little, she be fierce" type of women. Lisa ordered a beer. She hadn't had a drink since going out with Jessica and Holly. The whole night had unraveled in a way that made her not want to repeat the experience. But tonight was different. She had the Zoloft now. It didn't fix everything, but it made her believe she could handle a few drinks.

"So, how's life, Lisa?" Amber asked, sipping her beer, and

staring up at the baseball game playing on the television.

"That's a big question," Lisa said.

Amber smiled. Just lips, no teeth. "See, I knew I liked you. Honest. Some people you can just tell."

"What do you mean?"

"I mean you didn't just spit out a bull shit answer like, oh fine, because when is life ever just fine?"

"Maybe for a split second at a time," Lisa said, and drank some of her beer. It was flat but cold and easy to drink.

"My life is pretty complex right now. I got my kids and the youngest one's dad is around. I think you knew that," Amber said and Lisa nodded in agreement. "Anyway, dad number one is skulking around lately wanting to get back involved and my oldest, Victor, he's not interested. And I'm not super interested either, you know, but also it seems like a shitty thing to do to keep his dad away from him, even if he is sorta a scumbag. And Mike—that's my boyfriend's name— he's like a dad to Victor, but it just won't ever really be the same. Not with his real dad alive and well."

Amber kept talking and Lisa disappeared into her own head. She thought of her own dad and wondered why he never tried to reconnect with her. Then she realized, he probably had, and mom had kept him away. Lisa wasn't sure if she was happy about it or heartbroken. She felt a pang of regret even though none of it had been in her power to fix, or had it? She could've reached out. She could've gotten to know him. Wyatt would never know him. Wyatt might not even know his own father. How much of the responsibility was on Lisa to make sure that Bryan kept in contact? None, as far as Lisa was concerned. Bryan—Bryan was on his way to Cheyenne now, and as long as the checks kept coming, he could be dead for all she cared.

"Lisa?" Amber asked.

"Huh," Lisa said, snapping back to reality.

"Want another?"

"Sure. Sure, uh, I'll have whatever you're having."

"Two shots of fireball and two margaritas."

Lisa scoffed. "Whoa, I have to drive."

"Relax. We'll stop drinking after that and I'll bowl a game with you so we can sober up. Your babysitter is cool, right?"

Lisa had a vision of Cathy passed out on the couch and Wyatt screaming in the crib, face wet with tears, but she felt apathy instead of panic. The numbness confused her. She worried she was having a stroke or maybe a nervous breakdown. Nothing seemed to matter for a minute. And then she realized what it was. The alcohol. One beer and she was able to let it all go. She was able to stop feeling guilty. Wyatt wasn't crying in his crib at home. Her mom wasn't passed out. They were probably cuddling in bed, falling asleep peacefully. Lisa could have fun, live her life, be a twenty-one-year-old and not a mom for a few hours.

"Okay," Lisa said, hesitantly. "But I got the next round."

A shot and a margarita later, Lisa was laughing and throwing the heavy bowling ball down the waxy alley, watching it ricochet off bumpers and collide with pins. Life became a blurry home video. She was drunk but not wildly so. She felt like a warm blanket and a fond memory. Everything was good. Amber was the best friend she never had. Bowling was the greatest game on earth. Cathy was a great grandma and Wyatt was a happy go lucky kid.

When Lisa drove home that night, the road felt like a trampoline as the Jetta bounced along. She was in a cartoon land. The hard, steel edges of the cars moving alongside her were friendly and harmless. She thought about ricocheting off them into the Willamette River and sinking down into the black where it would be peaceful, and everything would be okay.

When Lisa woke up the next morning with a hangover, she remembered that moment and how sure she'd been that drowning in the river would fix everything. She stared at Wyatt and told herself that it couldn't be true. The other part of her thought about a place of peace at the bottom of a river and realized that death wasn't a way to escape, only disappear.

Months later, Lisa spoke on the phone to Amber while Wyatt sat on the floor, plastic toys in each hand, crashing them together and paying Lisa no mind.

"I swear to God sometimes he is deaf," Lisa said over the phone to Amber. "No. He's still not walking either. I know. I know. I'm trying not to worry. He hasn't been to the doctor for a checkup since his nine-month. I just got busy and missed the last one. Trust me, I feel bad. Bryan was here a month ago and freaking out because he read all the milestones, and now, he's like a goddamn expert. Yeah, well, whatever. I was going to take him in any way to get his shots. He's way behind."

Lisa talked for a few more minutes and then hung up the phone. She lay on the floor with Wyatt and picked up a toy. She crashed it into Wyatt's, making the sounds of a collision and Wyatt giggled.

"Hi, honey. Hi, baby," Lisa said staring into Wyatt's eyes. Wyatt giggled more but stared right past Lisa, making her feel invisible or inanimate. She grabbed Wyatt under the arms and pulled him face to face with her. His face contorted. His lip turned up and trembled. Lisa moved Wyatt back and forth in the air. Every time he tried to look away, she readdressed his gaze, and each time she did, Wyatt would look away. *Has he ever made eye contact with me?* Lisa wondered. Cathy walked through the side door just as Wyatt started to cry.

"Do you ever feel like Wyatt might be blind?" Lisa asked.

Cathy took Wyatt from Lisa's hands. She had a way of doing that. Taking over whenever she was in the room.

"What are you doing to him?" Cathy asked. She looked him over like she was checking for wounds. Wyatt stopped crying and started giggling. She spoke baby talk to him.

"I'm not doing anything. I was checking his vision," Lisa said.

"By making him cry?"

"No. Never mind."

Lisa started packing her things for work. It was Saturday so daycare wasn't open, but Cathy had continued her sober renaissance and offered to watch Wyatt on the Saturdays she had to work. Cathy lifted Wyatt into the air just as Lisa did. Wyatt stared right past her, but Cathy didn't seem to notice. She smiled and rubbed noses with him.

"Wyatt is perfect," Cathy said. "It's normal to be a little worried, but you're doing a good job."

"I know," Lisa said, trying to convince herself.

"I'm proud of you for getting your own place. And your job seems great. There is a lot of room to move up at a place like Fred Meyer."

Lisa nodded but secretly felt stupid for taking praise for things she was supposed to do. It was like, *Good job, Lisa, you breathe air. Way to go, kiddo.* It didn't feel right. That being said, she was doing more than almost anyone else her age. At least anyone she knew. No one had kids. No one was even married, really. She had a few friends on Facebook that had gotten engaged—Bryan included. Why she was friends with Bryan on Facebook was one of the great mysteries of the universe. But she was, and had seen his engagement post, and then proceeded to almost puke.

"It's just that sometimes I feel like he's a little off, or something," Lisa said.

Cathy spoke in a baby voice. "No, he's not. No, he's not. He's such a big healthy boy. Yes, he is."

"Even Janet said something."

"Janet? The woman from daycare? What does she know?" Cathy said, putting Wyatt back on the floor. "Don't you have to go to work?"

Lisa looked at her phone. "Shit, yeah, I do. Wyatt has food in the cabinet and milk in the fridge."

"Sounds good. Have a good day at work."

Work was dead. Lisa and Amber spent most of the shift chatting as Amber brought in carts from outside. Lisa stood at the checkout stand and wondered why anyone would use anything but the self-checkout.

These last few months had been Lisa's first taste of the drawl of daily work, and she was beginning to understand the banality of it all. Especially when it was something as mindless as checking people out at Fred Meyer. At first, she was happy just to have a job, and then she was happy to have a paycheck. It was freeing to be financial stable—with help from Bryan's paychecks of course—but now it all felt equally confining as she looked down the road of life and saw it stretched out toward the horizon: empty, flat, and joyless. Amber didn't share Lisa sentiment.

"This whole thing is bullshit," Lisa said.

"What whole thing?" Amber asked.

"This job."

"This job has benefits."

Lisa shrugged. "Lots of jobs have benefits. This job is benefitting from me more than I am benefitting from some retirement plan."

Amber opened a Snickers bar from the shelf in front of Lisa's checkout stand. She bit into it and talked as chocolate stuck to her teeth. "I feel like you haven't had very many jobs because this is a good one. It might not be like some Silicon Valley shit"—she said it like Silicone—"but I've had others, and benefits do not come standard. Neither does—"

"Why do you do that?" Lisa asked.

Amber narrowed her eyes, looking at Lisa sideways. "Excuse me?"

"I thought we were friends but then you do this thing where you talk to me like you're my mom or big sister or something. I know there are benefits. My point wasn't that there aren't good benefits here or good pay or whatever. I'm just looking for more. Aren't you?"

"More how?"

"I don't know. I want to travel. See the world. Climb some mountains in New Zealand or snorkel in Madagascar."

"You need to keep your head on straight and take this job one day at a time. You've got a kid to think about," Amber said, and disappeared outside to get more carts.

It was true. Amber was older. She'd seen more, done more, but that didn't make Lisa's experience obsolete. Lisa figured Amber felt the same but didn't want to talk about it.

That night when Lisa got home and put Wyatt to bed, she poured herself a glass of Diet Sprite and put three shots of vodka in it. It had become a nightly custom since the night at the bowling alley a few months back. It made her feel grown up. Go to work, come home, and have a drink. She had no reason not to. Wyatt was asleep, the bills were paid, Bryan was in Cheyenne with his soon to be ex-wife, and Cathy was happy in her little hole of a house, popping pills and lying half-awake in a recliner. Lisa sipped her drink. It basically tasted like Sprite, which Lisa liked, and she drank it quickly. She liked drinking every night. She knew there were negatives, or at least understood that drinking daily was frowned upon in open society, but she drank Diet Sprite, so she didn't put on any weight, and had a long time before it became a problem. Her mom had taught her that to some extent. Then again, it wasn't clear if the pills were always the problem or if Cathy was.

Lisa wished she could say that, underneath her drug fog, her mom was happy and bright and kind, but all Lisa could remember was that she was frazzled, quick to snap and depressed. Lisa hadn't known what to call it then, but she had been depressed. Lisa caught her crying while folding the same hamper of clothes every night for a few weeks. Lisa asked her what was wrong, and Cathy shouted, spanked her, and sent her to her room. Lisa hadn't realized until now what that was all about. Now she understood. To some extent at least. She'd never hit Wyatt, but she understood how lonely and hopeless life as a single parent can feel. Even though Cathy had been better lately—she was very sweet to Wyatt—it was tough to know who she even was anymore. Was she the past or the future?

The drinks at night not only felt like a reasonable reward to Lisa, but they helped her. Helped her sleep, feel calm, even get off the Zoloft. Lisa had been off the Zoloft for about three weeks now. She wondered if it had fried her brain, because she felt numb—and not the good kind—the lobotomized, hysterectomized kind. Sex hadn't crossed her mind in months. And now off the Zoloft, even though the idea of it happening felt like an impossible fairy tale, she thought of sex almost daily. She felt human again.

It had a few downsides. Or, rather, potential downsides. The other night she had two drinks instead of just one and woke up in a drunken stupor to Wyatt's cries. He'd been fine, but Lisa had trouble keeping it together. Plus, she had a wicked hangover in the morning—full blown headache, puking up breakfast—and the whole thing felt way too much like the night out with Jessica and Holly, something Lisa tried to forget. She put the glass down on the coffee table, and the beads of condensation dripped down the sides. She watched them gather and form a ring around the bottom before soaking into the wood. She turned out the light and went to bed.

It was another month before Lisa took Wyatt to the doctor. Her insurance changed since working at Fred Meyer and she had to go to a new office. She filled out the pre-visit paperwork and each question chipped away at what little confidence she'd retained.

Had Wyatt seen a dentist?

Were there guns in the home?
Did he take a multivitamin?
Does he do calculus and listen to Mozart?
Does he drink green smoothies and listen to NPR?
Was Lisa fit to be a mother, really?

She stopped answering questions and just wrote, See above. In the exam room, Wyatt started to cry, and Lisa tried to answer more questions she didn't know the answer to. Lisa had never taken him to this clinic before, and they didn't have the record for his vaccines. When the assistant suggested getting six shots in one day, Lisa shook her head.

"That's a joke, right?" Lisa asked.

"Well, he's due for six. The Haemophilus influenza B, measles, mumps, rubella, and, let me check the computer," the assistant said. She smiled at Wyatt and shushed him, like it was all a cute act he was putting on. That always bothered Lisa about doctors and healthcare people: they always seemed so casual in the face of distress. People screaming from pain, kids crying from needles, people scared for their lives. Meanwhile doctors and nurses and this assistant who wanted to poke Wyatt with six goddamn needles didn't even say a word when people were obviously upset and clearly terrified, Lisa thought.

"Three is fine," Lisa said.

"Which three—"

"Whatever three the doctor wants. Okay?" Lisa said and started bouncing Wyatt on her knee. When the doctor came in twenty minutes later, she didn't apologize for being late, said a quick hello, and started touching Wyatt.

"Hello, Wyatt," the doctor said. Turtle shell glasses framed her dark brown eyes. Her black hair was braided tightly behind her, and she had a thick accent. Wyatt started screaming but the doctor began clicking her tongue against the roof of her mouth and Wyatt giggled in response.

"Oh, there you go. There is the laugh," the doctor said.

"What is your name?" Lisa asked.

"Dr. Chowdry. Miss, Lisa? Is that right?"

"Just Lisa."

"Lisa. You have a beautiful baby boy here, just beautiful," Dr. Chowdry said, and continued clicking her tongue. Lisa felt an irresistible smile spread across her face as the guilt and worry gave way for a brief moment and she allowed herself to feel proud.

"Thank you," Lisa said, and let out a breath she didn't know she was holding.

Dr. Chowdry talked more about immunizations and milestones. She told Lisa she didn't see anything concerning today. Wyatt was a bit behind, but milestones are things each child hits at their own pace—some ahead of schedule and some behind. Lisa still wouldn't agree to the six shots though. Three sounded like plenty.

"I'd like to see him back in two months though. We need to follow up on the lack of eye contact and crawling. He should be crawling, and he should be making eye contact," Dr. Chowdry said in a way that Lisa felt like she was being scolded.

"Yeah, I know," Lisa said, her tone more defensive than she intended.

"Don't worry, Lisa. I am here for you one way or another. If there is something wrong, we just want to catch it early. We can't let these things fester," Dr. Chowdry said.

Lisa didn't respond. Her face felt hot as she thought about the word, fester. She didn't want Wyatt to fester. On the drive home, she started to think that Dr. Chowdry's compliments had been a ploy. The staff was probably talking about her in the hallway. Probably going through the papers and shaking their heads, jotting down notes. It had been a mistake to bring Wyatt there. The doctor wasn't an expert. Lisa doubted Dr. Chowdry even had any kids. She didn't know what it was like to raise a baby—alone. Lisa's fingers went numb. She gripped the steering wheel so tight her fingers lost blood flow. She took a deep breath and tried to tell herself that it all wasn't a huge mistake.

Amber texted her that night asking how it went. Lisa didn't touch the phone. She let it sit as she drank her second vodka and Diet Sprite. She felt guilty thinking she'd done something to damage Wyatt—to delay his growth and development. Lisa knew she hadn't, at least, she didn't think so, but the guilt came anyway. Her mind wrestled with the idea that she, the mother who was tasked with nothing but the protection of her child, had been the one to damage him. As her mind wrestled, it produced some of the same thoughts that had caused it to shut down in the past. The same thoughts that had made her go on the mind-numbing Zoloft. The same thoughts that made her want to leave this life, and never come back. The guilt made her angry. Angry at Bryan for being a deadbeat. At Wyatt for being born. At the world for fucking her over. But mostly, and most indiscriminately, at herself. Lisa turned off the lamp and sat in the dark. The house was quiet except for the ice cubes clicking against the glass. If she couldn't escape, maybe her mind could.

croatia: six

Lisa left the bar in a tearful rage. She was as mad at Tomislav as she was with the racist assholes that'd started the whole mess. She was mad at everyone. The world felt unfair—an unprecedented unfairness—at least it did in the moment, though she knew better. She knew how callous and unfeeling the world could be. This was just a taste of the sadness and anger it could bring. She started walking home. It was the middle of the night, or early morning. A few people walked the streets heading to work and a handful of drunks staggered around, crisscrossing the street in an attempt to stay upright.

Lisa pulled out her phone and dialed Luka's number. She wiped tears away and blew her nose on the sleeve of her jacket. The other side of the line remained empty and automated, echoing back each hollow ring but never leading to Luka's familiar voice. She hung up.

She wandered down to the docks, sat down, and stared out at the sea. It was black and oily. She tried to calm her mind, but it spun with a toxic, electric energy. The urge to harm herself flashed across her mind but she hadn't done something like that in years. Still. The urge fumed in the background while her anger slowly dissolved into pain. The exact pain she was trying to avoid. It crashed like a wave and carried an unshakeable feeling that everything that had happened to her was for a reason, and the reason was that she deserved it.

Her phone rang. It was Luka. She picked it up.

"Lisa? It's like four in the morning. Is everything alright? Do I need to come get you?" Luka sounded both tired and worried.

"Tomislav is such an asshole," she said.

"What? What happened?"

"He fired me. He fired me for the most bullshit reason. I was standing up for Angela and—"

"He fired you?"

Lisa paused. "Yeah. That's what I just said."

"Oh man. That's not good, Lisa."

"Really? Fucking shit. I know it's not good. But you haven't even heard why it happened."

Luka yawned. "Okay, tell me what happened."

"You seem like you don't even care."

"No. I just was sleeping. It's like four in the morning. I'm very sorry this is happening to you. Do you want me to come meet you?"

"Never mind. I'm sorry I woke you up. We can talk tomorrow night."

"Okay." Luka sounded relieved. "I will talk to Tomislav tomorrow, too. Maybe I can straighten this all out, get your job back. He owes me a favor."

"I don't want the job back."

"Don't you need the job? How are you going to—"

"Just forget I ever called you," Lisa said, and hung up.

Depleted, Lisa stopped walking. Maybe Luka was just like Tomislav and the men at the bar. Like Bryan. Like her dad. Like the world. She stayed on the docks until the first ferry appeared across the water. She rose out of the fog of rumination and realized she was cold and exhausted and ready to sleep. She walked the rest of the way home just as the sun started to come up. She hit her bed and fell asleep immediately. Her phone rang around seven. She ignored it, turned it off, and went back asleep to the sounds of cars and the sea.

She awoke to someone knocking on her door. It was Luka, looking annoyed and angry. His mouth was fixed in a straight line and his eyes had black watercolor brushes beneath them. She opened the door, but Luka didn't move. She rubbed her eye and stretched.

"Are you going to come in?"

"Did you turn your phone off or are you just purposefully ignoring me?" he asked, his face unchanged.

Lisa shook her head. "Just come in, okay? Just come in so we can talk."

"I've been trying to call you all day."

"My phone is off."

"I called and called and no answer. I don't know if you are hurt or on a plane back to America or—"

"I'm sorry. I'm sorry." Lisa grabbed Luka's hand. She squeezed it and kissed his cheek. "Come inside."

Luka came inside. His shoulders relaxed a little bit, but he still didn't smile. He sat on the edge of her bed. Her clothes were strewn on the floor and the bed. She hadn't realized how messy it was until she saw him juxtaposed against it. She started to pick up her clothes and realized how dirty everything else was.

"Don't worry about it, relax. Just sit down for a minute," Luka urged.

"I'm sorry. It's a total mess," Lisa said. Luka looked increasingly uncomfortable. His eyes avoided Lisa's and his hands rolled the comforter between his fingers. He stood up and walked toward the door.

"What are you doing?" she asked.

"I'll go. I'm sorry to bother you," he said.

"No, please stay. Or we can both go. I need out of here. Can I buy you a drink?"

"I don't know if you are in any position to buy me anything."

Lisa laughed. She wasn't sure why. She didn't want to, but the laugh escaped before she knew what she was doing. Her face flushed hot with embarrassment.

"I have money saved up. I'm not an idiot."

"You are not an idiot, I know. Now, Tomislav, that is something else. He is an idiot. Sounds like you really gave it to those guys."

Lisa was silent for a moment, and then said, "I did."

"Oh, I heard."

"And?"

"And I told Tomislav, '*Kretenski kmetu. Trebao si joj dati ratno odličje i odrezat liku kreditne kartice.*'"

Lisa pushed out her lips and scrunched her face. "I don't know what that means."

"I said the guy's a peasant! Cut up his credit card and you deserved a war medal for what you did."

"They did deserve it."

"Of course they did. They're lucky I wasn't there, or I'd take them down to the water and tie cinderblocks around their ankles."

They both stared at the floor, letting their smiles fade and silence sweep between them. Lisa felt alone in her thoughts. She still wasn't sure what the right thing to do had been. She'd done what she did and was okay with that. She was worried about getting another job, though. The tourist season was picking up, and many of the jobs she could do were already taken. And the savings she'd mentioned to Luka was nonexistent. She'd spent most of her money. Everything except the emergency fund. It was just enough money to buy her ticket home. If she spent that she'd be trapped. The only positive to come from the incident so far was that Luka was still on her side.

"I'm sorry, Luka," she said. "I'm sorry it's all such a mess. My apartment is a mess. My life is a mess. This isn't me. I'm better than this. I swear."

"I wouldn't change a thing about you," he said.

"I would."

They kissed and she felt happy for a second. It was gone before the kiss ended. She leaned back and opened her eyes, still in his arms. She worried he could read her mind and see her secrets. Luka's eyes were sad too—a stark contradiction to his smiling face. She hadn't realized that before. He was hiding something, too.

They headed down near the waterfront and sat outside watching the ferries unload and sailboats head out to sea. Lisa ordered some white wine. It was cold and tart and felt good going down her throat as the humid summer air drooped languidly around the edges of the city. Luka lit up a cigarette. The smell was nauseating and nostalgic at the same time. It made her think of her dad and of high school kids smoking by the river on summer nights. Luka pulled off the look. He was the cowboy, the rock star, the rebel, when he lit up. At least to her he was. It wasn't until he went through half a pack in a span of a few drinks that she saw it for what it really was. He was like an amalgamation of her parents. His fingers were busy on the plastic-coated cardboard pack searching for the next stick the same way her mom palmed child proof prescription lids—eagerly and effortlessly—subconsciously habitual and compulsive.

"I thought you quit," she asked, realizing now she hadn't seen him light up in weeks.

"You win some you lose some," he said, and shrugged.

Lisa sipped her wine and quickly ordered another.

"I don't mind that you smoke," she said.

"I mind. I'll quit. I just smoked today because I wanted to."

He dropped his cigarette into his beer bottle. She leaned over and felt the bare skin of his shoulder. It was hot from the sun beating down on it.

"Seriously, you do whatever you want. We should be able to be free with each other," she said.

It reminded her of her dad. It made Luka feel familiar yet mysterious. She would never admit to anyone that Luka's smoking reminded her of the dad she barely knew because, if she did, she'd feel dirty and a little ashamed. It wasn't some dad complex. She'd always carried a displaced love for her dad. And as much as she wanted to hate him—and told people she did—she never could. Her secret, yearning love was impossible to abandon because it belonged to someone who no longer existed.

Luka's friends dropped by their table and had a smoke or drank a beer. They'd start talking in English and after a few *Hi, how are you? and Are you liking Croatia?* they'd slip back into their native language and Lisa would sit and watch them converse, oblivious to the meat of the conversation. As the night grew darker and Lisa became drunker, the friends petered off and Luka suggested going out to a dance club or another café deeper in the city, away from the tourists and the docks. Lisa never gave a firm answer on whether she wanted to leave or not. She stared out into the black sea, her eyes glazing over until they teared up and the world became a wash.

"Do you think you're happy?" Lisa asked.

Luka opened his eyes wide, eyebrows raised in a comical look. "Oh man. We are going to get into some deep shit here." He grabbed another cigarette.

Lisa reached over and put her hand over his, the one holding the cigarette and about to light up, and he dropped it. "I'm serious."

He paused for a moment, their nystagmic gazes connecting. "I think I'm happy," he said.

"Why?"

"Because I know what being unhappy feels like."

"What do you mean?"

"I think when enough bad stuff happens to you, you begin to recognize when things are good, even when they aren't good enough, or could be better. I've personally been through enough bad shit to know when it's good. And life is good. It's good. I'm not blind. It's pretty straightforward, really."

Lisa blinked and felt like she might keep her eyes closed for the rest of the evening and her mouth would keep on talking. "I'm not talking about good. I'm talking about happy."

Luka waved her off. "Come on. What is the deal? Good. Happy. I don't think about these luxuries."

Lisa frowned at him. "These luxuries? This is life."

"I just don't know if I want to get so serious right now. I'm just trying to have a good time. Enjoy my time with you. Be happy. Right?"

"Life is serious, Luka."

"I know that better than anyone. I know that better than you." Luka's tone turned serious and intense.

"You don't know that. You don't even know me. We don't even know each other. I'm trying to know you, like, really know you. I just lost my job. I'm totally alone on the other side of the world, and all I have is you. And I know that's a ton to put on you, but I think we have something and I just, I want to know you."

Luka put his arms up and gave an exasperated look. "Okay, sure, Lisa. I want to know you too, whatever that means. But we can't force it, right? I can't just lay out my life story all in one go. Good relationships are built in pieces, and eventually they fit together, like a puzzle. We have to trust that each piece will fall in place at the right time and right place, and we won't know how it all works out until it's finished."

Lisa sucked her lower lip and bit it. "Don't fight this piece then. We'll have plenty of time to go out later, meet up with friends, and pass our time in pointless conversation. Just tell me, are you happy?"

Luka paused, and said, "No. But I'm not unhappy."

"So, you're in like a happiness purgatory," she said.

Luka lit up his cigarette, took a small inhale, and spoke through the smoke. "Sure, if that's the way you want to think about it. I like to think that I'm on the ladder of happiness. One rung at a time. I'm not trying to pretend I'm at the top, I just know I'm not at the bottom. This is a layover, not a prison."

"How do you know?"

Luka shook his head, "I don't want to get into all that. Sometimes the past is better left where it belongs. I just know."

Lisa stared at Luka. His eyes avoided her. There was something there. Something different than the burden she carried with her, always. He wasn't running from whatever it was. He wasn't trying to escape it. He'd accepted that it was part of him. A part he didn't like to visit. A part he'd love to amputate but knew better. It fueled him. It built him. She wanted to know more than he was letting on but tonight didn't feel like the right time to pry.

"I think of it as purgatory," Lisa said.

"So, you're saying you're not happy?" Luka asked.

"Did you think I was?"

Luka shook his head. "I wish I could say that you feeling that way makes me sad, but it doesn't. It just confuses me. You're smart, beautiful, young."

"If happiness was a formula, then I think I'd have figured it out by now. We all would have."

Luka shrugged.

"I don't mind being unhappy," Lisa continued. "I'm not in some deep depression. I've been there before. I know that feeling. This is not it. In some ways, it feels like the same despair, the same hopelessness, because I'm worried I'll never be happy again. I worry that maybe as a kid I used up all my happiness, and now I have no memory of it. Or maybe in the womb, I was bursting with serotonin, so happy to be unborn, until I came out and screamed at the world, and my brain was just spent. Depleted of all the serotonin. For good. I sometimes wonder if that's what's wrong with all the unhappy people. That they were faced with the harsh realities of the world at birth, and it sucked their brains dry. I think that the only way I can be happy is when I'm drunk. I don't mean like an alcoholic. At least I don't think that's what I mean. I don't feel some insatiable desire to feed an addiction. It's just the easiest and most reliable way for me to find that moment of peace, solitude. But I'm not alone, maybe I'm just away from my thoughts. When I feel like that, I'm happy."

"Away from your thoughts or away from yourself?" Luka asked.

"Maybe it's just being away from thoughts about myself."

Luka nodded. Lisa felt like he was trying to understand where she was coming from, but how could he?

"Is that the only way I can feel happy?"

Luka blew smoke out, staring at the starless sky. "You mean the numbness. 'Comfortably numb'. You know that song? Pink Floyd?"

"No, I don't know the song."

"You are describing the song."

"Well, I don't know the song. I'm just trying to describe when I feel happy."

Luka shrugged. "That doesn't sound good. I mean, that doesn't sound like you. I've known you for a while now, and I don't see you like that. Chasing the high. That sounds like a junkie or something."

Lisa sighed. "I'm not chasing it." Then suddenly, she thought of her mom, popping pills and passing out in front of the TV.

"I'm—it's not a pursuit. It's more of an observation. I don't even drink every night, Luka."

"Okay, okay. This is why I didn't want to get all deep and shit. I've had a few already," he said and then moved his chair over next to her. He put his arm around her and smiled. "You make me happy. I'm happy around you."

Lisa tried not to smile but couldn't resist. It spread across her face like a rainbow after rain. "How is that possible?"

"How is anything possible? It just is."

She leaned forward and kissed him and the numb—the void—was filled with something else, however brief, and she had hope that perhaps her life could be something more.

oregon: six

Lisa vacuumed while Wyatt pushed his walker around the carpet. She worried the sound was too loud for him, but he was almost two now, and it was probably fine. The vacuum wasn't on for more than a minute before Wyatt started to scream.

"It's okay, honey." Lisa said, continuing to vacuum.

Wyatt's mouth hung open like he was still screaming and shook, drool dripping from his lip. His fingernails tore at his scalp as his grip turned from earmuffs to talons. His skin flushed red as the shaking progressed from his face to his arms and down his body and legs. Lisa turned the vacuum off.

"Wyatt, stop. Stop, hon. It's okay. It's okay. The vacuum is off. Here, take your hands off your ears and listen. It's off," she said, but Wyatt dug his hands deeper into his scalp. Lisa could see his flesh turn white under the pressure. His eyes stretched open and darted around the room like he was following an erratic bee. Lisa tried to pull his hands down, but he resisted with such force that Lisa thought that maybe he was having a seizure and began to worry he'd bite his own tongue in half.

"Just relax. Relax. Hey. Can you hear me? Can you hear me? It's mommy," Lisa said. She kissed his head and rubbed his back. Wyatt's face became a dusky purple-blue hue. He looked like a child trapped under sheets of ice.

"Wyatt!" Lisa screamed and shook him. He didn't budge. It seemed like minutes went by. Lisa began to cry. She picked him up, held him tightly against her chest, and swung him back and forth like she did when he was a baby. Wyatt's grip loosened, and his chest expanded, letting air escape and then enter. He went limp in her arms, eyes wide open, his scalp bleeding.

"I'm so sorry that scared you," Lisa said. "I'm so sorry the vacuum scared you."

Wyatt was limp and silent. Lisa lay him down in his bed and looked at his scalp. There was blood mixed into his hair. He didn't flinch as she cleaned it with a warm, soapy rag. He didn't move when she kissed each wound and gently stroked his hair. Eventually, he closed his eyes and fell asleep. Lisa sat on his bed and watched him breathe. She worried he might stop just as suddenly as he'd started.

Eventually, some of the fear passed and she went into the kitchen to call her mom. Lisa wasn't really looking for advice, but Cathy was ready to dispense it. She told Lisa to take him to the emergency room immediately.

"How would you know what a seizure looks like?" Cathy said. But Lisa wouldn't take him.

They'd look at her clothes and his face and interrogate her with their paperwork. Their questions would be procedural on the surface but really trying to find out what kind of terrible life Lisa was giving him. Wyatt still wasn't talking, and Lisa hadn't been back to the pediatrician. She figured all they'd do was blame her anyway. Wyatt was moving at his own speed. The vacuum had scared him, but he was fine now. It wasn't a seizure. She should've warned him. Should've waited for a day he was with Cathy or at daycare.

"It wasn't a seizure, Mom. I'm sorry. I should've taken a second to calm down before I called you. He just had a tantrum. He's fine now. He's fast asleep," Lisa said.

"Lisa, listen to me. You need to take him in. He's done something like that with me before, too. He needs to be seen. If not the emergency room, then he needs to see his pediatrician tomorrow—next week at the latest. I'm worried about him. Maybe he has an ear infection that makes noises really bother him. I don't know. I'm not a doctor. But please don't ignore it," Cathy pleaded.

It was perplexing to have Cathy so involved in Wyatt's well-being. She'd been active since the beginning, yes, but it seemed to have multiplied exponentially. Cathy had been trying to do better since he was born. A little bit every day. She'd breeched sobriety, but Lisa felt it was just the tip of the iceberg. Cathy held a colossal portion of herself hidden beneath the surface. Part of her was still steeped in drugs. It would take a long time to dry out, if ever.

"You talk to me like I don't know what I'm doing. I was just calling to tell you about it," Lisa said.

"And I'm just responding to what you told me. Lisa, what do you expect me to say? These episodes he's having are not normal. What if they get worse? Then will you take him?" Cathy said.

"Not normal. Yeah, and how much was *not normal* when I was growing up? I don't seem to recall you having that same concern when I was a kid. There was a lot of stuff that was *not normal*. You remember the cutting, Mom? Did you ever take me to the doctor for that? We both know you went to the doctor plenty. Different doctors and different medicines, always changing but always the same. Remember those times I tried to finish making dinner because you fell asleep, and I burned my hand so bad you kept me out of school for a week. You never took me to the doctor. You weren't scared then. Do you remember slamming cabinets so hard that they broke off their hinges and then you'd blame me for it? I remember—"

"Stop. Lisa, stop. Why are you doing this? I feel like you're lashing out for no reason."

"Are you saying it's not true?"

"I'm saying that I don't know what the point is. I'm talking about Wyatt. My grandson. Your son. I'm worried about him."

"The past dictates the future. How do you not see that? If there is something wrong with Wyatt then there is something wrong with me, and if there is something wrong with me, it's because of you," Lisa said and hung up the phone.

Mom must get off on this shit, she thought. Getting all worked up like something was wrong with Wyatt. There was nothing wrong with Wyatt. Lisa was doing her best. She was doing a hell of a lot better than her mom had done for her. Sometimes, Lisa wondered why Cathy even ended up a mom. Had Cathy wanted her? And then, the answer came to her—of course she hadn't. Dad hadn't either. She'd been a mistake, just like Wyatt. An unwanted child that they'd cobbled together their best efforts to care for, and her dad eventually had said enough was enough and disappeared forever. And Cathy had tried. She'd tried but failed.

The vacuum was done until he was older. It wasn't a seizure. It wasn't even a big deal the more Lisa thought about it. He was fine. Lisa was fine.

The second tantrum happened at daycare.

Lisa pressed the phone hard against her face. She was standing at the checkout stand, A customer was waiting impatiently, but Lisa didn't care.

"What's going on? Does Wyatt have a fever or something?" Lisa asked.

Janet's calm voice said, "Lisa, no. He's fine. I mean, he's going to be okay. I don't want you to worry but I'm taking him to the emergency room. We're on our way right now."

"What?" Lisa shouted.

"What's going on?" the customer said. "Where is the manager?"

Amber walked up from behind Lisa. "Chill out dude. Something is wrong with her kid, I think. Is something wrong with your kid?" Amber asked.

Lisa nodded, almost in tears.

"I got you," Amber said and winked. "Go figure it out."

"I'm on my way, Janet. Where are you taking him?"

"Randall Children's," Janet said. "He's going to be fine. I'll see you there. Drive safe."

Lisa almost hit two cars on her way out of the parking lot. Once she got on the road, she took a few deep breaths and tried to calm down. She was too worried to cry. She felt a pit in her stomach not knowing why Wyatt was being taken to the emergency room. Did he fall and break his arm? Was there a pencil in his eye? Was he bleeding? Crying? Unconscious? Lisa slammed the palm of her hand against the steering wheel in frustration for not asking Janet what was wrong. *If it was something simple, Janet would've told me,* Lisa thought. Suddenly, her worry for Wyatt shifted into worry for herself. She started to think of why Janet would take him to the emergency room and not tell her why. Maybe she wanted a neutral territory, a place to lay bare all her grievances against Lisa as a mother. Lisa sped up, hoping to leave as little time as possible where Janet would be alone with Wyatt.

"Where is he?" Lisa said, louder than she meant to, when she arrived at the front desk of the emergency room.

"Where is who?" the woman at the desk asked.

"My son. Wyatt."

The woman ushered Lisa back to him. She pulled back a sliding glass door adorned with animal stickers meant to distract from the fact that her child was in the hospital. Lisa saw Wyatt lying on a bed, a bandage wrapped around his head. Janet sat next to him, stroking his hand. They both were looking up at a television screen bolted in the corner. Janet smiled. Lisa ignored her and rushed over to Wyatt's side. She kissed his bandaged head, kissed his cheeks, his chest, his arms, and his hands. He squirmed away, never making eye contact. His gaze locked on the cartoons playing on the small screen.

"What happened?" Lisa asked.

"Maybe we should talk outside," Janet said.

"If you think I'm leaving him now, you've lost your mind." Lisa gripped Wyatt's hand tightly.

"I just worry it might upset him," Janet said. She looked old and tired and ready to cry.

"I'm his mother. I'm here now. Just tell me what happened. Wyatt will be just fine."

Janet began to explain what had happened at daycare. Some of the older kids had been playing a game where they messed up each other's hair. One of the kids—Janet purposefully kept the name from Lisa—walked up and rubbed Wyatt's head. Wyatt had been playing with blocks, quietly per usual, and once his head was rubbed, the kid also accidentally kicked over Wyatt's blocks. Janet went over to make sure Wyatt was okay and found that he was shaking, red faced and holding his breath. The story was all too familiar to Lisa. What she thought was just a one-time response to the vacuum, was being told to her in a play-by-play, almost exactly as it had occurred before, except this time Wyatt wasn't pushing his fingernails into his scalp, this time Wyatt beat his forehead with a block. It was soft at first, at least according to Janet, but then again, Lisa wasn't sure she could trust anything Janet was saying. When Janet went to try and calm him down, Wyatt started hitting himself harder. When Janet tried to take the block away, Wyatt bit her.

She showed Lisa the mark. Lisa put her hand over her mouth when she saw it. It looked like something a wild animal would do.

"Oh my God, Janet," Lisa said.

"It's okay," Janet said. "I love my kids. I know this is part of the job. But when he bit me and I tried to pull away was when he really did the damage."

Janet got up from her seat and pulled back the bandage on Wyatt's head. He had a large goose egg—a red and purple bump—with split skin across the front, jagging down toward his eyebrow. Blood oozed out with the bandage removed. It wasn't deep but the skin had separated significantly.

"I don't know what set him off."

Lisa put her hand on the wound, feeling the pulpy flesh on her child's head. Wyatt swatted her hand away, still staring at the TV.

"It sounds like he was set off by that boy touching his hair," Lisa said.

"Yeah. You're probably right, but still. It's not a normal—"

"It's not normal?" Lisa asked, and then again, louder, "It's not normal?"

"That's not what I meant," Janet said.

Wyatt moaned and slapped the bed. Lisa stroked his head.

"I'm very sorry that Wyatt bit you, but I think it's time you left," Lisa said.

Janet nodded and walked toward the door. She turned around before leaving, opened her mouth to speak, but thought better of it. Lisa slumped into the chair next to Wyatt. She was glad to be rid of Janet. She hadn't seen the doctor yet and was hoping to avoid the whole "head bashing" talk. Lisa was in uncharted territory. Really, she had been since the beginning, but with this second outburst, she was starting to worry something really was wrong with Wyatt. It hurt to think that. She had so many complex emotions about Wyatt. He was her baby. She loved him, cherished him, worried herself sick about him. But he also was a burden, not just in the work of caring for him, but because of the responsibility—it weighed heavy on Lisa's mind. Even now, in the emergency room, Lisa had this sick feeling that she'd done something wrong, and the doctor would come and question how she could've let this happen. How could she have prevented this? Not taken him to daycare? Not been at work?

When the emergency room doctor saw Wyatt, he didn't scold Lisa. He was busy and Wyatt was low on his priority list. They put some sort of gel on his head before the stitches were placed. Wyatt was surprisingly calm. The nurse informed her that she'd given him sedatives before Lisa arrived. He had been throwing such a tantrum that they were worried he'd hit his head again. Lisa wanted to be mad but was surprisingly thankful to have not witnessed it. Wyatt was calm. He breathed through his mouth, eyes barely open. He looked so much like Bryan usually, but at that moment, he looked like Lisa. The green eyes, the blonde hair. She kissed him on the cheek.

"Almost time to go home, baby," she whispered.

The nurse came in with the discharge paperwork and told Lisa she was free to go. Lisa held Wyatt in one arm and grabbed the paperwork with the other. On the top, in the portion labeled "Patient Instructions", it read: **Head banging may be a sign of a more serious psychiatric disease. Please follow up with your regular pediatrician.**

Six months later, Lisa was struggling with the remote with one hand while restraining Wyatt with the other. He writhed beneath her, screaming, and trying to slam his head against the floor. She got the TV on and managed to press play. The fish movie, *Finding Nemo*, the one where he loses his dad and then finds him again all the way across the ocean. It was the only thing that worked. One day, they watched it six times. She fed him his food while his eyes were trained on the screen. Changed his diaper and his eyes never left the movie. But she was thankful for it. She felt blessed by it. Without the movie, she didn't know where they'd be.

Wyatt was two and a half, maybe closer to three, Lisa wasn't sure. She'd lost track of time since she had quit her job at Fred

Meyer and the days had started to blend together. Bryan's job was apparently everything he'd said it would be, and after Lisa screamed at him over the phone for withholding funds from her and Wyatt, he eventually sent her what they were owed. It was enough to live off, thankfully, because Lisa had to stop working.

She'd grown tired of Fred Meyer but enjoyed the freedom it gave her. After the incident at daycare, Lisa didn't have much of a choice but to quit. Cathy had filled in for a while, but the tantrums slowly became more frequent and she was at a loss. Lisa never brought him back to the emergency room. She never brought him to his pediatrician again either, and because of that, Cathy refused to see Lisa or Wyatt. She told Lisa that she wouldn't be a part of her life if she was going to mistreat Wyatt like this. Lisa had blown up on her and they hadn't talked since.

Wyatt's body went limp against Lisa's as the movie started. Her hands loosened their grip. He stopped screaming too. Lisa's arm began to burn and throb as his fingernails dislodged. The fish acted like people, made little villages in the coral, and took their kids to school. Lisa and Wyatt both shut down their brains for a minute after the struggle—the screaming and kicking and biting—and thought about the movie instead of what they'd both endured. Lisa carried Wyatt off the floor and wiped his sweaty hair out of his face.

She'd gotten used to taking him down onto the carpet when it happened. Sometimes it was once a day. Sometimes she'd lose count. She *had* to restrain him. She'd tried letting it run its course—his tantrum, or fit, or whatever it was called—but Wyatt essentially destroyed the house and hit his head against the wall hard enough to leave behind bruises and cuts. So, she restrained him as gently as she could but firmly enough to keep both of them safe. She kept his fingernails short, watched out for his teeth, and moved the fragile objects out of the living room. But the head banging was scary and difficult to control. Wyatt struck the walls with such force that it was disturbing to watch. Lisa thought that every part of his body must have been telling him to stop. When Lisa hit her head, it elicited an immediate withdrawal from whatever had struck her and an unconscious, primal movement of her hands to create a helmet. Wyatt had the opposite reaction. It made no sense to her. If Lisa didn't stop him, he'd keep going until he knocked himself unconscious. She used to cry and beg him to stop, but when that didn't work, she reminded herself that he did not have control and it wasn't his fault. She'd grab him in a bear hug and lay on the carpet until he either ran out of energy or she put the movie on. The bites and kicks and screams were more endurable than the head banging.

Lisa carried Wyatt from the floor over to the couch and lay him down. He'd urinated through his diaper. His pants were darker on one leg to about the knee. It didn't seem to bother him. Neither did the teeth imprints on his arm, still sunken and red and covered with saliva from his own mouth. He stared, wide-eyed, open mouthed, looking like he had on sedatives in the ER. That was what *Finding Nemo* was. A sedative. Watching the talking fish was calming in a way that Lisa would never understand, but it worked.

She'd tried other movies. She tried singing. She'd tried books, and car rides. She'd tried shutting him in his room and holding the door closed. She'd tried candy, sticker charts, begging, pleading, and screaming. She'd even tried spanking him, once and only once, but it wasn't effective and left Lisa feeling dirty and confused. Wyatt's instincts drove him to hurt himself and in response Lisa had hurt him more. She still cried sometimes at night when she thought about it.

Lisa poured herself a vodka and Diet Sprite and brought Wyatt an apple juice. He snatched it out of her hand and drained it in seconds. He held out his hand and moaned, quietly at first but then louder. Lisa took a long sip off her drink; she was thirsty after holding him down. He was surprisingly strong for his age. She went to grab Wyatt another juice box. She handed it to him. He slammed it and seemed satisfied. Lisa slouched back into the couch and drank her cocktail. She would change his diaper and pants later. He didn't mind and it would just turn into a struggle. Lisa was all done with struggling for the day. It was two in the afternoon. This was the earliest she'd started drinking but she didn't care. She was going to do what she had to do, and what she had to do right now, in that exact moment, was drink.

The fish were swimming all the way to the bottom, into the dark. Lisa wondered about places like that—holes, trenches, upside down mountains miles under the sea. For her, that part of the movie was the most important because Wyatt and her connected on some intangible level while it was on. Like their brains synched together and sparked a shared thought. She wished it was when the orange fish reunited with his dad and everyone lived happily ever after, but that wasn't it. It would never be that part. In the dark, something in Wyatt's eyes changed. She'd stood right in front of him and watched it happen. Like whatever magic might be down in the darkest part of the ocean might also be in the deepest part of his mind and she would watch it light up. When the fish reunited with his dad, Wyatt's eyes did nothing. They looked dead, like dried out lichen.

Sometimes, when Wyatt had a break down for the umpteenth time that day, Lisa closed her eyes while she held him on the carpet and pictured the two of them at the bottom of the sea, so deep that light could not penetrate, and in the dark, she'd feel an overwhelming, invisible pressure. She'd picture them all alone, at the peak of an upside-down mountain, with billions of pounds of pressure crushing them from all sides, and then she'd cry—her tears spilling into Wyatt's blonde hair—and gasp for air, but there would be none, and she'd be thankful that at least she was not alone.

Lisa had gained almost fifteen pounds over the last few months, eating delivery pizza or Chef Boyardee ravioli. Things she could get at gas stations or convenience stores while Wyatt waited in the car. She only shopped at places where she could still see him through the window. Taking him inside was not an option. She'd tried it and would never make that mistake again. It was too much of a risk. Lisa showered every third day at best and had trouble keeping up with the laundry. She didn't want to be seen in public. She didn't want Wyatt to be seen. Both of them had bruises and bite marks. Wyatt would probably be snatched by Child Protective Services before Lisa could bag her groceries.

Lisa picked up her phone, stared at it for almost a minute, and then put it back down. *Mom abandoned us, she thought. I didn't abandon her. It's up to her to reach out.*

Later that week while Wyatt was napping and Lisa was attempting to clean up, the doorbell rang. Lisa winced at the sound, hoping it wouldn't wake Wyatt, and went to open the door. It was Cathy. She stood there with grocery bags in both hands.

"So," Cathy said.

Lisa didn't respond. Part of her wanted to break down crying. She felt like someone had finally come to rescue them. The other part of her wanted to armor up, slam the door in Cathy's face, and tell her through the thick wood that they were fine and she could go to hell. But Lisa knew they weren't fine. The wave of emotion Lisa felt when Cathy showed up affirmed that. She opened the door all the way and took a bag of groceries from her.

"You aren't going to say anything?" Cathy said, still standing outside.

Lisa took a deep breath, closed her eyes and started to cry. Cathy dropped the grocery bags and hugged Lisa.

"Just come inside. We can talk. It's fine. Just come inside," Lisa said.

Last time Lisa had seen Cathy, she pulled an ultimatum. Lisa had come home from work to pick Wyatt up, and Cathy had been waiting for her, sober as a trial lawyer. Cathy told Lisa that Wyatt had another fit—a tantrum, an episode. Lisa nodded in understanding and said she was sorry, but Cathy wasn't looking for an apology. She reached out and held Lisa's hand. *He needs to see a doctor, she had said. There's something wrong.* Lisa again had nodded in understanding, knowing there was something wrong but something innate within her told her that bringing him to a doctor would only do harm. What was wrong with Wyatt was almost certainly because of what was wrong with Lisa. In a way, she felt that his illness was penitence for the mother she'd been. She damaged him somehow, with her hate and selfishness, or simply with her lack of love. She didn't need a doctor to tell her that. Lisa thought that Cathy must feel that way too. In some way, Cathy must realize that Lisa was broken before she ever got the chance to be a good mother herself, and the only one to blame for that was Cathy. But Lisa wasn't interested in tracing back the genealogy of toxic parenting. The damage was done.

When Lisa told Cathy that she would never take Wyatt to the doctor again, Cathy freaked out. She'd tried scolding Lisa and then tried to reason with her. She tried to explain that maybe Lisa wasn't in her right head and not thinking clearly. But Lisa told Cathy that she wasn't going to change her mind. *The best thing I can do for Wyatt, Lisa had told her, is try to love him.* Cathy had argued that it wasn't love. It was bordering on abuse. That was when Lisa said some things that weren't really true and later regretted. She'd said other things that were true but still regretted the way she'd said them. In the end, Cathy wasn't willing to participate in Wyatt's life if Lisa wouldn't get him help. *If I made a mistake with you, Cathy said, let me make it right with Wyatt.* But Lisa had taken Wyatt and left without saying another word. That was almost three months ago, and now Cathy was here with groceries, sober, and with her own agenda.

Cathy helped her put the groceries away in silence. Lisa felt like she was judging her, noticing her dirty clothes, her extra pounds. Lisa had a strong urge to kick her out. She hadn't asked for the groceries anyway.

"Where's Wyatt?" Cathy asked.

"Napping," Lisa said.

"I tried to get your favorites at the store. I grabbed some grape juice and cheese sticks for Wyatt. I got you some—" Cathy trailed off while sifting through the fridge.

"I'll look later."

"Okay."

Once the groceries were put away, Lisa leaned against the counter and crossed her arms. Cathy looked around the kitchen, trying to avoid Lisa's gaze.

"Something is different," Lisa said.

"With what?" Cathy asked.

"You're off your pills. I know you were cutting down before, but you're completely off, aren't you? This isn't you. Bringing groceries over. Look you're shaking." Lisa pointed to Cathy's hand as it trembled slightly.

"I don't know what you're—"

"Oh, sure you do, Mom."

"Lisa, I don't understand why—"

"Did you think you were going to bring groceries over here and pep talk me with your new sobriety?"

Cathy clenched her jaw and her eyes teared up. "What did I do to deserve this? I'm trying to help you."

"Thank you for the groceries. We are doing just fine." When Lisa said fine, the fallacy of the statement caused her lower lip to tremble. Cathy grabbed Lisa's wrist.

"You're not," Cathy said.

Lisa turned her face and tried to pull away. Tears streamed down her cheek.

"Even if you won't admit what's going on with you, it's time to stop pretending Wyatt is okay. I know he's not. You know he's not. He needs help," Cathy said.

Lisa pulled her wrist loose. She sat down on the couch, wiping away hot tears with the sleeves of her shirt.

"You know just how to hurt me. Was that what you came here to do?" Lisa said.

Cathy sat down on the couch, "Honey, you know that wasn't my intention. You're a mother, Lisa. You can't be so selfish. All this talk about me and you. That's not what this is about. It's about Wyatt."

"And what was it about when I was a kid?" Lisa asked.

Cathy stood up. "Lisa, I refuse to go back there. I refuse to have you change the subject so you can berate me about the past."

"You think I pretend that Wyatt is okay? Do you really think that's what I'm doing every day? Look at this shit." Lisa lifted her shirt, showing bite marks and bruises. Cathy didn't say anything.

"This isn't pretending. This is living. I am fully aware that there is something wrong with Wyatt. I am facing it every day," Lisa said. Her nails dug into her palms. Her vision blurred with tears.

"It doesn't have to be like this," Cathy said.

"It is like this."

"It doesn't have to be, sweetie." Lisa sat down on the couch next to Cathy. "There are professionals and doctors and people that specialize in this kind of thing."

Lisa felt sick to her stomach hearing Cathy say this kind of thing, meaning a *thing* where the parent was fucked up. An issue of aptitude. Lisa was trying her best but, in the end, she knew it was doing Wyatt harm. She felt all she'd done was cause Wyatt harm. Even at her best. Even holding him in a bear hug and smelling his hair while he bit and scratched her. Even when she used to sing to him in bed as he fell asleep in her arms. She knew why. It wasn't just because she was a bad parent. It wasn't just because she didn't have what it takes to be a good parent. It was because Lisa didn't love Wyatt. Lisa didn't love anyone. She didn't know what love was. And how could she be a mother when she couldn't even understand love? Couldn't even express it? She couldn't even conceptualize it. After her mom, dad, Bryan, and Wyatt. All these things that were supposed to equate to love. They were so different and yet all the same. That couldn't be love. It was impossible for that to be love.

"Is this love?" Lisa asked. Cathy had continued talking, stroking Lisa's hand and telling her they could get Wyatt help.

"Is what?" Mom asked.

"Is this love?"

"Right now?"

"All of it."

"I'm not sure what you mean, sweetie."

"It can't be. I was sure it was going to be different." Lisa felt in a dream state. The room wobbled. Cathy's face looked like it was behind stained glass. Wyatt screamed in the background and everything stabilized along the shrill frequency.

"I have to—" Lisa said.

"Let me get him," Cathy said.

Lisa sat on the couch alone and wiped the tears off her face. A cold reality settled over her. It felt like wet clothes that stuck to your skin. It was the same feeling Lisa had when she was frozen in the shower, except this time, instead of ambivalence, she felt confident that her decision was already made, maybe always had been, and she'd been dodging her destiny all along. Lisa wasn't sure she believed in destiny. She liked to believe that life was made up of freewill and endless possibilities, but this was different. Her course felt set. Cathy was in the other room singing softly to Wyatt, and Lisa felt like an invader. She felt ethereal—like a memory suppressed—or maybe the world was ethereal, and Lisa was the only real entity. She wasn't sure. She felt dizzy again, like she needed to lie down and wake up from a nightmare. Something inside told her what she needed to do. Something innate, that felt intangible and simultaneously concrete. It showed an open path while throwing shade over other potential routes. She tried to reason with the feeling. Tried to reconcile with what it meant. But in the end, it only solidified, and Lisa felt its unbreakable permanence in her heart. She had to leave Wyatt. She had to never come back.

croatia: seven

"How about a trip?" Luka asked.

"A trip? A trip where?" Lisa asked.

They were walking home from Luka's work after his shift ended a few hours prior. The sun was setting, painting pink and orange across the sky. It was still warm enough for the shorts and the tank top Lisa wore, even with the breeze coming off the sea.

"Wherever. Just a trip. Where do you want to go?" Luka asked. His smile held through the words. He was excited and it excited Lisa to see him happy.

Things had been going well between them. They were dating or going steady or something like that. Something exclusive and intimate. They'd connected physically a few more times, mostly sweaty kissing on the dance floor or loose hands in the alleyways, but no sex. And Luka hadn't pressured her. He seemed fine with how things were going. Plus, it was more than the physical. Obviously, the physical part was fun—it made Lisa feel young and sexy and normal, basically the opposite of everything she'd felt in Oregon—but Luka was a kindred spirit. Their hearts connected on a level Lisa had never experienced before. She was sure Luka felt it too. Neither of them talked about it. It was something invisible and electrifying that resonated between them. Something more mystical and nebulous than love.

"Paris?" Lisa said.

"Paris?"

"Yeah."

"Is that where you want to go?"

"Sure. Well, not really. I don't know. It's not something I've thought about. I wasn't a big traveler before. I just picked Croatia because of Instagram, honestly."

"How about a trip here?"

"Here? Like Rijeka?"

"No, here like Croatia."

Lisa smiled. "I'd go anywhere with you."

"How about Zadar?"

"Don't know anything about it."

"It's beautiful."

"Seems like everything here is. But why there?"

Luka shrugged. "It's the next stop down the coast. We hit Zadar, then Split, Montenegro, Antarctica. And after that—"

"Wait," Lisa said. "Hold on. I don't like making plans like this if we aren't actually going to do it, so let's not get too far ahead of ourselves. How would we even swing this?"

"Swing it? It's swung."

Lisa laughed.

"Is that not a saying?" Luka asked.

"Nope."

Luka waved his hand. "I'm ready to leave that job. I'm prepared to move on to bigger and better things. Today will be my final day as a rental car salesperson!" Luka shouted and raised his fist defiantly. Lisa laughed again.

"You're crazy."

The walked in silence as dusk settled in, their fingers intertwined, arms swinging as wide as their smiles. Luka's apartment was down the street. They went up the stairs to the third floor.

"You're coming in I'm assuming," Luka said.

"You assumed right."

"It's a mess."

"Well, how else would it be?"

Luka laughed. "Right. Sure."

He opened the door and led Lisa in. She'd never actually been inside his place before. There were two bedrooms to the left of the main hallway, and one of those walls were made of cubes of glass, dividing the bedrooms from the living room and kitchen. It wasn't messy. She glanced into one of the bedrooms and saw clothes on the floor and across the bed. They weren't Luka's. It had to be his roommate Davor's stuff. Lisa had only met him once and they'd both been drunk and tired. He came across as arrogant and talked way too much. She wasn't sure if that was a fair assessment or not, but when Lisa had mentioned that she found him rude, Luka shrugged and said, "Davor is Davor."

"It's nice. Now I'm embarrassed we always hang out at my place," Lisa said. She sat down on the couch. It was old and worn and she sunk down deep into it.

"I started from the bottom now I'm here," Luka said sarcastically.

"Hey, say what you want, but this is nice. This is as nice as. . ." Lisa trailed off. She'd almost said it was as nice as the basement apartment she'd shared with Wyatt but caught herself. She'd never given Luka much backstory. He only knew that things weren't great back home and that she was from the Pacific Northwest. She wasn't sure that he knew what the Pacific Northwest was, but he never pried. She assumed everyone outside of the US knew all the states and the small intricacies that defined them, but since being in Croatia, a country she'd never heard of or noticed on a map before, she realized that every state that wasn't New York, California, or Texas was vague territory.

"Nice as? Nice as the Ritz? The Hilton? Daddy Warbucks. I knew it. Little Orphan Annie, you're home," Luka said.

"It's as nice as you need. Or I'd need. I guess I don't know what you need."

"Just you." Luka winked.

"You are cheesy as hell."

"But it works."

Lisa picked up the remote and turned the TV on while Luka sliced some fruit and peppers. The TV came on to a random Croatian music video full of earnest, folksy pop innuendo. Lisa turned it off.

"What will Davor think if you quit your job?" Lisa asked.

Luka set the food down on the small coffee tablet in front of the couch.

"Why would I care what Davor thinks?" he said dismissively and took a bite of an apple slice.

"Are you serious about the quitting thing?"

"I'm serious about the quitting thing."

"Okay, well, if you quit your job and you don't have a steady stream of income, won't your roommate worry how you'll pay rent?"

"Are we talking about you, or are we talking about me?"

"I'm good," Lisa said, knowing it was a lie. She barely had enough to pay next month's rent. After that, she had nothing. But Luka didn't know that.

"Davor was given this apartment when he married Ivana," Luka said, taking another slice of fruit.

"Davor is married?"

Davor wasn't hideous and that was probably the best way to describe him. He was balding—and not in the good way—sloppy in dress and in her single encounter with him, abrasive. Though, he had a nice smile and seemed to really care about Luka. Still, she couldn't imagine him being married.

"No, I just said he got the apartment when he was married. Now he's not but still has the apartment. The point is, he doesn't pay rent and so if I stop paying, what's he going to do?"

"I don't know."

"He will have less money to buy women drinks who don't want them. He'll get over it. Plus, I have a plan. I'm not flying by the seat of my pants. I have a grand scheme."

"Oh yeah?" Lisa said, raising one eyebrow.

"I have money, Lisa. I've had this money saved up and had the chance to spend it a million times, but each time the chance presented itself, something told me, 'No, Luka. Not this.' But then you came along and decided to get fired, and I realized that this is it. This is what you want, Lisa."

"You want to spend your money on me?" Lisa asked. "How romantic."

"Not on you," Luka said. "With you, or. . .I mean. . .I don't know what I'm saying. I was joking around, but seriously, I have some money and I want to spend it. I want to take you on a trip."

"I'm listening."

"Not a vacation. I don't want to have to worry about when I need to come back to some bullshit job I don't want or need. I'm serious. We should go to Zadar and live our lives. We don't ever have to come back. The next place we go, we'll decide once we're there." Luka's eyes lit up as he talked, and then, with a convincing American accent, "Maybe New York City."

Lisa smiled and averted her eyes. Luka's gaze was intense and yearning for commitment. She wasn't sure what she was hesitant about. Maybe it was being stuck away from the city she knew with a man who barely knew her, or maybe it was the thought of her secrets unraveling—money, Wyatt.

"You don't want to go?" Luka asked.

"No, I do," Lisa said, feeling a surge of confidence. "I do."

"Okay. Tomorrow? You want to go tomorrow?"

"What about Angela?" Lisa asked.

"What about—what about Angela? I guess. I don't know. What about her?" Luka looked confused and slightly deflated.

"I mean. If we're going to skip town, I'd like to see her. Maybe she wants to come to Zadar with us. You like Angela, right? You'd be okay with her coming?" Lisa distracted herself with food while Luka took a while to answer.

"Sure. I mean. If that's what you want. We can invite Angela," Luka said.

"We don't have to. I just thought—"

"No, no. You're right." He looked over at the front door, thinking about something else. Lisa was worried she'd blown it with the Angela thing and now regretted it. She wasn't even sure why she mentioned it. Some part of her was scared to be alone with Luka. Not that she was scared of him. She was scared of herself.

"I'll ask Davor if he wants to come," Luka said.

"What? No. Why would you want to do that? You don't even like hanging out with him," Lisa said.

"Davor is like a brother to me. You don't abandon family. You have to accept them. It's okay to hate them, but you can't abandon them."

"Right." Lisa got up and paced in the kitchen.

"Davor's not that bad. It's not like I want to be alone with just you and Angela. Maybe Angela and him will hit it off. You never know. Love can strike anywhere."

"Right."

"I feel like you don't want to do this. I thought you'd be happy."

Lisa stopped pacing. "I am. I am happy. It's a great idea. Let's go tomorrow. I'll text Angela. I'm sure she'll want to go."

"We will see Davor tonight. Will you stay over?"

That night Lisa went to bed before Davor got home. She heard Luka and him laugh and argue in the living room and out on the balcony, smoking cigarettes and drinking Ožujsko beer. Angela texted Lisa back and was excited to go. Lisa left out that Davor was going. Angela didn't know Davor and Lisa didn't elaborate about who he was. We don't abandon family. That stuck with her. Of course it did.

It made Lisa think of her dad leaving. How he'd abandoned her. She had so few memories. She remembered how he used to fall asleep watching TV with his socks halfway off his feet. She couldn't remember his face but for some reason she could picture his socks halfway off his feet perfectly. She wondered why he left. Did he think he was doing the right thing? In some way, he probably did. Maybe he was as toxic as Lisa.

Her mom had stuck around even in the worst of it—when Cathy was at her worst and recently when Lisa was too. She had her faults, but Cathy never gave up. Cathy never ran away. Lisa didn't want to abandon anyone. Luka was the only family she had now. She would stomach Davor. She would do whatever it took to be with Luka. Maybe even tell the truth.

oregon: final

Lisa absent-mindedly scrolled through Instagram and liked things at random. It had only been two days since Cathy had brought over groceries and confronted Lisa, and the deadline was now rapidly approaching. Cathy had convinced Lisa to take Wyatt to see a doctor and Lisa had agreed. Really, she had accepted it as inevitable more than agreed that it was the right thing to do. It seemed like the *only* thing to do. She knew things were bad. She'd accepted that Wyatt wasn't well. She'd accepted that what she had tried to do—even with her best intentions—was not helping and, when viewed from an outsider perspective, was probably doing harm. And she'd had the opportunity to see it from an outsider perspective over the past few days. Her mom had taken Wyatt. She'd framed it as an opportunity for Lisa to catch her breath, and Lisa had allowed it. She needed it as bad as Wyatt did. Some time to herself would allow her to see things more clearly. She finally had time to clean. She cleaned up the snack fragments strewn across the floor. She vacuumed the carpet that smelled like sweat and saliva. She washed her sheets and took out the glasses on her nightstand, still sticky with Diet Sprite. Then she sat, alone and quiet, and tried to think. She tried to think of a way forward.

In the end, it all added up to one simple conclusion. Although Wyatt was born from her body and shared her DNA, they were toxic for each other. It made her feel guilty to think of it that way, but that was the conclusion she found herself making. Maybe things would've been different if Bryan had been someone else, and maybe Lisa would be someone else and then so would Wyatt. In this alternate timeline, they all would've been their best selves and instead of poison, maybe they would've been each other's antidote. But Lisa was pretty sure that was the same as happily ever after, which was to say that it didn't exist and never would because it was a made-up fantasy to help people deal with their inherent caustic nature and the reality that they would never be with anyone, let alone happy forever. Lisa was poison, and with Wyatt, she was something worse—a vacuum or a void—where a viable future for both of them disappeared.

Lisa continued to scroll through Instagram, the images fleeting as they rolled from bottom to top, teasing fantastical lives transfixed within photo frames and impossibly saturated with color and fantasy. An azure sea flashed with legs fanning out toward the bending horizon. Lisa pictured herself there—the sun warming her legs, the ocean calm and inviting. Some sort of drink in her hand that people only drank in hot weather and near the ocean—and definitely never in Oregon. She clicked on the photo and read the description:

Life doesn't get better than this—Hvar, Croatia.

She didn't know anyone in Croatia and realized it was an ad. Lisa usually instinctually scrolled past ads in her feed but for some reason this one stuck. She searched for Croatia, having some faint recollection that it was a country in Europe, maybe near Europe, but did not know how she knew that or why. Maybe it was an Anthony Bourdain episode she'd watched back when she binged his show and wanted to travel the world. She'd always pictured herself going to someplace warm and exotic like Jamaica or Fiji, maybe Australia, but instead had only ever made it to Canada. Canada had been disappointingly similar to Oregon, and while she'd crossed some physical border to get there, her imagination had not. The trip left her with a sense that maybe the whole world was like Oregon or Canada and equally stale. But she knew in her heart that wasn't true. Still, the idea that beaches and foreign languages and exotic foods were a plane ride away seemed impossible.

Lisa had flown on an airplane once. Cathy had taken her to Disneyland with her one and only boyfriend, Ralph. It was a short and easily forgotten trip, like Ralph, but Lisa remembered the plane ride. She'd been scared for takeoff but had read somewhere that the way some people get over that fear was that they picture the city they are leaving was about to blow up or something along those lines, and so they *have to* take off. Instead of climbing into the sky and thinking about falling to her death, Lisa was supposed to imagine she was being saved. Lisa had tried to think about a volcano erupting or an atomic bomb going off, but it didn't work. Instead, she pictured her dad waiting for her in California, and all she had to do was get on the plane and hold on, because when it touched down again, her dad would be waiting. She'd cried during the takeoff. Ralph laughed callously and patted her hand thinking she was scared, never realizing that they were tears from joy not fear, knowing her dad wasn't waiting for her. But the thought of it, even for a second, gave her joy, however fleeting.

Lisa's laptop screen was flooded with pictures of Croatia. Perfect turquoise seas clear enough to make boats look like they were floating in the air. Old, stone houses with pastel siding scattered along mountainsides. Red-roofed buildings grouped around an ancient church steeple. Sailboats with their blinding white sails contrasting with the almost neon-like colors of the sea. The pictures filled her with a sense of wonder. It was a place she hadn't known about. She hadn't known anyone who'd been there. No one that planned to go. It represented the world she'd been hoping to explore. The one where everything was different and maybe better—a world where she could start over again. Though her heart stayed in place, anchored by guilt and duty, her soul floated away and entertained the prospect of being free, being new, being anything or anyone, as long as it was different from who she was now.

She looked at flights. She was putting in dates and choosing between lay overs in cities like Paris, Zurich, and Amsterdam. Names that were in movies or books, not real life. Certainly not her life. She worked at Fred Meyer and got pregnant at nineteen. That was supposed to be it for her. And now with Wyatt, with his developmental issues, where was her future? Maybe they'd take Wyatt from her. Would she ever be able to live with herself? Wyatt, living his life out in a foster home, or worse, some sort of facility. She'd die from regret and shame, alone.

Lisa wasn't sure they would take Wyatt, but she was sure that things wouldn't be the same once they went to that appointment. The appointment was with a psychiatrist—a special kind at Doernbecher Children's Hospital at Oregon Health and Science University. Lisa had looked him up. Beneath his many degrees from fancy schools, there were words that frightened her, like autism, traumatic brain injury, and fetal alcohol syndrome. Words that frightened Lisa. They meant there was no fixing what was wrong and there was no going back. Not to mention the way the doctor would look at the two of them. He'd blame Lisa for what Wyatt had become. They didn't know how much Lisa had sacrificed. How much Lisa had done. She didn't want to go. She didn't want Wyatt to go.

Lisa found a flight and picked out her seat assignment. She knew it was a fantasy, but something about keeping the fantasy going made her happy. She selected one of the seats near the window, just behind the wing of the plane. There were more seats in the plane than she thought possible. The price was astronomical. To afford it Lisa would have to use all her savings. She changed it to a one-way flight and the price dropped considerably. The mouse hovered over the "Purchase Ticket" button. Lisa closed the laptop and walked away.

Two days passed. Wyatt was back in the house and his behavior had been better since his stay at Cathy's house. He had his appointment in the morning. Lisa had come to terms with it. He was going and she hoped her mom was right—that it was the right thing for him. She liked the idea of Wyatt being happier. More in control. She didn't know if it was possible, but she hoped that maybe Cathy knew what she was doing.

That night Wyatt bit into a microwaved piece of chicken that apparently was too hot. He screamed and threw the bowl of beans, spilling most of them on himself and breaking the bowl. They went to the carpet like they always did. After he calmed down, Lisa took a warm, wet towel and cleaned the beans off his face and hair while he watched the fish movie. The blue water made her think of Croatia again.

"I don't think I'm good for you, babe." Lisa spoke softly to Wyatt while she ran the warm rag over his cheek.

"I don't know if you are good for me either. I think it's okay to say. I've been so scared to say it, but now that it's out there,

I feel better. Maybe those kinds of secrets poison us from the inside, and then they're let out like a puff of black smoke. I think it's okay to admit that we're bad for each other and still know that there's no bad in either of us."

Wyatt stared blankly at the television. His eyelids dipped toward closing with each gentle wipe from the washcloth. Lisa felt tears tapping her cheeks like unexpected rain. Wyatt turned to Lisa. He made a sound like he was upset and tried to wipe the tears off her face. Lisa wiped her face with the palm of her hand.

"It's okay, sweetie. Mommy's okay."

Wyatt went back to watching the movie.

"Sometimes, I think maybe we're just two magnets turned the wrong way. Too much the same. I like to think things would be different if your dad were around, but honestly, I don't think it would be. I don't think it has anything to do with him. It's always been me and you since the day you started to grow inside of me. Even then, I could feel the push. You were repelling me, or maybe I was repelling you. Either way it was there. Something invisible separating us. And I know I did this to you. I'm not sure how or what exactly, but I know it was me."

Lisa began to cry again. Wyatt didn't turn his head. He sat calmly on her lap. She kissed his ear and he leaned back into her chest. Lisa wrapped her arms around him.

"But two wrongs don't make a right. I've been trying to fix things, but I've only made it worse. I don't expect you to understand it. I don't expect you to forgive me. I remember hearing once that if you love something, give it away. I wasn't ever sure what that meant until now. I'm still not sure what love is, but I just want you to know that—"

Lisa's voice cracked as emotion overcame her. She gripped Wyatt tightly. She couldn't believe the words that were spilling out, but they wouldn't stop.

"I want you to know that in the morning I won't be here anymore, and you have to know that it's for the best." Lisa hugged Wyatt closer. He'd almost fallen asleep, and she smelled his blond hair as it tickled her lips and nose.

"In the morning, I'll be gone."

It was midnight at the Portland International Airport. Lisa pulled her bag along the security line and tried not to think about anything. She tried to make her mind blank and clean like a freshly washed cutting board. She nervously tapped her foot and bit her lower lip.

"Hello," the TSA worker said, never actually looking up at Lisa.

"Yeah," Lisa said and handed him her passport. She'd gotten it before, thinking she was going to take a trip to Cancun after graduation, but the trip never became a reality. Their summer job money was spent on eating out, makeup and clothes—all meaningless, pointless things to Lisa now. But she'd kept the passport, luckily.

"Where you headed to, ma'am?" the TSA worker asked, shining a red light on her passport.

"Croatia. Well, first to Amsterdam. Then to Croatia."

The TSA worker looked at Lisa for the first time and gave her a cold, dead stare.

"Have a nice trip," he deadpanned.

Lisa felt a cold sweat pour out from under her armpits and around her ears. She walked past the worker and toward the departure gates. Her phone vibrated. It was her mom again. Lisa ignored it and put it back in her pocket.

She'd called Cathy before leaving, saying there was an emergency and she needed her to come watch Wyatt for the night. Cathy unleashed a barrage of questions that Lisa dodged for the most part. Now Cathy kept calling. Lisa wondered if she'd found the note she'd written to try and explain everything. It basically said that Wyatt was hers now. Bryan hadn't had a single bit of correspondence in almost a year since he'd moved to Wyoming. Just the checks. Lisa had noticed his wife was pregnant before she'd deleted him from her Facebook. She'd put that in the note. Lisa didn't want Bryan to have anything to do with it. She figured if he found out that she'd left, he'd flip his shit, just for show. But in the end, he'd be happy that Cathy was taking care of Wyatt. Plus, if Wyatt got diagnosed with a developmental delay or something worse—there were much worse things Lisa had found out after spending some time reading parent discussion boards and researching the names of some of the diseases—Bryan would do more than just forget about Wyatt. He'd renounce him.

Lisa's gate was down the terminal on the right. She could see the number now, twenty-four. It was ominous in a way Lisa couldn't quite put her finger on. The terminal felt cold and barren at this time of night. The lights from planes and the runway illuminated the ground outside but the sky above was a deep, starless black. As she got closer, she noticed the gate was packed full of people. It would be another thirty minutes or so before they'd start boarding. Lisa's phone rang again. It was her mom. What if something was wrong with Wyatt or what if something was happening with the house? What if it was a fire? A burglary? Was Wyatt alive? Was he safe?

"Are you okay, miss?" a man with a thick, black beard asked.

"What? Yeah. Yeah, of course. I'm fine. I'm fine," Lisa said, cracking a smile between tears. "Thank you, really. I'm fine. Fine."

The man gave her a look that said, *suit yourself*, and nodded before turning away. Lisa's phone vibrated again. She threw it into the trash. Wyatt was Cathy's now. Not hers. If the house was on fire, Cathy would handle it. She would do better than Lisa ever could. Wyatt was safe. Wyatt was home. Lisa was gone.

She'd gone back and forth since the day he'd come home with her from the hospital. Lisa believed that there was something to that—the pull to leave. That was what she'd thought about these last few days—the pull. It was protective for both of them. If there was a God, which Lisa believed there probably was, maybe it was his plan or message. Or maybe it was Lisa's own soul, selfish and empty, content on dragging Lisa along for the self-destructive ride as it careened like a comet through any semblance of a normal, honest life. Whatever it was, Lisa knew it wasn't going away. Leaving was only going to get harder. She was not going back. She was not. Going. Back.

Lisa sat down at a bar surrounded by televisions. There were two men sitting next to her on stools chatting each other up about business this or business that. They'd both loosened their ties and looked like they were on beer five or six. Lisa signaled to the bartender and ordered a shot of vodka and a White Claw.

"You alright?" the bartender asked. She had black hair, black lipstick, and black eye shadow.

Lisa handed her a crumpled twenty-dollar bill. "Yeah, thanks. I just get emotional before riding planes. Nerves and shit. You probably see a lot of that, right?"

The woman shrugged, opened the can of White Claw and placed the shot on the bar top. She handed Lisa her change. Lisa slid over a dollar tip and slammed the shot of vodka. The businessmen stopped talking and chuckled as Lisa made a face after the shot. She wasn't used to drinking it straight. She grabbed her White Claw and sat down at a table closer to the window. She watched the planes take off and land, suddenly appearing from the cloudy darkness and disappearing just as quickly. She was crying but didn't care. She felt a phantom vibration on her thigh and checked for her phone and then remembered it was in the trash. *Wyatt is safe. Wyatt is home. Mom will take care of him. This is the right choice,* Lisa said to herself.

"This is the right choice," she whispered to no one and brought the can to her lips, drinking it quickly. The alcohol kicked in fast but gave her a full feeling like she needed to belch or vomit. She cried quietly until the final call for boarding. She walked down the jetway. Her mind felt like a forest after a fire—fragile, broken, and charred—and the rush of alcohol thundered down like fresh rain on the embers, washing the burned remnants toward the sea. She reached her seat, feeling half psychotic, half ecstatic, and completely devastated. A young boy moved into the middle seat next to Lisa.

"Oh, please no," Lisa said, louder than she meant to.

"No, Michael, this row," the child's mother said and led him down a few seats behind her.

"Jesus Christ," Lisa said. She'd made it this far but was not ready to sit next to a kid the whole goddamn flight. She was committed to her resiliency but had her limits. A woman in her late seventies with another woman, maybe her sister, sat next to her. They both had the same Portland hippiness to them. Patchouli and weed. Crystals and chakras. She buckled her safety belt as the plane began to taxi toward the runway. She wasn't scared the plane was going to crash. But wouldn't that be fitting? She was fighting a torrent of anxiety as the plane started moving on its way to another country—another world for all Lisa knew. She gripped the seat armrests, closed her eyes, and tried to take a deep breath. She didn't think about her dad waiting for her on the other side. Instead, she thought about Wyatt waking up in the morning: healthy, normal, without his fits and tantrums, healed and happy because Lisa was gone. As the plane began to accelerate and lift off, she felt selfless, and as the jet took to the air, she felt like she'd just delivered the antidote to Wyatt's suffering, and if the price was never seeing him again, she would pay it.

Portland disappeared and the plane shuttered upon entering the dark clouds. Some people on the plane made nervous conversation. The lights dinged with seat belt warnings. The two hippy women were asleep already, snoring slightly louder than the jet turbines. Lisa stared out the window, watching the dark vapors passing at alarming speeds. Suddenly, the plane stopped shaking as it broke through the clouds. Everything felt weightless as they continued to climb. Outside there were a thousand stars, brighter than Lisa thought possible. Her emotions overwhelmed her. Seeing the stars made her feel grateful for the experience and feel melancholy for the idea that she'd already missed so much. Not anymore. Her life was starting anew in this very moment. This nightscape was only the beginning. If Wyatt was free from her, she was also free from him, and she would live her life like she'd been given a second chance.

croatia: eight

They headed out early the next morning. Davor drove. He had a used BMW 5 Series he bought in Germany and wanted to make sure everyone knew. "They treat their cars like little children. Little genius children. Send them to the right schools. Feed them the right food. Always gentle with them. Never rough," he said. It seemed to creep Angela out even though he was joking. His jokes were long and unending. He went on with the BMW child prodigy analogy until Luka told him to chill out and he quickly shifted the conversation to something even less interesting: soccer. Soon, the two of them were arguing over the best attacking midfielders in the Champions League and switched to Croatian. Lisa and Angela got a chance to talk.

"I never got to thank you for that night," Angela said.

"Oh. Don't worry about it. You'd do the same for me," Lisa said, waving her away.

"Oh, I don't know. I like to think of myself as tough, but I'm not tough like you. I don't know if I'm the type of person who would stand up when the time came. It's hard to admit something like that to yourself, but I think it's true. I admire that about you. You know what's right and what's wrong and you're willing to fight for it."

Lisa squeezed her hand. "Glad you're here."

"I was surprised you invited me. That night, you were so angry."

"Let's not talk about that night. Okay?"

"Sure," Angela said. "Silly me. It was the last time I saw you. I've been missing you."

"Well, yeah." Lisa said, letting go of Angela's hand. "Me too."

"Plus, men are pigs, and you couldn't stomach this ride alone, could you?" Angela said in almost a whisper. "Right, Davor?"

she said, louder.

"Right! When a beautiful woman speaks, a man agrees!" Davor shouted.

Lisa and Angela both burst out laughing.

"Make yourself a little harder target, brother. These girls are smart, and we must keep our senses about us," Luka said.

"Smart women may intimidate some men, but to me, I find it sexy. Big brains, big—"

"C'mon man," Luka said.

"Big skulls! Big hats! What? You're my babysitter? The joke police?" Davor spat. The two argued in Croatian until Lisa stepped in.

"Can we just enjoy the ride? Pick something to play," she said.

"What are you in the mood for, Lisa?" Luka asked flipping through his phone. Lisa looked out the window, watching the blue shimmer in the early summer sun.

"Something like that," she said, pointing out the window.

Luka nodded knowingly. Davor turned up the music and Lisa leaned back in her seat and rolled down the window. Warm, sweet air blew her hair around her face. The music and the coastline rolled by and Luka and Angela were within arm's reach. It was enough to make anyone happy. For Lisa, achieving happiness was an event. It was like the world came together and patched an unfixable hole in her heart. And the longer it lasted, the more in awe she was. Hopeful, too, but also realistic. No matter how good the present patched her up, she'd never be the same—never be healed. Still, the moment was a welcome distraction from the heartache.

They arrived in Zadar by midday and checked into their rental. The city was a maze of hills and small streets. They'd circled three times before finding the apartment. Angela looked ready to get out of the car. Davor had not proved himself to be any more likeable than the brief interactions she'd had with him before. He was harmless, really. More obnoxious than abrasive. He was just a guy who didn't know how to socialize, especially not with women. But if Luka cared about him, Lisa would try. Luka wasn't giving his love out to just anyone, so there had to be something to it.

Inside the apartment, there were only two bedrooms. Lisa

put her things on one bed and Angela stared at her nervously.

"I'll be on the couch then," Angela said.

Lisa didn't say anything. Luka was still outside unloading the car with Davor. The couch wasn't really a couch but rather a large chair that would make for a few very uncomfortable nights for Angela.

"Are you crazy? We'll share the bed. The boys can take the other room and the couch," Lisa said.

"Oh no. I couldn't do that to you and Luka," Angela said. "I'm just along for the ride. I'm not trying to get between you two."

Lisa persuaded Angela to put her things in the room and said they'd finalize everything later. The point was that they were here and ready to explore. Luka came in and saw Angela's things in the bedroom with Lisa's. He cocked his head at Lisa.

"So," he said.

"Don't worry about it," Lisa said. "We'll figure it out."

"Sure. Of course." He threw his things in with Davor in the other bedroom.

Lisa walked over and hugged him from behind. She got up on her tiptoes and kissed him on the back of the neck. She didn't say anything. She just swayed back and forth. His demeanor calmed her, like the Zoloft had, but instead of making her feel numb, she felt alive.

"I have to protect her from Davor," Lisa whispered in Luka's ear.

"Ah," he said.

"It was your idea. Remember?" Lisa said.

"It was," Luka said, a shy smile showing. "I do have the best ideas. This is way better than being alone."

"Everyone ready to head down? I think we can walk to Old Town from here," Angela said. She'd changed into a blue dress and put makeup on. She looked beautiful. She always looked beautiful. Davor kissed his fingertips and threw them into the air.

"My God, we need a carriage for this princess," Davor said.

"Now I know where you get it from," Lisa said to Luka. The walk down was farther than they thought. Lisa wore heels, which turned out to be a huge mistake. She'd only worn them a few times in her life, but everyone was dressing up nice, so she'd given it a chance. Halfway down, she was cursing herself as she slipped and almost fell into traffic. Cars zoomed around narrow, winding roads. There was no sidewalk and nothing picturesque. It was all identical, white apartments and houses with dirty walls and overgrown fig trees. She began to wonder if the apartment posting had been lying when it mentioned that everything was "within walking distance." Eventually they passed by a crumbling wall, then a gate, and a park with green grass and a stream flowing through it. Everyone was out despite it being midday in the middle of the week. Either no one worked or everyone was a tourist. Lisa couldn't tell and didn't know if it mattered. The city felt alive and vibrant the closer they got to Old Town and the water's edge.

Old Town was the original city. It was hundreds of years old, encapsulated by a stone wall at the edge of the Adriatic. The four of them walked over a small footbridge, through the stone gates, and into cobble stone streets. The streets were too narrow for cars. They were built for people, maybe carriages, but were never meant to be driven on.

It was late afternoon. The sun was directly ahead of Lisa and she held her hand up to shield her eyes. They started walking through the labyrinthine streets. The smell of gelato, sweat, and stone hung in the air. Lisa brushed her hands along the buildings, feeling the immensity of time that had passed on the grain. Portland was a speck compared to the life this city had lived. Lisa's life was less than a speck. An atom. Nothing she'd ever done or would do mattered in the scheme of things. *So, give yourself a break*, she thought.

They walked down the crowded main street, passing gelato and trinket shops. People were drinking beer, red wine, and mint-muddled mojitos at the sidewalk bars. Lisa peered into an Internet café, and for a moment, she thought of home. She thought of Mom and Wyatt. She wondered if Mom had tried to reach out. Maybe an email or a Facebook message. She'd avoided these places because of the temptation to check. She'd worked so hard to try and put the past behind her. She didn't like it when it came roaring back at random. There was no point to checking the messages. She wasn't going home. What was done was done.

They headed toward a tower with beautiful, ornate windows etched from the stone at each level. Lisa wondered how big the tower must have seemed to the people who watched it being erected. How majestic and awe-inducing it must've been. It still was to some extent. Not for its height though, but for its age and beauty. Anything that looked remotely similar seemed faux and artificial, usually because it was.

"That church looks exactly like the one from *Indiana Jones*," Lisa said.

Luka looked at the church and then around at the other buildings on the street. "This church looks like what?" he asked.

"The one from *Indiana Jones*," Lisa said again.

"I thought that one was in Petra," Angela said.

"No, not that one. The one where the whole X marks the spot and then they go down in the catacombs and there's rats," Lisa said.

Luka nodded, obviously lost but not wanting to admit it. "You are totally right."

"Never mind," Lisa said, shaking her head and laughing. "You Europeans have no culture."

"No culture! Look around you. This is. . .," Davor started, waving his hands emphatically.

"It's sarcasm, bruv." Angela said.

"Let's go to the boardwalk," Lisa said, and they all turned off the main street toward the water. A cement walkway stretched the whole side of the city along the Adriatic. It was full of people, just like the main street, but it didn't feel compressed or crowded with the open sea air spilling in. The sun was dipping toward the horizon, casting oranges and pinks like fireworks in slow motion. Lisa held Luka's hand and they walked ahead of Davor and Angela. Lisa glanced back briefly. Angela was smiling and staring out at the sea. Davor was nervously licking his lips and looking like he had something to say but didn't know how to bring it up. Lisa wanted to tell him to keep his mouth shut and they'd all benefit, himself included, especially if he ever dreamed of having a shot with Angela. Lisa knew he didn't. Still, she liked the quiet, nervous Davor better.

They continued on the boardwalk. The seaward side gave way to stairs descending into the water. Lisa heard music between the gentle lapping of waves but wasn't sure where it was coming from. She began to realize it was coming from the stairs themselves. The stairs had pipes built into them. Luka had mentioned this to her, but she hadn't quite grasped the concept. They were a sea organ. As the waves rolled in, the water entered the pipes creating sounds beneath the concrete boardwalk. It was haunting in a way: the sea creating music. It was perpetual and resonant—a never-ending symphony as the tide ebbed and flowed. To Lisa, it was another reminder of her infinitesimal existence when measured on the arc of time, and she knew that there was no room for regret or misery because time would not wait, and if she tried to stand still, consumed by regret, life would pass her by.

"Like Beethoven. You hear it? Beautiful. It's beautiful music," Davor exclaimed and started waving his hands like he was conducting an orchestra.

Luka laughed and shook his head. He said something to Davor in Croatian and they both began laughing harder. Lisa blushed, knowing it likely had nothing to do with her, but she still felt self-conscious.

"It's creepy," said Angela.

"It's pretty in a sad way," Lisa said.

"Sure. That too, I suppose," Angela said, and took a few quick steps to walk next to Lisa and Luka instead of Davor.

"Take it easy on him," Luka whispered into Lisa's ear. "He's doing his best. That's just who he is."

"This is us taking it easy," Lisa said. "I promise." She kissed him on the cheek and took Angela by the hand over to a dock. White goals stood in stark contrast to the green-blue water. Men lined up along the dock with rubber caps and Speedos.

"Heard they do it a lot here," Angela said. "Not bad." She lifted an eyebrow and smiled at Lisa.

Lisa turned back toward Luka. "Is this like a normal thing here? Water polo?"

Luka nodded and lit up a cigarette. He passed one to Davor. "No one plays water polo in the US? People only play volleyball in jeans, right? Like in *Top Gun*?"

"Hemingway said the greatest sunset in the world is right here, in Zadar," Davor said, pointing to the diving orange globe.

"Hemingway was a clod," Angela said.

Lisa stopped walking and stared out at the horizon. With the sound of the sea organ and the pastel streams, Lisa thought it was the most beautiful moment she'd ever experienced. At the end of the boardwalk, there was a huge circle of glass. Beneath the glass were small LED lights faintly coming to life in hundreds of different colors. People were scattered all over the top of it. Lisa and the others joined in.

"It responds to the sunset. Sunrise too," Angela said.

"Where's Luka?" Lisa asked.

They both looked around but found themselves in the middle of a gathering crowd, unable to see Luka or Davor. As the sun disappeared, the lights erupted, blinking out random patterns in a rainbow of light.

"It's pretty," Lisa said.

Angela said something but it was drowned out by the sound of speakers blaring electronic music. There was a troupe of breakdancers drawing the crowd away from the circle of light.

"Sorry, what did you say?" Lisa asked.

Angela opened her mouth to say something but stopped. Her eyes darted back and forth like something inside her was going to burst.

"There they are," Angela said, pointing.

Luka and Davor were standing near the end of the street in a small cul-de-sac at the edge of the sea. A white car was holding up traffic. As Lisa and Angela got closer, they heard Luka arguing. Someone got out of the white car. He was a muscular, white man with long hair to his shoulders and a fuchsia tank top. He moved quickly, purposefully, like an apex predator as he rounded the front of the car and confronted Luka. Luka was taller, but the man was stouter, angrier. Davor was standing a few feet behind Luka with his fists clenched, balancing on the balls of his feet in silence.

"What's going on?" Lisa shouted. The man was in Luka's face now, their foreheads almost touching.

"*Toplo bih ti preporučio da odjebeš iz Hrvatske prije nego što se neko sranje dogodi,*" Luka said calmly but assertively. The other man laughed, wiped his nose with his thumb and finger, and put a hand on Luka's shoulder. Luka swiped it away, and Davor took one step forward.

"Stop it," Lisa said, moving between the two men.

"*Ko je ova kučka? Tvoj telohranitelj?*" the long-haired man said. Bass thundered from the small white car.

Luka shouted and Lisa pushed him away from the other man, her face pressed into his chest, her arms trying to control his. The man laughed again and got back into his car. Luka spit over her head. Lisa turned to see the man almost get back out of his car, but a woman inside grabbed his arm and they drove off. The stalled traffic's collective horns grew into a crescendo before the cars started moving again.

"What the fuck, Luka?" Lisa said. "What are you doing?"

"Don't question me. You don't even know," Luka said. His face was red and tight.

"Fucking shit, guys," Angela said.

"Listen, you don't even know what happened. You came up here at the end, so just don't worry about it, okay?" Davor said.

"I'm worried about it," Lisa said. She was almost shouting now. Her cheeks were hot.

"Let's take a break, yeah?" Angela said. "C'mon. Everyone let off some steam."

Lisa stood in front of Luka. "What was that about?" Luka stomped past Lisa. She followed. "Come on, Luka. What was that about? I don't like it when you aren't straight with me."

Davor intercepted Lisa as Luka walked ahead of them. He tried to tell Lisa that everything was fine and started making bad jokes. Lisa was quiet. She was angry but not quite sure why. She just wanted Luka to talk to her. Davor caught up with Luka and put his arm around his shoulder as they walked.

"Men," Angela said.

"I guess," Lisa said.

They followed Luka and Davor back into the city center. The streetlights were on, and all the restaurants and bars were open and full of people. They sat down at a sidewalk bar at a tall metal table and ordered drinks. Lisa faced out toward the street and stared at people walking by. Somehow, all she could notice were the families with children. A frequency illusion. She was subconsciously seeking out all the women with children. She couldn't unsee the kids. Luka reached out to hold her hand. She let him but didn't turn around. She hadn't seen that side of him, and it scared her. Less because he was angry and about to fight, and more because she wondered what other parts of him she hadn't discovered yet.

Davor locked Angela into a conversation about soccer. He mostly berated the English and added an apology each time he said, "Shit-eating Premier League." Angela pretended to like Arsenal—only to make Davor angry. Lisa caught one of Angela's coy smiles that let Lisa know she was having fun with him. Their drinks came. Luka let go of Lisa's hand and Lisa faced the table again.

"*Živjeli*," Luka said, lifting his pint. "To friends and adventures."

They each clinked their glasses. When it was Lisa and Luka's turn, their eyes connected, and Luka's face softened. His eyes became sad and kind again. They took a drink. Luka leaned over to whisper in Lisa's ear, "You don't need to worry. I got everything under control."

"That's not what I'm worried about," Lisa said, loud enough for Davor and Angela to hear.

"What isn't?" Davor asked.

"You guys getting into fights. I don't need that. We don't need that. Everyone just needs to put their ego away tonight. We're here to have a good time, not get arrested," Lisa said.

"What was the deal anyway?" Angela asked.

Now Luka turned away from the table and stared out at the people passing by.

"Mr. Sensitive," Davor said and punched Luka in the shoulder.

"You know what? You wouldn't—never mind about it, ladies. It's done," Luka said.

Lisa's eyes narrowed. "Why are you being like this? I've never seen you act like this."

Luka threw his hand up. "Alright. Okay. So, that guy was Serbian. He—"

"How do you know he was Serbian?" Angela asked. Davor and Luka scoffed. "I'm just wondering because he appeared pretty damn inconspicuous to me."

"License plate. The fact that he spoke Serbian. My point being that he comes to our coast, to our city—one of the few places left untouched from what those Serbian dogs did in Slavonia—and he acts like he owns it. He was holding up traffic to watch the sunset. No thoughts for anyone around. If you think—"

"Why is it your job to step in, Luka?" Lisa said.

"This is the part you will not understand. It is everyone's job to step in. Everyone must do something," Davor said. He had his hand out like a hatchet and he chopped in the air as he talked.

"It may be better if we do not speak about these things," Luka said, waving his hand dismissively.

"What did you say to him?" Lisa asked.

"I told him to move his car and that he was not welcome here," Luka said. His eyes stared past her and Lisa could see a hint of his anger simmering beneath his words.

"Well, you actually said that you warmly recommended for him to get the fuck out of Croatia before some shit happens," Davor said.

"That's some macho bullshit," Lisa said. "Don't get stabbed over that."

Angela shrugged. Davor shook his head. Luka's face tightened, and he looked like he might flip the table over. It alarmed Lisa.

"Or not," Lisa said. "I just don't want you to get hurt."

"Luka's father was killed by the Serbians back home," Davor said. "You don't know shit about it. If his father or my father or the older boys from our school had not stood up then, where would we be now? This whole country would be overrun with Serbians and they would shit all over it. We don't—"

"Enough," Luka said.

A silence fell over the table, but the tension was deafening.

"I'm sorry," Lisa said. She touched his face with her hand and kissed him. His lips held firm at first but after a few seconds they loosened and opened, their tongues spilling into one another. "Right then," Angela said. "Who's up for a round?"

She produced a tin box from her purse. Everyone, including Lisa excitedly agreed. Angela and Lisa went to the bathroom first and then handed the box over to Luka and Davor, who fought about the idea of going to the bathroom together until they did. They finished their drinks and ordered another round. Davor talked louder and faster, but Lisa was feeling so good that she didn't mind. She was in love, not just with Luka but with the world. Every time Angela and Davor started talking about some random subject again, Lisa took the opportunity to kiss Luka. She felt warm and numb and weightless.

The waiter brought another round. Angela drank her beer and kept talking. "Get a sailboat first. Or a private plane. What am I saying. Get yourself a fucking jet, okay? Well, if you can't get a jet, you find a friend who knows a friend who has a jet—whatever you have to do. Get something that can take you across the world because the ultimate dream, the fantasy, is to go back and forth across the equator chasing summers. Because there really is nothing better. We spend the whole year waiting and waiting and talking about how terrible the winter is, how miserable it is to be in the fucking dark. Every year, it gets dark at five o'clock and I find myself saying the same thing: 'How in the hell is it dark already?' So just be done with that. When it starts getting dark early, or cold, or even hints at leaves changing, you hop on your jet or sailboat, or whatever, and you go to Argentina, or Chile, Namibia or Botswana—"

"Madagascar," Luka said.

"Wherever," Angela said. "Perpetual summer. Right, gents? How is that not the dream? I bet you could have a quarter of the cash you have now but twice the health and happiness."

Lisa took a long drink from her cider and placed the glass down harder than she meant to, causing it to splash. "That would mean you prefer sunlight and warmth over people or things."

"If I had a jet, I'd take it to Brazil to start recruiting some of these young athletes to Croatia," Davor said.

"Sunlight and warmth are what moves me. That's why I left my cold, grey island and came south," Angela said and laughed.

"Jets seem like a nuisance. I prefer to travel by land. A sailboat though. Never given it much thought," Luka said.

"Brother, you could reinvent yourself. Spearfish off the coast of Tortuga. Meet ladies in Fiji. Get a new name, like Bartholomew Arriba. Or Mickey Rattlesnake," Davor said.

"Francis Undergarments," Angela said.

"Eugene Thunderclocks," Lisa said.

"Who's that guy by the manta rays? It's Bruce Cocknockers," Davor said.

They all laughed, including Luka. The talk about reinventing yourself sparked something in Lisa's mind.

"There's this park in Idaho where people ride their bikes and have picnics and kids go on field trips, but it's actually the site of the largest public hanging in US history," Lisa said. She surveyed the faces. They still had the smiles from the earlier laughter but seemed unsure how to react to Lisa's story. "I'm serious. You wouldn't know unless you looked into it but it was the largest public execution in American history."

Lisa started telling them the story about the hanging. The unjustness of it. The pseudo-trials. The blood thirsty townspeople. When Lisa stopped talking, she realized she didn't know how much time had passed. No one had a smile on their face anymore. Both Davor and Angela looked distraught with her story. Only Luka appeared not only interested but also calm and understanding. It was like they were communicating through telepathy or something.

"And you know what? I thought it was nice. My friend Jessica and I smoked a blunt in the bathroom and they had an old replica town with canons and butter churners we played with. There's moms pushing their kids in strollers and kids playing tag in the grass. I saw some people LARPing. You know, the people who dress up like knights but with football gear. They look like a walking medieval bouncy castle with all the pads on their body and weapons. They were LARPing on this hallowed site. Just let that settle in there for a second. But my point isn't that we should be outraged by the LARPers, because we should be, it's just not my point. The reason I'm telling you about this place is because there was a time when I felt so depressed. About everything. About who I was. Who I'd been. Who I was becoming."

Lisa paused. Luka's eyes encouraged her to continue.

"But then, I was walking through this park, and I looked around at a whole class of kids, second graders or something close to that, and they were so psyched to be there because they had no idea what went down and I just had this wave of reassurance. Because it reminded me that nothing is sacred and nothing is remembered. If that place can reinvent itself, then nothing is impossible. The past is dead, and the dead are forgotten."

croatia: nine

They continued drinking late into the night. Luka ordered another round of rakija for the table. Angela tried to wave him off, but he insisted. Lisa was seriously intoxicated but in a good way. The part of her brain that managed her memory was still working, barely. Lisa and Luka kept making out every chance they got until Davor or Angela pried them off each other. It was then that Lisa finally admitted to herself that it was stupid to bring them along. There was something happening between Luka and her. They were connecting on a deeper level and were revealing things to each other that Lisa hadn't said to anyone. The drugs and alcohol freed her, and likely Luka too. She'd never heard him talk so openly. He'd lost his father too. Not in the same way. She wasn't even sure Luka would find the two situations comparable—one died heroically fighting an enemy and the other abandoned his wife and kid and fell victim to cancer. Lisa felt a punch in the gut when she thought about abandoning Wyatt. *You didn't abandon him, you saved him*, Lisa told herself. Would Luka see it that way?

Angela offered more coke and only Davor took her up on it. Davor likely thought this was his chance with Angela, but Lisa thought not. She'd seen Angela interact with men—women too for that matter—she was interested in sexually, and there was a significant difference between that and what she was doing with Davor. She had two smiles. Her fake smile only used half her mouth. It made her look devious and flirty. But when Angela was actually interested, her smile stretched across her whole face, showing her perfect, straight white teeth, and her tongue pressed against the roof of her mouth or along her incisor. Angela hadn't flashed a real smile toward Davor since she'd met him. Lisa, however, had caught plenty. Luka too. And that was okay. She wasn't even sure what it meant besides that Angela found them both attractive. Nothing wrong with that.

When Angela and Davor left, Luka and Lisa were alone, finally. She straddled him on the chair, their tongues pressing messily against each other's teeth. Lisa had trouble kissing because she kept smiling which broke the seal. People walking by whooped and yelled. Some told them to get a room. They didn't care. They were right on the brink of becoming blackout drunk and reveling in the moment.

"You know what supersymmetry is?" Luka said.

"Symmetry that is super?" Lisa said between kisses.

"It means a lot of things. In physics, it's a set of ideas that help explain the universe."

Lisa laughed. "Luka, you are so weird."

Luka pulled back and looked into Lisa's eyes. "I know I'm weird, but I just thought of it. Because it's this idea that for every particle there is a hidden one that fits perfectly together with it. Balances it out. Makes the laws of the universe work."

Lisa pulled Luka's hair gently. "College boy, what are you trying to tell me?"

"Let's get a hotel," Luka said. "I can find something."

"You're so sexy," Lisa said, smiling while she stroked his hair. Her whole body felt like Pop Rocks.

A car horn beeped rapidly in succession and then became one continuous wailing sound. Through an alleyway on the edge of town, Lisa saw the white car from earlier.

"Stupid guy," she said.

Luka's eyes locked on the car.

"Don't worry about it," Lisa said, grabbing Luka's cheek and turning his head. "It has nothing to do with you."

Luka forced a smile and the horn beeped again. He moved Lisa's hand away from his face and stood up. The man in the white car shouted something from an open window. Luka threw his chair out of the way.

"Stop. Stop. He's trying to set you off," Lisa said, standing in front of Luka. His eyes glossed over. He couldn't see her. Lisa wanted to slap his face and tell him to knock it off, but she didn't. She moved out of his way. Luka walked like a prizefighter toward the ring, all shoulders and chest. At least people here didn't carry guns like in the States, Lisa thought. She was really drunk, and that kept her from having much thoughtful discourse on the actions unfolding before her. Davor and Angela returned, laughing loudly until they saw Luka walking toward the car. The man got out of the car. He threw his hands up and started shouting. Davor sprinted after Luka. Luka continued his steady pace toward the man. He wasn't shouting. He wasn't running. He walked with purpose, arms held stiffly to his side with his fists clenched.

"What the fuck is he doing?" Angela said.

"I don't—I couldn't stop him. He's all messed up," Lisa said. "Luka, stop this shit! It's stupid!"

Luka didn't turn around. The man was yelling louder now and pointing at Lisa. He was speaking Croatian or Serbian or Italian, Lisa had no idea. She didn't know if Luka understood him or not, but nothing she or the man said made any impact on him. Davor caught up and stood in front of Luka, holding him back with one hand while pointing and shouting at the man with the other. The man cocked his right arm way back and threw a punch at Davor, who ducked at the last minute. The punch was sloppy and hastily thrown. It was meant as a knockout—a haymaker. This man wasn't a fighter. He wanted to hurt Davor—lay him out. It grazed and bounced off the top of Davor's head, sending the man stumbling toward the ground with his unhinged momentum. Luka grabbed a handful of the man's tank top and delivered a solid fist to the man's cheek. It made a slapping sound that made Lisa wince from twenty yards away. The man fell to the ground, blood spilling from his nose and mouth. Lisa started to run toward the fight, but Angela grabbed her wrist.

"You'll only make it worse," Angela said.

Luka was shouting again. He spit on the man. Lisa felt like she was trapped in a nightmare. This couldn't be real. This couldn't be the sweet, gentle, sexy, loving man she'd anchored her future to. Could it?

The man got up and tackled Luka to the ground. They both hit the cobblestone street hard. Luka threw a few misguided punches that ricocheted off the man's shoulder and side. After a short struggle, the man ended up on top and threw a wild flurry of punches at Luka's head. Luka had his arms up but plenty of blows still got through, slamming Luka's skull against the street. Lisa wriggled her wrist away from Angela and ran toward Luka. Davor kicked the man in the ribs twice. The second time caused the man to buckle and fall over next to a bloodied and dazed Luka. Davor grabbed the man by the shirt and pulled him to his feet, tearing his shirt in the process. The man was still trying to catch his breath, spitting blood with each breath. Davor kicked him from behind and sent him stumbling forward. He was badly injured or drunk or both because he didn't put his hands out as he fell limply onto his chest and face. He got up slowly and half-crawled, half-tumbled toward his car.

"Mother fuck!" Davor screamed.

The white car drove away with squealing tires. Luka was still on the ground. Lisa ran over just as Luka was lifting himself off the road.

"Jesus Christ! What were you thinking?" Lisa shouted. Luka turned his face to look at her. His right eye looked like someone injected red paint into it. His nose was leaking blood, and his left cheek was swollen and turning purple. Lisa felt tears falling from her eyes and rolling down her cheeks. She recoiled slightly and covered her mouth with her hands.

"Jesus, Luka," she whispered into her hand and backed up slowly.

"I had to, Lisa. You don't understand," Luka said.

"That guy deserved it. Fucking Serbian thinking this is his town," Davor said. Luka rose up with Davor's help. He had his hand around Luka's hip like he was a wounded soldier. She shook her head and walked backward.

"Seriously. It's over now. It's fine. We'll go get a drink and an ice pack. Everything will be fine," Luka said, letting go of Davor and hobbling toward her. She moved away.

Lisa thought life had played a giant trick on her. Like someone reached down and switched Luka out with someone else—someone brutal and unstable—and now that the violence had ended, they were trying to switch him back out again. She felt alone and abandoned for the first time since coming to

Croatia. She didn't recognize anyone. She didn't know anyone. She was a stranger in a country of strangeness. She thought of Wyatt, home in Oregon, crying like she was now, unable to explain what he was feeling, but crying tonight and every night because Lisa—his mother, the only person in the world who should never abandon him—had abandoned him.

"I have to. . .," Lisa began and then turned and walked away. Lisa heard them yell something after her, but she burst into a sprint and disappeared into the receding shadows. She ended up in a poorly lit back street that smelled like garbage. She kept walking, hoping that she'd find her way to the main street again, but things kept getting darker and narrower. She tripped on a piece of cobblestone and almost landed on her face. She caught herself on her hands. The smacking sound made her nauseous and she quickly got up. There was a white, crumbling staircase ahead, leading onto the old city wall. She ascended the stairs and sat with her legs dangling off the side of the wall. She stared out at the people walking across the lighted walking bridge to ride taxis back home. Lisa thought about taking a taxi back to the apartment but felt better sitting on the wall. The night was warm and beautiful, and she was very drunk. She also didn't want to have Luka come home in a few hours and then have a whole discussion in the middle of the night. She was okay with sleeping on the top of the wall. She lay back and closed her eyes, and for the first time since arriving in Croatia, she had the thought that she needed to leave. It was brief but disturbing. Something about the turmoil of the night made her realize that being here wasn't an answer, only a delay. She pushed the thought away and fell asleep.

Lisa woke to Angela shaking her shoulder. Lisa looked around confused and then saw that the footbridge had gone dark. The whole old town was silent.

"What time is it?" Lisa asked.

"We've been looking for you for hours. I convinced Luka and Davor to go back to the apartment. He was really hurt. I think he has a concussion," Angela said.

Lisa felt a pang of guilt but then said, "He did it to himself."

"Yeah. He feels really bad. I thought he was going to cry for a minute. Didn't seem like his typical thing. He got caught up in it. The whole Serbian-Croatian thing."

Lisa rubbed her face and tried to wake up. Her neck was stiff from sleeping with her head on her knees. "Serbian-Croatian thing. I've known him for months and never heard him mention it."

Angela sat down next to Lisa and pulled her knees in to her chest too. It was colder now. The silence was eerie. "I've heard of it. Lots. I saw some of it on TV but was too young to know what exactly was going on."

"You mean the war?" Lisa asked.

"Yeah. It wasn't all straightforward. They were all one country for years. Serbia, Croatia, Slovenia, Bosnia. When they started breaking up, Serbia invaded and everyone started killing each other. Neighbors. Coworkers. Families. It wasn't all good guys versus bad guys. Not that it ever is. I just know that a lot of the soldiers were normal, everyday people. People who tried to defend their homes. Their families. If Luka's dad died doing that, I can imagine he probably has some PTSD because of it."

Lisa stared at the water for a long time, not answering. When she finally spoke, her voice was dry and raspy. "That was a long time ago. I can't believe he just snapped like that."

"Men are like that," Angela said. "They're always like that."

Not Luka, she thought. Her and Angela sat on the old city wall, letting long periods pass between their sentences, enjoying the night as best they could. There were times when everything around her slowed down, and Lisa saw things in a new light. Life moved so fast that sometimes she lost context, but as she sat on the wall, running her hands over the ancient stone, she was very much aware of her place in the world. Not so much where she fit in, but the space she occupied. She could envision a camera zooming in from space as it rapidly closed in on the two of them, finding them here in Zadar, a world away from home.

The next morning, Angela raised her head from the bed she shared with Lisa and smiled. Lisa was already awake. She felt exhausted but hadn't been able to sleep. Part of her wanted to wake Luka from his drunken and concussed stupor, kiss him on the lips, and tell him that she'd lost her dad too. The other part of her wanted to cut ties immediately, catch a train to Split or Zagreb with the last bit of her money, and find a new job.

Or maybe end the whole charade and fly back to Oregon. But she knew she wasn't brave enough. She wasn't dumb enough either. Luka was a good man. That was what she realized by the time midmorning rolled around. She'd tossed it back and forth in her head and come to the conclusion that Luka was who he said he was. He was loyal, fierce, loving, and kind. That didn't mean he didn't make mistakes. Even if he didn't realize it was a mistake, she knew it wasn't a decision he was going to repeat. She didn't try and pretend to understand the reasoning behind it. Some things had too much baggage—too much history wrapped up in them to explain in words. But she understood. In the moment, she'd been too surprised and shocked to see it, but as she'd reflected on the night, she remembered the look in his eyes as he transformed into a scared child right in front of her. The fight was like losing his dad all over again.

Angela hugged Lisa in the bed they shared and nuzzled her face against hers. Lisa laughed. It reminded her of sleepovers at Jessica's house when they'd all sleep in a tent, dew scattered across its nylon walls, in her backyard and wake up in a jumble of arms and legs.

"Good morning," Angela said. Lisa sat up. She smiled at Angela and got up to find Luka. Luka was up. It was almost one in the afternoon. He was putting ice cubes into a washcloth and placing them over his cheekbone. Lisa walked up and put her arms around him from behind. Luka stood still. Lisa pushed her head into his back and squeezed. Luka gently lifted her hands and walked into the living room.

"What is it?" she asked.

Luka sat down on the couch, kicked his feet up, and pressed the ice onto his face. Lisa walked over and sat on his legs.

"How are you feeling?" she asked.

"Like I got punched in the face," Luka said, his voice nasal and congested.

"Let me see." She pushed the ice rag away and looked down at his bruised face. The left side was a pool of purple and yellow just below the eye. His lower lip was split but it appeared to be minor and already healing. He had the same scared look on his face. It was unnerving for Lisa to see him like that. It wasn't him. Or rather, it wasn't who he'd been. Luka was the stable one, the calm one, the we-will-figure-this-out optimistic one. She gently touched his face and lip and then kissed him. At first, he didn't respond, but then his lips gave in and reacted to Lisa's like they normally did. Davor opened the door to the bedroom.

"Glad to see Luka take you back," Davor said. "I thought after last night, you know, maybe—" He waved his hand at Lisa. "Never mind. I see that you have fixed the problem."

"Take me back?" Lisa said.

"Yes, of course. You really hurt his feelings last night. Both of us actually. We fight to protect the honor of our families, our country, and you throw a fit and run off and—"

"Shut your mouth, Davor. Are you having a laugh?" Angela said.

"This is no laugh. This is serious. Luka, we talked about this last night. I hope Lisa apologized to you. It wasn't right."

"You've got to be shitting—"

"Angela," Lisa said. "Enough."

Angela closed her mouth and folded her arms.

Lisa kissed Luka on the hand. "I'll always have your back, but I can't have shit like that in my life."

"We don't need to do this in front of them," Luka said. His voice was hoarse.

"Maybe we need some time apart," Lisa said.

Luka's eyes widened. "Why would you—"

"We'll talk tonight," Lisa said. "When everyone isn't hung over and still hotheaded." She spoke the last words to Davor.

Lisa and Angela left the apartment. They walked down to the center of the city again. Things were busy. Cars flew by. People were walking, talking, drinking, and laughing. The midday heat kept people in the shade or in the water. Angela suggested they catch a ferry out to one of the nearby islands to go for a swim. They'd brought their swimsuits but jumping off the boardwalk with the sea organ echoing didn't feel relaxing, especially not with the crowds growing.

Instead, they caught a ferry to Mala Rava with a handful of tourists. They'd asked the ticket man where the best beach was and got an answer that involved the most expensive ticket and a three-hour ferry ride. Angela picked Mala Rava at random because she liked the way it sounded and so did Lisa. They both kept repeating it to each other, laughing as they accentuated the *l* and the *v*. The ferry was slow and hot. They drank tiny bottles of cold white wine as they leaned over the steel railing, watching the sea go by below. They passed between multiple large, narrow islands visible from the boardwalk of Zadar. They appeared to be sparsely populated and mostly flat. A stone house sprung up here and there. So did a dock or small marina. The sailboats were ubiquitous. For every private, secluded cove appearing along the island's edges, there were twice as many sailboats. The ferry passed between two islands and turned right toward Mala Rava. The sailboats and houses started to dissipate and gave way to low hills flush with greenery and blue crystalline water that turned turquoise as it met jagged, rocky coastline. There were innumerable private coves and beaches devoid of sailboats or swimmers. As the ferry passed by, Angela and Lisa tried to memorize the coastline, decided where they'd spend the day, and then changed their minds a dozen times as each inlet revealed increasingly beautiful water and privacy. Lisa could take it or leave it with the privacy, but Angela was adamant about it. She didn't want to share the beach with anyone. It would be better for swimming. The water would be cleaner. *It's a much better experience*, she had said, and Lisa believed her.

The ferry docked and they hiked toward a private cove with a backpack full of sangria. It was early afternoon now and the walk was miserable. Lisa was hung over and tired and Angela had stopped talking after about ten minutes of walking. Finally, they made their way through some short, twisty-branched trees and down a steep scree hill toward the sea. The trees stopped and they found themselves staring at a small, half-circle inlet about forty yards wide, flanked by a terraced cliff of shale that gave the beach a sliver of shade. In the shade, Angela opened the bottle of sangria and took a long drink. She handed it to Lisa. Lisa's mouth was dry and her forehead was covered in sweat. It felt good in the shade. The bottle of sangria was cold and covered in moisture. She took a big drink like she was downing Gatorade. The sangria was cheap and tasted like Hawaiian Punch mixed with boxed wine. In the moment, it was exactly what Lisa wanted. She drank more and took her shirt and shorts off, finally feeling cool in only a bikini. Angela took her shirt off too, and her sweaty skin shimmered in the midday sun. Angela took some of the sangria and passed the bottle to Lisa. Lisa downed another drink, letting some of the sugary wine spill down her chin. She wiped it away with the back of her hand. They both hobbled over the small, hot rocks until they gave way to coarse, rocky sand. The water was so clear that Lisa saw straight to the bottom at almost fifteen feet out. They waded in, their sweat-covered bodies immediately cooled by the water. Lisa swam until she got used to the temperature and treaded water about twenty yards from the shore. The sangria was starting to take effect, and she felt good and relaxed. She was happy she'd taken the day with Angela. As much as she wanted to move on with Luka, there was a lot to unpack emotionally. Out here on the island, though, there was nothing but sangria, the sea, and sun.

Angela swam past her toward the open water and Lisa followed. After a few minutes of swimming, fear crept through the euphoria. Lisa shouted to Angela, "Don't you think this is far enough?" but Angela laughed and kept swimming. Lisa laughed, a nervous, not-sure-why-I'm-laughing laugh.

"You're crazy!" Lisa shouted. It was unlikely that Angela heard her with the kicks and splashes. Lisa looked at the shore and then back at Angela.

"Fuck it," she said to no one and swam further. When she finally reached Angela, she was out of breath and her arms and legs felt drained. Angela looked relaxed, peaceful.

"How deep is it out here?" Lisa asked. She looked down at her legs twisting underwater. Somewhere deep beneath their feet, the water went from clear to blue to green to black.

"Are you scared?" Angela asked.

"It's really deep. Jesus, what are we doing out here? Look how far away the shore is. I don't think I've ever—"

"It's okay to be scared," Angela said and moved closer.

"I'm not scared. I'm being sensible. I like swimming but I'm not trying to die."

Angela swam up right in front of Lisa so that their faces were almost touching. The salt water was so buoyant it took minimal effort to stay afloat. Lisa could feel the waves from Angela's treading feet and hands.

"Being scared makes you feel alive. Right?" Angela said.

Lisa felt transported, like the two of them were floating above the earth instead of in it. She thought of Wyatt. His face was hard to picture. She could only capture it in single frames. Single expressions. The memories weren't sharp enough to construct a free-form amalgamation of all the snippets of time she'd spent with him. That part of her was disappearing so quickly it made her question whether it had been real. Part of her believed that this moment was just as real as the others, whether she liked it or not, but the other part recognized the implausibility of the two lives she'd lived ever intersecting. Maybe this was a dream. Maybe her past was a nightmare. Maybe it was all make-believe.

"I'm freaked out, Angela," Lisa said. "Let's head back."

Angela smiled. "I sometimes forget that you're just a kid."

"You don't have to be a kid to drown," Lisa said. "C'mon."

Angela cocked her head at Lisa. "The whole world is open to you, but I wonder sometimes if you're too scared to get what you really want."

Lisa's heart started beating faster. She felt like the current was pulling her farther away from shore. "What? What are you talking about? I'm getting tired. I want to go back."

"It's a metaphor, Lisa. Don't you see? You're afraid to explore. To branch out. You don't know what you want just like you don't know what you're missing."

"Whatever," Lisa said.

She started swimming back to shore. By the time the water was shallow enough for her to stand, she was nauseous and tired. She stopped at the edge of the water to catch her breath and resist vomiting up the sangria. The sun was hot now that half her body was out of the water. She used her hand as a shade and squinted out at Angela, who was floating on her back out in the open sea. Lisa sat, letting small waves cover her legs. A few more minutes passed, and Angela made no attempt to come back to shore. Lisa had half a mind to pack up and leave her. She felt a flurry of responses to Angela but the biggest was confusion. She felt gaslighted. Angela was supposed to be on her side. She was hoping this was her opportunity to finally find someone who understood her, but

Angela acted like Lisa had no agency. Lisa thought they were equals, but Angela thought Lisa was a child. Lisa threw a rock into the sea and drank more sangria. Angela didn't swim back for another ten minutes. Angela lay back on the fine, smooth rocks, letting everything below her chest be submerged.

"I've always loved doing that. I think it's important to get to the point where you're a little nervous about whether you can get back safely or not. Where your mind starts wandering and worrying about what's going on below you and your heart races. Was your heart racing?" Angela asked. She smiled as she squinted from the sun.

"What's your deal?" Lisa asked.

Angela shrugged. "No deal."

"Why did you say I don't know what I want?"

Angela picked up the sangria and drank. "Well, I just mean there's a lot out there for you if you'd just look."

"No riddles, please."

"Okay," Angela said. She rolled over onto her side, propping her hand up on her elbow. "You saw who Luka is. You were petrified. It was like the night in the bar. We know who these men are. And yet, this morning you're ready to go back to him? I just don't think you need to be scared. Luka is not the one for you. Isn't that obvious by now? I worry you're too scared to see it. Worried you'll be alone. But you won't. You'll have me still." Angela reached out and put her hand on Lisa's.

"I know what I want. You don't know anything about me." Lisa pulled her hand away.

Angela let out a single laugh. She let her head fall back and opened her mouth wide. "If there's one thing I know about you, it's that you don't know what you want."

Lisa pulled her knees into her chest. "I'm being serious. I'm not sure about a lot of things, but I am sure about Luka."

"Is he your first boyfriend?"

Lisa squinted at Angela. "Why are you pushing so hard about this?"

Angela sat up and threw her arms in the air. "It's so obvious! If you could see it from my perspective, you'd see it's so obvious!"

"Okay," Lisa said. "Sure. And who should I be with? Are you some Casanova? Some all-knowing matchmaker?"

"I see you, Lisa. I know what you're like inside. But it's true. You're just a kid. A beautiful, intelligent, fiery girl. How could you know what you want? But that's okay. Just don't make the mistake of following a lie."

Lisa got up with the bottle of sangria in her hand. She drank the rest of the bottle and threw it against the rock cliff. Glass shards scattered into the sea and shale.

"You don't know me," Lisa said. "You think you do, but you have no idea."

"Okay," Angela said. "I don't know why you're getting upset. I'm trying to help you."

"Luka knows me."

"I think that's a naïve way to think."

Lisa folded her arms.

"No one knows anyone," Angela said. "If there's one thing you two have in common, it's that you're both lost. You don't even know who you are, so how could someone know you?"

"If we're both lost then, what does that make you?"

"Listen, maybe it was wrong to bring all this up. I wasn't trying to make you angry."

"No. So, what does that make you?"

Angela ran a hand through her wet hair and turned to look at the cliff. "Free? I don't know. I feel like everything is getting all mixed up."

"I want to go home." Lisa grabbed her bag.

"Just wait a second. I'm trying—"

"Maybe we should go separately."

Angela's eyes teared up. "I never meant to hurt you. I want to help you."

"I never asked for your help."

"Lisa, I'm sorry. I—"

Lisa threw the bag over her shoulder and started making her way up the trail. "Whoever you think I am? You're wrong."

She left Angela alone on the beach.

On the ferry ride home, Lisa sat in the front while Angela stayed in the back. Lisa would look back every once in a while, but Angela had moved to a lower section and Lisa couldn't see her anymore. When they pulled into Zadar and started to disembark, Lisa saw Angela moving quickly ahead of her.

"Hey, wait," Lisa said.

Angela kept moving. Lisa jogged over and put a hand on her shoulder.

Angela turned and gave a polite smile. "It's okay. We don't have to do this."

"Maybe I overreacted," Lisa said.

Angela shook her head. "I shouldn't have said anything."

They walked together back toward the apartment. It was empty when they arrived. Lisa tried to act like everything was normal, but it wasn't, and Angela felt it too. Angela went and grabbed her bag from the room, told Lisa no hard feelings, and kissed her on the cheek.

Lisa watched Angela leave and felt conflicted. She liked Angela. Not in a romantic way, but as a friend, and yet here was another friend she felt betrayed by. Lisa started to question whether it was something she was doing. Was it the people she attracted or the people she was attracted to? Plus, for all the talk about Angela not knowing who Lisa was, it only seemed to affirm that Lisa didn't know who she was. How could she know? She'd been perpetually reinventing herself since leaving Oregon. Adapting and changing. Living it up. All while holding onto the fact that she was a mother who had abandoned her child. She liked to frame it that she'd left for his sake, but lately she had this feeling that it was all a selfish lie. It made her nauseous to think about what Luka would think if he knew what she'd done. Maybe it was something in her DNA that drove her to leave. Something genetic that she'd inherited.

These thoughts disturbed her. Lisa assumed it was all happening behind closed doors in her mind, but when Angela called her out, she realized how obvious it must all be. She existed under false pretenses. Everything felt like a diorama that Lisa had moved to the side of and was seeing it all shallow and fake. What she thought was vibrant and beautiful might actually be nothing. She had to talk to Luka. That was the only way to really know.

She walked from the water up the hill to the apartment. Davor's BMW was gone. Lisa put down her things and took a shower to wash off the salt from the sea. She dried off and lay on the couch and to watch TV while waiting for Luka and Davor to return. She wasn't sure what to say. She wasn't sure where they stood.

Around midnight, Lisa woke up to the door opening. The TV was still on. Luka walked in. His face was partially lit by the white-blue light of the TV. His bruises had grown. The swelling had decreased. He sat down on the couch next to Lisa. He smelled like cigarettes and white wine and fresh air.

"Where's Davor?" Lisa asked.

"Home. He went back to Rijeka," Luka said.

"He did?"

"Where's Angela?"

Lisa rubbed her face and tried to brush her hair out with her fingers. "She left too."

They both stared forward, watching the television. It was late-night Croatian news. They showed clips of a soccer player leaving a club and driving off in a Lamborghini or Ferrari or something.

"How are you? Your face still looks pretty bad. Anything serious?" Lisa asked.

"I believe the modeling career might be over. Hollywood needs to look for a new fresh face. This Slav is officially roadkill," Luka said.

Lisa laughed. "That's good to hear. That you're not hurt seriously."

"Been through worse."

Lisa turned to him. "Tell me about it."

"What?"

"Tell me about when it was worse."

Luka gave her a sideward glance and shook his head. "You're always trying to get real serious and shit."

Lisa felt Angela's words echoing in the back of her skull. "I'm worried I don't know you. I'm worried we don't know each other. I don't know what we are doing. Do you? Do you know what we're doing?"

Luka shrugged. "I thought we were just living our lives."

"Okay, but it has to be more than that," Lisa said. "What happened the other night really scared me."

"I wasn't trying to—"

"No," Lisa said, putting her hand on his. "Not because of what you did. I mean I wasn't happy about it, but because I didn't know why you did it. I felt like you just became another person right in front of me, and that scared me."

She paused. "But I've been thinking about it. It's not that you became another person, it's that you were that person. You are that person, and I just didn't recognize you. It scared me."

"The person I am scares you?" Luka asked.

Lisa rubbed her eyes until she saw falling silver sparks in the darkness of the room. "Level with me."

"I'm leveling. I'm level. You're freaking me out with this stuff." Luka stood up from the couch and paced in the kitchen. Lisa stood up and followed him. She walked up to him and put her arms around his waist. He reluctantly put his arms around her shoulders, and she pressed her head into his chest.

"I love you," Lisa said quietly, as if she were whispering it into his heart.

They swayed together, squeezing tight in the dark kitchen, slow dancing to imaginary music. Luka kissed the top of her head and said, "I love you too. I have since I met you. It's impossible, I know. I tried to tell myself that, but it's true."

She led him into the bedroom and stripped off all her clothes. Luka did the same. In the dark, under the covers, they made love.

Lisa woke up a few hours later. It was dark and late. Or early. It was hard to tell. She rolled over and her naked body bumped into Luka's. She felt him turn. His hand went to her hip and then onto her lower back. Her hands found his face in the dark. Her fingertips ran along his sandpaper stubble. She couldn't see anything at first, and then his face slowly came into view. His eyes were open, shining with faint, ghostly slivers of light.

"When we were kids, me and Davor, we loved to go to this marketplace in Bosnia. My hometown, SB, Slavonski Brod, it's right on the border. There's a small bridge between the two towns, Slavonski Brod and Bosanski Brod, and you just walk over and you're there."

Lisa stroked Luka's hair while he spoke. "Me and Davor liked to go to Bosanski Brod during the summer, when our parents were working and we could get into trouble. When we were eleven or twelve, we started sneaking things over from the Croatian side and sold them. It was nothing really. Not like drugs or guns. It was real small time, silly stuff. Like cough medicine they didn't have in Bosnia. Or certain players' jerseys, stuff like that. It was great. We'd take the money we'd earned and go buy cigarettes and fake Adidas shoes from the flea market. But then one day a cop found out. He shook us down for what we had to sell and the money we'd earned. I remember being really scared because he kept talking about our accents and how he knew we weren't from there, but I knew what he meant was that he knew we were from Croatia. Even though before the war we were all part of Yugoslavia, he didn't like that we were from SB. This wasn't too long after the war and there were many parts of Bosanski Brod that were still completely demolished, buildings and streets—entire blocks in some places. Not to mention the people who'd been killed or hurt by the bombs. We had our share too, but it was different there. I could tell by the way the cop was talking to us that he was mad about it, really mad, and felt like somehow, we had something to do with it even though we were very young when it happened—the war."

Luka paused for a while and Lisa was unsure if he was going to go on. He turned onto his back, took a deep breath, and continued. "Anyway, this cop handcuffed us and took us to a bombed-out building with rebar sticking out of broken concrete and most of the roof missing. Davor was crying. He even pissed himself. He was just a kid. We both were. But I wasn't going to cry or piss myself. If he was going to kill us, then I had to be brave like my dad had been. But he didn't kill us, obviously. He beat us with a nightstick. Broke my arm and head. Broke Davor's ribs and punctured his lung. I had an eye like a rotten, pulpy fruit for about two months and a skull fracture right here," Luka said and pointed to the side of his head. Lisa reached up and touched the spot, feeling a hard lump.

"Someone found us and left us on the bridge. Our moms

found us that night and took us to the hospital. I was there for weeks. Davor not quite as long." When Luka stopped talking, she heard his breathing accelerate and his teeth grind.

"Sometimes, life feels full of stories like that. They're just spilling over the brim of what we can handle. Like the world's reached critical mass with bad energy and now it keeps accelerating exponentially," Lisa said.

"It's not. You're good. We're good," Luka said and turned to kiss Lisa's shoulder and bare chest.

Lisa thought of Wyatt. She thought of what she'd done. She'd been telling herself that it was good that she'd left, but for whatever reason, it all became clear that it wasn't. The decision appeared very black and white now. It was bad, or evil, or selfish and mean. It was against nature, for a mother to abandon her child. It was against the rules of love. At first, she couldn't figure out why it became so clear then realized it was because of Luka. Admitting her love for Luka had opened her heart and made her see. It made her see what she'd done. What she was still doing. I'm not good, Luka, Lisa wanted to say but didn't. Instead, she grabbed a handful of his hair and pulled his lips into hers and lost herself in his body.

Lisa woke to daylight streaming through wood shutters. Her hair draped over her eyes in tangles. She pushed it to the side and rolled onto Luka's outstretched arm. She found her way to the soft spot she fit perfectly into—just below his chin, between his neck and shoulder. He smelled like sweat, cigarettes, and sunburns.

She got up and took a shower. The water ran down her body and she traced it to her C-section scar, letting her fingers travel along its smooth edges. She thought about how she'd made Wyatt doing the same thing she'd done with Luka last night and how it seemed impossible. What she'd done last night she'd never done before. Sure, she'd acted out the motions with Bryan, but the connection she felt with Luka was incomparable. She stood in the doorway wearing only a towel. Luka was still asleep. His body sprawled out, half tangled in a sheet.

"Does Davor hate me?" Lisa asked.

Luka lifted his head from the bed, looked at the sunlight streaming through the shutters, and rubbed his face.

"Good morning," he said.

Lisa sat down on the bed. "Because that story you told me last night made me think about how important he is to you. I knew he was, but I didn't realize how much you'd been through."

"Davor is my main man," Luka said, yawning.

"I know. That's why I'm wondering if he hates me. I know he was upset with the way I acted when you got in the fight."

"He doesn't hate you."

"You sure?"

"Yes, I'm sure. Why are you so worried about people hating you? Even if Davor hated you, why would you care? He's an idiot. I love him like a brother, but he is an idiot."

"I just don't want people you love hating me."

"Ah, speaking of that," Luka said and walked out of the room.

"What?" Lisa asked, but Luka closed the door to the bathroom. She could hear him brushing his teeth. She got dressed and waited for him in the living room.

"Speaking of people I love," Luka said, not missing a beat, "I got a call from my cousin, Kata last night. She is getting married this weekend. It was on hold because her mom was sick but now it's back on. Would you like to be my date?"

"I've never been to a wedding," Lisa said.

It was partially true. She'd never been to one as an adult, only a kid. She remembered dancing with her dress over her head and drinking more punch than she could ever have at home, but she'd never gone to one as an adult. Most of the people she knew back home weren't married, and Lisa had missed the weddings of those that married right out of high school because she'd been too busy caring for Wyatt. The idea of attending one sounded romantic and fun. Meeting Luka's family was intimidating to say the least. She felt like they'd just shed Angela and Davor, and now they were going to throw his family into the mix.

"This will be a good wedding. You've never been to a Slavonian wedding. To say that it's a party would be an insult. It's a crazy love fest. Kata said they booked the resort in the woods that Tito himself used to stay at."

"Who is Tito?" Lisa asked.

Luka laughed. "Jesus Christ, Lisa. How long have you been in this country? Did you just pick this place on a map at random? Tito was the leader of Yugoslavia."

"Right. Like you know the American presidents."

"We study American history in school as a matter of fact. Washington, Lincoln, Roosevelt."

Luka lit up a cigarette and Lisa followed him out onto the balcony. It was already hot outside of the air-conditioned house.

"Want to swim today?" Luka asked.

Lisa thought about Angela and their time on the island. "No. Not really. It's pretty hot though. Don't we need to leave for this wedding?"

"Not till this weekend. It's what? Tuesday? We've got time."

"How far away is home?"

"Slavonski Brod?" Luka exhaled a plume of smoke and looked around like he might be able to point it out. "Far. Well, not far for you. How long does it take to drive across the US? Eight days? Twelve?"

"No idea," Lisa said. She wanted to go back inside. The heat was intense.

"I'd love to do that. In a Chevy Camaro. Or a Pontiac GTO."

Lisa laughed. "Those cars are shitty. More like a BMW or a Mercedes."

Luka waved her off, cigarette in hand. "No, no. You've got it all wrong. That doesn't match the feel of it. If you're going to drive across the US—New York City to San Francisco—you need an American muscle car. Route 66."

"Pretty sure they get bad gas mileage."

"You're crazy."

Lisa put her arms around his waist. "So, what car should you drive in Croatia?"

Now it was Luka's turn to laugh. "A Yugo."

"Why is that funny?" she asked.

"You'd have to see it to believe it."

"Can we go back inside?" Lisa asked.

Luka raised an eyebrow. "You didn't get enough of me last night? You'll drain my life force, woman."

Lisa nodded. "It's hot."

Inside, they talked more about driving to Slavonski Brod. It was about four hours if they shot straight through Zagreb.

They could rent a car and it would be no problem, but they still weren't sure what do to for the rest of the week. Luka mentioned staying in Zadar, but Lisa had had her fill. She was ready to leave Zadar behind. Part of her felt guilty about not working and spending all of Luka's money, but he didn't seem to mind. He told her that this was how he wanted to spend the money. Part of her had a feeling that the money had something to do with his dad, but she was too afraid to ask. It was none of her business. She thought maybe he'd left it for Luka. Maybe he'd taken Luka's mom on a similar trip when they were this age and Luka had just been waiting for the right girl to come along. Those were the kind of thoughts Lisa had when she wasn't feeling guilty. That maybe she was the right girl. She liked thinking like that, and when everything was going right and memories of Wyatt weren't playing on a nightmare loop in her head, she was able to.

"What about Sarajevo?" Luka asked.

Lisa cocked her head at him. "What about it?"

"You want to go?"

Lisa knew almost nothing about Sarajevo except something vague about the Olympics and the war. "Isn't that in Bosnia?"

Luka nodded.

"Is there a reason why I'd want to go there?"

Luka stared at Lisa for a long enough time that she felt her face get hot. He looked at her like he didn't know her.

"I'm sorry," she said.

"No, don't be sorry. I forget about you sometimes," Luka said.

"Forget about me?"

"I forget you haven't travelled. There are a lot of things you don't know."

"Okay you prick. I know a lot more than you give me credit for."

"Sorry, sorry," Luka said. He seemed to snap back from whatever fugue state he was in. "I don't mean that. Yes, Bosnia is a place you'd want to go. I'd love to show you. Sarajevo is a beautiful, amazing city."

"Is it safe?" Lisa asked.

"It is with me."

The next morning, they headed out. Their plan was to stop in Split overnight and then drive up to Sarajevo the next day.

Without Davor's BMW, they had to rent a car. Cars were expensive and Luka was not particularly fond of the drive between Zadar and Split. Instead, they found a ferry that would take them the whole way. They figured it was the best way to experience the coastline. It was about a four-hour trip, and they caught the afternoon ferry.

The day was hot. Lisa guessed it was close to one-hundred degrees. The only thing that made it bearable was the breeze coming off the water. Once on the ferry, they rushed inside to the bar where the air conditioners pumped out arctic air. Bumps stuck out on Lisa's bare arms, and Luka shuffled in place to keep warm. Luka ordered them a few Karlovačko beers, and they sat on the plastic molded seats and drank them.

"Man, it's so cold," Lisa said, sipping the beer that felt the same temperature as the air.

"We'll go outside soon," Luka said. He kissed Lisa. She wasn't expecting it, and before he could pull away, she put her hand behind his head, opened her mouth, and felt his tongue meet hers.

"Are we a thing now? Look at this public display of affection," Luka said. His face flushed red.

"I said I loved you," Lisa said. "Was that not clear enough?"

"Right. I'd forgotten. Thank you for the reminder."

Lisa thought about her first ideas of romantic love. Not prepubescent attraction or flirting but real love. The most concrete memory came from watching the movie *Titanic*. Jack and Rose had fallen in love in only a day or so, but it felt real. It seemed real. Almost like *Romeo and Juliet* except for the whole suicide thing. But Lisa never thought *Romeo and Juliet* seemed very realistic. Killing yourself wasn't love. There was no afterlife. There was nowhere to be together forever. But in *Titanic*, Jack sacrificed himself for Rose. He froze to death so she could live. That seemed like real love. She realized that some part of her must of held onto that more than she realized. She'd engrained it into her personality—the idea that love meant sacrifice. She'd tried to sacrifice for Wyatt, and though it wasn't a romantic love, it was something. She'd wondered if she ever truly loved Wyatt and realized now that she had. The love was strong. It punished her for not attending to it. It broke her heart but never left it. It was something she would always carry. With Luka it was easier. It was romantic love. It was split-second, sacrifice-everything-before-you-realize-what-you're-doing love.

"If this ship sank, would you save me?" Lisa asked. She pulled her knees to her chest and wrapped her arms about them to keep warm.

"Whoa. Take it easy. It's not good to talk about ships sinking, especially when you're on them," Luka said.

"I'd save you, even if that makes me sound like a crazy girlfriend or whatever. I mean it. If there was only one life jacket, I'd want you to have it."

Luka smiled with only half his mouth. "You're so crazy. That's why I love you. I'm just trying to have a *pivo* here and you're talking about ships sinking. So morbid."

Lisa took another drink. "It's not morbid. People die, Luka. It's okay to think about it. It doesn't make you a bad person."

"I know it's okay to think about. I just don't want to think about it."

"I think it's a sign of just how out of control I'm feeling. I don't know if there's anyone else in this world that I would say something like that to," Lisa said.

"I know what you're saying," Luka said quietly. He wiped a tear from his eye.

"Why are you crying?" Lisa asked.

"You're talking about dying for someone you love, and it just made me think." He paused. "Made me think of my dad."

"I'm sorry." Lisa put her arm around him and rubbed his back.

"This is why I don't like talking about all this sad shit," Luka said. He brushed another tear off his face like it was burning his skin. "He'd be happy though. He'd be happy seeing us here. Not talking about morbid stuff but being together—me and you. Out travelling. He'd like that."

They clinked their glass bottles together and decided to go out on the deck to try and warm up. They drank their beers and walked back and forth on the deck, watching the blue water sparkle and the pale slate and emerald islands pass by. The more beer they drank the more Luka talked. Lisa thought he must've taken her words to heart and was now was divulging everything. But it never felt like too much. If anything, it felt like he'd sprung a leak and Lisa was getting a glimpse into just how much he held. She soaked in every detail as he relayed stories from his glory days playing soccer, to stories about partying in college. Lisa did her best to tell her own stories but was still guarded. Luka never pushed. He accepted her vague recollections, free of too much detail like he knew, or at least understood. He was okay with whatever he got.

Still, she felt like they were building the scaffolding of their relationship out of cheap lumber and shoddy concrete, except Luka didn't know, and that was the point, but Lisa didn't know if she could keep it from him forever. Part of her wanted to blurt out that Wyatt was broken and it was her fault and she'd abandoned him in Oregon. A few times when the beer had really loosened her mind and she felt desperately in love with him, she almost did blurt it out. She knew it wasn't time. Would it ever be time? Probably not. They loved each other but their future seemed impossible. They were like Bonnie and Clyde or Jack and Rose. They had to live in the moment. Lisa wanted to. She was trying. Her past was always chasing her.

croatia: ten

The ferry pulled into the harbor at Split as dusk brimmed on the horizon. The waterfront was lined with tables and bars. Women wore high heels and dresses, and the men wore button-ups and slacks. The air smelled like wet stone and dirt despite its metropolitan feel. They walked toward their hotel—a small house sandwiched between restaurants along a narrow curving street. It was indiscreet and seemed like any other house or building except the sign out front. When they got to their room—before they even looked around or made sure the TV worked—they instinctively tore off their clothes and jumped into bed. Lisa's face pressed between Luka's chin and shoulder as their bodies moved together. She ran her hands through his hair and their feverish pace slowed. She kissed his neck and he curled into her and began moving faster again. She felt his anticipation building as it rose within herself, mirroring Luka's. Just before he finished, her pleasure was overtaken by an immense wave of sadness. She gripped him around the neck—just behind the ears—and forced his eyes to meet her own. The rushing feeling was like a pre-seizure aura, an unexplainable warning siren wailing for their impending doom. She wanted to scream, *I love you. Please don't leave*, but he finished before she said anything, collapsing next to her in the bed. She rolled over, instantly grateful she'd said nothing but unable to shake the feeling.

"What if the boat is sinking?" Lisa whispered.

"What? What?" Luka said. He kissed the back of her shoulder and moved up her neck.

"You said it's bad luck to talk about it, but what if it is sinking?"

"Did I do something wrong? Was that not good for you? I thought—"

"Luka," Lisa said, turning over to face him. "How is this going to work out?"

Luka smiled. "How is it going to work out? It's working out great. You're beautiful and sexy and I love you. What's there to work out?"

Dread built in her chest. Luka knew what she meant. He had to. He wanted to deal with it the same way he dealt with everything else, but Lisa couldn't. She had too much riding on this relationship for it to fail. She'd bet everything on their love. If it was doomed, she needed to know.

"Would you live in America?" Lisa asked.

"Would I—would I live in America?" Luka asked himself. "I've never even been there."

"What if that was the only way we could be together?"

Luka threw the sheets off and put on his boxers. "If it was the only way we could be together then how could we be together here in Croatia? Things are going fine."

"I don't know why you always have to blow me off whenever I'm trying to talk about something serious."

Luka put his clothes back on and Lisa pulled the sheets over her naked body. "I'm a total stranger here," Lisa said. "I'm thousands of miles away from my home and I'm traveling with you and now we're driving up to a wedding and I'll meet your family." Lisa wiped away a tear forming in the corner of her eye. "You might not realize it, but our future is very uncertain."

Luka came back and sat on the edge of the bed. "I mean it's all about perspective, right? I know it's serious stuff. I didn't decide that things should get so heavy. I didn't choose to fall in love with you. Did you choose? It's out of our hands. All of this. Everything that you always want me to talk about. Happiness. Sadness. The future. Love. I have no say. You might think you do but you don't. You want me to move to America? You want to live in Croatia for the rest of your life? How can we answer that? All we have is now. All we can decide is today."

"How are we going to make it if you don't make a conscious decision about anything?"

Luka lowered his head and didn't speak for a few seconds. "I don't know what's going to happen, and I'm in love with you. It's possible for both of these things to be true, and for us to be happy. The future is always shifting no matter how much we may plan. My dad had his entire life planned out and then it disappeared in a second. Less than that even." Luka paused. "I'm not ruling anything out, but I'm not making promises I can't keep."

Lisa started to cry. Luka bent over and wiped her tears with his fingertips.

"My baby didn't die, Luka," Lisa said, her lips trembling. "Before we take this any further, I need you to know."

"Okay," he said. His eyes were big, like the room had gone dark and he was looking for something he'd lost. "Okay."

Lisa took a deep breath, wiped her tears, and exhaled. She told him everything. She told him about Bryan. About Wyatt. About how she'd refused to take him to the doctor. About the fish movie and hugging him on the carpet. About the bite marks, the spilled food, the crying, the screaming, the Zoloft. She told him about leaving. That was the hardest part. For a long time, she thought that telling someone about having a kid with a developmental disability would be the hardest part, but it wasn't. Admitting that you'd given up was.

Luka sat and listened. He didn't say a word. He didn't make eye contact. Every once in a while, he'd reach out and touch Lisa's hand but otherwise he sat still and silent. Lisa finished, feeling exhausted and empty, but also healed, like she'd been cured by bloodletting and, in the process, had bled out. Luka still looked lost and confused.

"I don't know what to say," Luka said. "I mean, I had a feeling something like this was going on. I knew something had happened. I don't know what to say."

Luka trailed off. Lisa felt her heart breaking and wanted to run. After a moment, he spoke again.

"A lot of the time I think I know what's right and what's wrong, but the older I get, the less I understand. I love you. Knowing this changes nothing. It only makes me love you more."

His arms encircled her. She felt his breath on her face and his hand on her head, brushing her hair gently like Lisa would do to Wyatt after an incident. She collapsed in his arms and entered a state somewhere at the absolute intersection of sleep, death, and waking. Paralytic catatonia, except it wasn't just that. Time stopped moving. Their impossible, continuous blossoming into the present froze and she knew that this was the power of real love. This was what she was able to give to Wyatt. Even if he didn't understand it or want it, she could give this to him the same way Luka gave it to her. Soundless, wordless, incomprehensible, and all-encompassing love that made time and life and death—all of it—stop. Not only stopping their perpetual march toward eternity but changing the linear progression all together. True love made reality an illusion.

When time started up again, she wanted to ask him what he thought, what he would've done, but Luka stayed silent, and Lisa knew it was stupid to ask questions there were no answers to. They made love again, slower and less frantic this time. Afterwards, Lisa cried, not because she was happy or sad, but because she felt both completely exposed and absolutely safe.

Lisa woke up once in the middle of the night to see if Luka was still there. She'd dreamt that he'd only pretended to be okay with it all but was actually disgusted by what she'd done and had made off in the night. But he hadn't. He was asleep on his back. His arms sprawled out like he was falling. She'd studied his face in the dark to try and see if there was something that would give away what he was dreaming about, but there was nothing.

They woke up early and walked the streets of Split with coffee in their hands. In the old town, there was an ancient wall, similar to what she'd sat on in Zadar with Angela. It weaved between stone buildings, outlining where the palace grounds used to stand. They'd kept the wall, but the rest had been filled in. Inside the walls, the buildings were old and plain with green shutters. Chairs and tables spilled out into the narrow streets. Sometimes, they'd come to a small alleyway that Lisa would take Luka down just so they could be alone in the city for a moment, and Lisa would touch the walls and the street and think about the countless lives that had stood on the same corner. Luka watched but he didn't share her same earnest interest in the dead.

"It's the same people that are here now. Look at the people living," he said.

They stopped for lunch and then afterwards went to find a

car to rent. The cheapest option was expensive enough, but Luka wanted to rent an Audi.

"We don't need that," Lisa said.

"We don't need anything," Luka said. "Why not? Who is telling us no?"

Lisa glanced at the salesperson who winked at Luka. "It's just a lot of money."

"Money is just money. There's always more of it to get. My dad saved this money for me. He wanted me to spend it on something special. There were so many times in my life when I could've spent it but I never did. It never felt right. But this trip. All of this. This feels right."

Lisa could think of more reasons why they shouldn't spend more than they needed to, but she didn't say anything else. Luka seemed intent on renting the Audi. Growing up near Lake Oswego, she'd been in plenty of nice cars that rich kids borrowed from their parents. It meant nothing to her. She always imagined the better ways they could spend their money. Save the bees or the rainforest or something like that. But Luka wanted it for the pleasure of the moment. At least that was what Lisa thought. She wouldn't deny him that. It was his money.

They headed back to the hotel to pick up their things and planned to head out after. In the lobby, Lisa noticed two computers sitting unused for guests. Something came over her, urging her to go over. She told Luka she'd meet him upstairs and sat down at one of them. After telling Luka about Wyatt, she felt healed but fractured. Like she'd been ignoring an injury for so long that when she finally looked at the open wound with jutting bone, she couldn't stop poking it. She knew her mom must've tried to reach out. The messages were waiting for her. Lisa hadn't told her much in the letter she'd left. Only that she was leaving. That it was the right thing. That Cathy was the right choice and that everything was going to be all right.

Lisa logged onto her Facebook. Sure enough, the messages were there. She checked the first one sent the same day she'd left. Her mom was angry. Maybe hurt was a better description, but to Lisa, she couldn't help but read the words like she was being shouted at. "Lisa, how could you" was how her mom opened up the message. Lisa felt a pang in her stomach and almost didn't read on but took a deep breath and did anyway. Her mom went on about how hurtful this had been to both her and Wyatt and how she hoped this was a long weekend and she'd be back soon. Lisa skipped a few messages. A few from Amber asking what had happened. One from Bryan that Lisa deleted without opening. Lisa noticed a message from a month ago—the last one in her inbox—from her mom. It detailed how she'd taken Wyatt to the developmental specialist and how the doctor had given a preliminary diagnosis and was hopeful for Wyatt. Now there were speech therapists, psychologists, social workers involved. Everyone was working together with a single goal in mind—to give Wyatt the best life possible. Lisa cried tears of hopeful joy and immense sadness while reading the message.

Near the end of the message, Cathy wrote:

> *This wasn't your fault, Lisa. I hope it wasn't guilt that drove you away. Being a parent is hard, harder than anyone can imagine until they are one. There were times when I wanted to run. Times when I've had to face the guilt of the mother I was. It's never pretty. It's always painful. But leaving doesn't let you leave. Not really. If you have a good heart, then you can't just forget.*
>
> *Do you remember when you found that dead squirrel out front? You were pretty young, five or six. I tried to shield your eyes and lead you inside, but you wouldn't leave. You said it wasn't right to leave it squished in the street, so we grabbed a dustpan and you swept it up with grace and care. You dug a hole in the backyard, buried it and cried about every night for the next week. That's who you are Lisa. I know you haven't forgotten. If I had to guess, you are starting to remember.*
>
> *Wyatt hasn't forgotten either. He doesn't quite know what's broken, but I can see it in his eyes. He looks for you around the house. He wanders around in the mornings like he's waiting for something.*
>
> *We love you, Lisa. We need you. Come home.*
>
> *-Mom*

"You ready?" Luka said.

Lisa scrambled to close the window on the screen.

"Are you crying?" Luka asked. He put their bags down and put a hand to Lisa's cheek. Lisa hastily wiped her face.

"Yeah. Yeah," she choked out. "Gimme a minute." She ran into the bathroom.

Lisa looked at herself in the mirror. Her freckles had gotten darker, along her forehead and flanking her nose. Her mascara was smeared from the tears. She flashed back to when she was crying in the bathroom at work when she found out she was pregnant. Was she even the same person? The memories felt so foreign that Lisa thought maybe she was going insane. She wiped her face and threw up a little in her mouth. The acidic bile burned the top of her mouth and she spit it into the sink. She rushed out of the bathroom.

"What is it?" Luka asked.

"I shouldn't have done that," Lisa said, as much to Luka as herself. "What was I thinking?"

"Done what? I'm gone for a minute and I feel like everything has changed."

Everything had changed. The gnawing feeling just below her breastbone was the same feeling she had when she first thought about leaving Wyatt. Something had changed in the last few minutes. Something drastic and heavy—intangible yet visceral. She didn't know exactly what it was or what it meant.

"I'll tell you later," Lisa said. "It's not important now."

"Seems pretty damn important. You were just crying, and you seem real upset still," Luka said, running a hand through his hair.

"It was my mom. She wrote me about Wyatt. She's written a lot and enlisted other people to reach out to me too. It was—it was hard to read."

Luka nodded, knowingly. "Did you write back?"

"Of course not," Lisa said. "What would I say?"

Luka shrugged. "I don't know. Say anything. It's like you said that night. There are no right answers. Silence seems a little brutal, I feel. I'm not trying to be out of line, but I think saying something in response makes sense."

Lisa stared at the floor. "I shouldn't have told you," she mumbled.

"Okay, you know what? You're right. You do what feels right, Lisa. I'm not trying to fuck things up between us." He grabbed her by the shoulders, forcing their eyes to connect. "They'll probably never understand. Your mom. Wyatt."

"Just stop, Luka. You're making it worse," Lisa said and pushed his arms away.

Luka tried to explain further but she eventually shut him up with a kiss. They started their drive to Sarajevo in the Audi that Luka no longer seemed excited about. They drove in near silence from Split to the Croatian-Bosnian border. Lisa thought more about her mom's messages. She was struggling with the idea of writing back. Was it cruel to not respond? Lisa liked to keep the reasons she left Wyatt separate from the reasons her dad left her, but she couldn't. Would she have been happier if he'd written? What if he'd said things that she wasn't ready to hear? Like, *Dear Lisa, I'm a bad person who treats other people badly and I don't have time for you* or *Dear Lisa, I fucking hate kids and I never want to see you again.* No. In many ways it was easier to make up a story about her dad than it would've been to hear the truth.

The gnawing feeling gripped Lisa's stomach just below the rib cage as they waited at the border. Luka turned the car off while they waited and even with the windows down the car was sweltering. Luka slammed his palm down on the wheel.

"What the fuck!" he shouted.

"It's fine," Lisa said.

"Who are all these people? How close could they be looking at the passports? Are people trying to sneak into Bosnia?"

Lisa wiped sweat off her forehead and put her hands around her abdomen, trying to quell the gnawing nausea.

"Just chill," Lisa said.

"I'm chilling. These people are messing things up for us."

"I'm going to throw up." Lisa unbuckled her seatbelt, opened her door and leaned out. She felt a rush of heat from her bowels into her throat, but nothing came up. Luka reached over and put a hand on her shoulder. She sat back in her seat and closed her eyes. Luka rolled the windows up and turned the AC on.

"Goddamn. Sorry. I hope it's not heat stroke or something. It's not, right? Are you dizzy?" Luka asked. He revved the engine trying to get the AC going faster.

Lisa took deep breaths, filling her belly up with air and pushing it out, slowly, through pursed lips. Cold air began to blow through the vents and the line moved forward. The feeling disappeared as quickly as it had arrived.

Whatever was holding up the line had been removed and they passed across the border easily. On the other side they found themselves on a small highway with green hills growing into distant mountains. Luka powered the Audi around the corners and Lisa felt a mix of fear and excitement until eventually telling Luka to slow down. Luka played some music, and they started talking about bands that had shaped their childhood. Luka liked Radiohead and Rolling Stones and went on a long rant about Nirvana and Pearl Jam. Lisa felt embarrassed about the pop music she'd grown up listening to and pretended to like the same things as Luka. Outside, the mountains on either side of them began to rise up toward the sky. The road twisted along next to an impossibly glacier blue river. Huge slabs of granite lined both sides of the mountains, like someone had taken a massive knife and peeled away the trees and dirt leaving smooth, steep rock faces that jutted upwards. Lisa held Luka's hand and felt thankful to see such beauty.

"I didn't think it would be like this," Lisa said.

"Like what," Luka said.

"Like, beautiful. It's beautiful here."

"It is really nice in this place."

"But what about the war? I guess I pictured it to be all ruined or something."

Luka stared out the window at the mountains looming. "Not here. Here, it's perfect."

The road followed the river as it emptied into larger lakes and pools surrounded by small towns and roadside restaurants. Darkness began to fall as they entered the serpiginous city road. Traffic came to a standstill and Lisa rolled her window down to let the night air replace the stale air-conditioned interior. It was humid and smelled like gasoline and the river. The cars moved slowly. No one was honking and Lisa wondered if there was a crash up ahead. They passed identical cement apartment complexes until a dim light began to glow ahead of them. It was a soccer field lit up and filled with players. It looked like half the town was there. Maybe the whole town. Traffic inched past as the drivers whooped and hollered for the players on the pitch. The cars started to disappear as they left the town and Lisa fell asleep.

She woke to the sound of a commuter train clanging. She opened her eyes to an old green train speeding through the city alongside them.

"We're here," Luka said, gesturing to the tall buildings in the distance. The city was darker than she expected. There were clouds covering the sky and a faint mist that dimmed the streetlights. They drove through the anachronistic city of Soviet-era architecture, shiny glass skyscrapers and ancient brick buildings. They continued up a steep road into the mountains. The road narrowed, and Luka kept glancing at his phone trying to find the address. They ended up circling past the house twice before parking. Lisa got out. The house was unusual. The street was full of similar-styled cement houses with red roofs, but their house had a purple roof and multiple ornate, distinguishing characteristics. Someone had put a lot of time and effort into a rental. Lisa got out and immediately had the urge to go to sleep. She grabbed her bag and made her way toward the front door.

Luka poorly executed a British accent. "Oh, excuse me, miss. Lisa, is it? Let me take your bag. You look exhausted."

Lisa gave a sleepy smile and put her arm around his waist. He carried her bag inside. They made their way upstairs to the bedroom. The house was just as uniquely decorated as the exterior, with sharp angular furniture and sparse things purposefully placed around each room. The bedroom had a black, furry comforter, and a full-length mirror with a hand-carved wooden frame from someplace like India. Lisa lifted the comforter, got into bed, and closed her eyes. She fell asleep faster than she ever had.

Lisa woke up in the middle of the night. She shot straight up into a sitting position like a mousetrap going off. She gasped for air. Her eyes scrambled to find something familiar in the room. She turned and heard Luka snoring next to her. His bare back was barely visible in the dark. She got up and opened the blinds to let the street glow in. She searched her mind to try and find a source of panic. A nightmare? A memory? No. It was too obscure to materialize. She looked back at Luka who hadn't moved. She couldn't remember falling asleep. What time was it? When did Luka go to sleep? Everything felt foreign and unsafe. Her mind was awake and moving at an unnerving speed. She tried to take a deep breath. She closed her eyes and tried to concentrate. Was it Wyatt? Mom? No. It would make sense if it was, but it wasn't. The nauseous feeling came over her and she almost doubled over on the floor. Cold sweat and stomach pangs enveloped her. Her heart raced.

"Luka," Lisa whispered and then again, louder, "Luka, please wake up. I think—I'm worried I'm getting sick or something."

Luka sat up and got out of bed. His hands found Lisa's face before his eyes could.

"You're sweating. Or are you crying? Turn a light on or something, I don't know what is going on," he said, blindly reaching for the lamp. With the light on, Lisa crawled back into bed and Luka held her in his arms until her heart rate normalized and the stomach cramps dissipated. She woke up again a few hours later. She looked out the window. It was still dark. She got out of bed and paced the room, too worried to stop moving. She didn't want the nausea and pains to return. What was wrong? What was happening? Luka sat up from bed.

"Lay down. You still look sick," he said.

"I can't," she said.

"You can't?"

Lisa's bare feet on the cold floor grounded her. She pressed her toes into the wood. "It's fine. You don't have to get up yet. I need to leave though. I need to go."

Luka threw off the comforter. "I'm coming with you. It's fine. The sun will be up soon. We'll go have breakfast."

They left the house and found themselves in a wet fog. It was near dawn. Some hint of emerging sunlight could be seen through the clouds as slivers of orange filtered through the mist. They made their way down a steep hill. The fog started to disappear as the sun rose in the distance. Lisa noticed the mountains surrounding the city, looming over it from all sides, like the buildings were placed in a punched-out bowl of forest. On the opposite end of the city, Lisa noticed something strange.

Across the hillside were white markings scattered across a hillside. They were arranged in some sort of grid.

"What's that?" Lisa asked, pointing.

"Graveyard," Luka said.

Once he said what it was, Lisa noticed them everywhere. They were pools of white posts in a sea of red roofs. She'd never seen them so prominently placed in a cityscape. They made their way down the hill and into the narrow streets. It was quiet and cool, but the sun had burned up the fog and clouds, casting a soft, yellow glow on everything.

"I don't know anything about this place," Lisa said. "I feel stupid walking around a city I don't know anything about. Weren't the Olympics here?"

"Yes," Luka said. "And World War I started here with an assassination. And when the Serbians attacked, this city was under siege for a while."

"What do you mean *under siege*?" Lisa asked.

"I mean that there was artillery along all the mountains there," he said and pointed to the forested ridges in the distance, "and snipers, and they lobbed shells into the city center, and snipers picked people off trying to shop for groceries at the markets. For like, almost four years. Or more. I'm not sure. A lot of people died."

"That's terrible." Lisa looked around as if she would notice something to suggest that the impossible atrocities had actually taken place.

"Terrible things happened all over. But it's true. What happened here was bad. It's a miracle the city survived. It could've been decimated. I mean it was decimated but there were things left. The soul of it lived."

They walked in silence until they found a coffee shop. They went inside and ordered some Turkish coffee, which Lisa had never had but was pleasantly surprised with. The coffee was jet black and thick, like ink. It tasted fantastic and Lisa liked drinking it out of the small cup. They sat at a table outside and watched the street come alive.

"Do you think people think about the war?" Lisa asked.

"What do you mean?" Luka said.

"Like, do you think they think about it every day? Do they

look at a chip on a building—or a scar on some stone—and think about what happened here?"

Luka drank his coffee. "No. In SB, there are scars from the war everywhere. Bullet holes on the buildings, shrapnel in the hillsides, but we don't see it anymore. It's gone. In the past."

"I don't think I could live in a place like this. I feel something here. Something sad and old."

"It's like your story you told, Lisa. The one about the place where bad things happened but then it became something else. A place has to reinvent itself if it wants to survive."

"What about Hell, though?"

Luka laughed. "What about Hell?" He looked around and lowered his voice. "What did you have nightmares about last night?"

"I mean that in the history of time, yes, things are forgotten and reinvented. Tragedies become nothing more than stories. There's no weight to them. But within the span of a lifetime, I don't know if things can be forgotten or reinvented. I think if you are bad you go to Hell. In Hell, you don't get to reinvent yourself. You just suffer for what you did—forever."

"Hell is not real. The only real thing is the moment, the present. Right now. This," Luka said, gesturing to himself and Lisa, "is real. Everything else is perspective."

"Do you think the people who carried out the siege in this city thought that?"

Luka took a sip from his coffee. "Sometimes you get on this kick and it's hard to figure out how to talk to you." A moment passed. People walked by on the street, on their way to work, or breakfast, or aimlessly wandering. "The people who carried out the siege? I don't know—how could I know what they thought?"

"Do you think we pay for the sins we commit in life?"

"I don't know if I believe in sin." Luka grabbed a cigarette from his jean pocket. Lisa drank her coffee and stared at the table. She thought of her dad and wondered if abandoning your family was enough of a sin to go to Hell over. The pang of nausea hit her again. She searched her mind, trying to find the root of the guilt and restlessness, expecting to find the messages from her mom bouncing around in some dark crevasse in her head, ricocheting off the walls and causing silent damage, but she found something else. The nausea, the stomach pains, the gnawing ache—they were because she was thinking about leaving Luka.

"I love you," Lisa said. "Sometimes I want to tell you that all the time. Just in case."

"In case of what?" Luka asked.

"It's the last time. My last chance."

Luka leaned forward. "Do you think I'm going to die or something?"

"Or disappear."

"Or disappear . . ." Luka looked up thoughtfully. "I'm not going anywhere."

"Then I'll say it anyway. I love you."

Luka leaned further across the table and Lisa met him. They kissed. It made Lisa want to cry, but she didn't. Something had already started to pull them apart.

After coffee and breakfast, they walked down to the city center. They shopped and looked at intricately handmade Turkish coffee sets. Someone tried to sell them a trip to go zip-lining in the mountains. Luka considered it for a while until Lisa reminded him of the wedding they had to make, and they moved on. They stopped for some hummus, red pepper, cheese, and a sausage called ćevapi. Afterwards Luka took her to a fountain in the middle of a square.

"What is it?" Lisa asked as they came up closer to the fountain.

"Sebilj," Luka said. "There's a legend about it. We have to drink the water and then I'll tell you."

Lisa looked at the fountain that resembled a half-pagoda, half-phone booth, with an emerald dome and small faucets on each side. People walked up and drank with cupped hands. They both scooped a handful of water and drank it. It was cold and clean tasting. Lisa wiped her face.

"It's good," she said.

"We will return here together," Luka said.

"Oh yeah?"

"That's the legend."

"That we'll return?"

Luka nodded. "Together though. If you drink together, you return together. Either in this life or the next. We will be back on this exact spot."

Lisa looked at the fountain and then back at Luka. "I thought you didn't like thinking or planning too much in the future."

Luka led her back into the streets lined with coppersmiths and cafes. "I'm not planning. I have no control. It will just happen."

Luka went to have a beer and Lisa sat on a bench inside the grounds of a mosque. It was quiet and the trees were beautiful. She couldn't shake the feeling she had being in the city. Since she'd been here, she hadn't been able to sleep or feel at peace without thoughts of death or the afterlife. After they'd drank from the fountain, the nauseous pang hit her again. She ignored it this time, knowing what it meant. Now, alone, she couldn't help but think about how improbable their love was to begin with. From across the world, both with their baggage, trying to live in the moment. She figured that must've been how the city survived. One day at a time. Once the bombs stopped dropping and the shots went silent, the people here held the past in their heart, but that was where they kept it. They lived a day at a time.

croatia: eleven

They left Sarajevo early. Lisa slept most of the way and by mid-morning they were almost at the Croatian border. She woke up to bombed-out houses scattered in the tall grass. She wondered if she might take Wyatt here one day. It was something she daydreamed about in the rare times she was able to think about Wyatt and not feel terrible. She wondered about him as an adult, or a teenager. She really felt like he'd turn out okay. Without her something deep inside Lisa whispered that he could be cured. That it was the poison she exuded with her love. She daydreamed that one day he'd be a man and they'd come together, and he'd understand. Then perhaps they could have a life together. A life less about being a mother and a son and more about being two people who loved each other. Maybe she'd take him here and show him things he'd never seen before.

"Who exactly am I going to see at this wedding?" Lisa asked.

"Everyone," Luka said. "Except Davor. Well, maybe Davor will be there. Everyone else though."

"It's your cousin's wedding?"

"Kata," Luka said. "She is marrying Marko. I knew Marko a little bit growing up, but he hung out with—"

"Is your mom going to be there?"

Luka paused and turned to Lisa. "Of course."

"Does she know about me?"

"She knows I'm bringing a girl."

"Oh my God," Lisa said, rubbing her face. "She doesn't know I'm American? Or that I'm jobless and having you pay for everything?"

Luka laughed. "I think we'll leave that part out."

Lisa kept rubbing her face until she saw little gray and silver stars.

"It's okay to be nervous," Luka said.

"I know it's okay," Lisa snapped. Luka flexed his jaw muscle. "Sorry," Lisa said. "What's your mom's name? I should at least know her name. I feel like a total imposter rolling into this wedding like this."

"Zara. And you don't need to worry about her. She knows how I am. She respects my choices. If I tell her we're in love, she will love you as well. That's how it works. Even if you were not who she was hoping for, she would treat you like family. You will see. I don't know how it is in America, but here, once you are family, you will always be family."

Lisa paused. "That sounds nice," she said but wasn't sure she believed it.

In the distance, a city emerged, and past it, a bridge. It was Bosanski Brod and the bridge on the Croatian side, Slavonski Brod. As they crossed the border, the Croatian officers essentially waved them through once they saw the American and Croatian passports. Slavonski Brod was small, at least to Lisa. There were no tall skyscrapers, only small apartment complexes and a soccer stadium. The river beneath the bridge was calm and beautiful, with small beaches where people sunbathed and swam. Luka turned down a street and sped through the center of the city. There were no tourists here. People walked with purpose not leisure.

"That's where I grew up," Luka said, pointing out the window at an apartment complex. Lisa spied an inconspicuous building three stories high with large windows and a brick façade. There were bullet holes the size of tennis balls and larger slashes that Lisa could only guess represented shrapnel from bombs or mortars across the brick and stone. She wanted to ask Luka more questions. Was he in the apartment when the gunfire went off? The bombs? How exactly did his dad die? But she knew the answers didn't matter. They never did. Morbid curiosity never yielded satisfaction and yet she still yearned to ask. She yearned to know him. Know his trauma. His fears. His memories. But she loved him without having to know. All she really wanted to do was tell him that she was sorry it happened—all of it—but knew that it had made him into the man he was today, and without it, they may have never have met. She felt selfish thinking that way. As if all the suffering had taken place so they could be together. Wyatt's issues. The war. But she knew the world didn't work that way. Their love was for them and them only. The world would follow its entropic chaos toward the future. There was no plan. There was no destiny. There was only now.

Luka kept driving and the city disappeared behind them.

"This isn't Slavonski Brod?" Lisa asked.

"We're going to Grandmother's house. It's close," Luka said.

The city gave way to a small town, single streets lined with houses and gardens or farms stretching back for acres behind them. The houses were identical brick-colored, single-story buildings with a single driveway. They passed a sign for local honey and another for fresh flowers. Luka pulled into the driveway of one of the houses.

"This is it," he said and got out before Lisa could ask any questions.

Lisa stepped out of the car and into a dry heat. The yellow grass crunched under her shoe. Kids ran from the side yard to the gate. She could hear laughter and Croatian folk music playing. Luka was flanked by a swarm of young children before he could even get to the gate. Lisa smiled. For the first time, seeing children didn't bother her. She liked seeing Luka interact with them. Their eyes tracked his movements like he was a celebrity they couldn't believe was there. Luka picked up a couple of laughing boys and carried them over his shoulder into the yard. Lisa didn't move forward. She stayed and had half a mind to go back into the Audi and hide in the backseat, but Luka returned, childless and laughing. He picked her up in both arms—not over his shoulder but in his hands like a groom would for his bride—and carried her into the yard. The children clapped and cheered. Lisa's face blushed as she slapped on a nervous smile. Someone shouted and Luka put her down. A woman hurried over, gave Luka a playful slap on the face to which he pretended like he was going to pick her up as well. The woman turned to Lisa and said, "Welcome. Welcome. We are so happy you are here."

She was about five foot two, thin, with black hair,

sun-kissed skin, and dark, almond eyes. Her voice was raspy and comforting.

"Mama, please. Give us some rakija, we've been driving all day," Luka said.

"Are you his mom?" Lisa asked.

"Zara," the woman said and gave Lisa a hug. Lisa hugged her back. Zara smelled like spices and flour.

Zara disappeared inside the small house and returned with two rakija, a lemon beer, and a plate of grapes. They downed the rakija and Luka joined some other young men gathered near a grill where the smell of cooking meat emanated. Lisa never had time to protest. Zara put a gentle hand on her shoulder and led her around and introduced her to everyone. She called Lisa, Luka's *friend,* which gave way to knowing looks from the women, and the happy children saying that they were Luka's *friend,* too. After they'd made the rounds, Zara led Lisa over to a long table covered in a blue tablecloth beneath a lattice swarming with grape vines. At the head of the table was an old woman, plump with short gray hair, a huge, unflinching smile, and a soft, kind voice. Grandmother, Lisa was sure.

"It is so nice to have you here, Lisa," Zara said, offering Lisa the plate of grapes. "My Luka is usually so secretive about his life, but he has not shied away from telling me about you."

"That's nice to hear. What's he said?" Lisa grabbed one of the grapes and chewed slowly. She turned to see where Luka was and realized he had likely left her on purpose. To be alone. With Zara.

"That you are beautiful, which you are. That you're American, and that you are looking for adventure."

Lisa gave a polite laugh that almost exploded into something inappropriate. The rakija was hitting her harder than expected. She wondered what Luka had actually said to have Zara describe her as *looking for adventure.*

"He didn't tell me that you were in love," Zara said.

Lisa almost choked on the grape.

"I—he didn't?"

"No, but I can tell. When you raise someone from a baby to a man, you can tell when his heart is swept up."

Grandmother began talking. Zara laughed and turned to Lisa. "She likes you," Zara said, gesturing to Grandmother. "She says you look like her sister when they were young."

"Thank you," Lisa said. "Your home is beautiful."

Zara translated.

"She says of course, you are welcome anytime. She is wondering if you and Luka will be here for long?" Zara asked.

"Not sure," Lisa said. "We don't have a plan, really."

Zara translated again and Grandmother laughed. Grandmother got up and kissed Lisa on the cheek and went inside.

"She's going to go make a bed for you both. In case you need to stay," Zara said.

"Oh," Lisa said.

"It's a bit overwhelming, isn't it?" Zara asked.

"Yeah." Lisa ran her hand through her hair and looked for Luka again. "But everyone is very nice."

"So, tell me what you are doing with Luka," Zara said. One eyebrow was raised. She shifted her posture, crossing her legs and leaning her head on her hand.

"What I'm doing? I'm—not sure what you mean," Lisa said. Her voice cracked. Despite her small stature and warm welcoming demeanor, Zara was intimidating. She wanted Zara to like her. She wanted Zara to be impressed with her. But Lisa felt devoid of anything impressive or even likeable. The kids ran by the table as they chased each other—a tornado of giggling energy. Zara shooed them away before they knocked over the bottles on the table.

"I don't mean anything by it," Zara said. She smiled as she spoke. Her teeth were crooked but white. "It makes me very happy to see Luka happy. There have been times—well, I'm sure you have seen even in the short time you've been together; Luka is not always this happy. He looks like whatever he's been looking for—to fix that part of him—he's found."

"We found each other," Lisa said. She sipped her lemon beer. "He's a wonderful person and he's done a lot for me. More than anyone, really. Luka has been very good to me."

Luka plopped down on the chair between Zara and Lisa. He kissed Zara on the cheek and Lisa on the lips. The three of them went silent for a moment. Luka eventually broke it by sarcastically telling Zara not to harass Lisa. They entered into an easy conversation, talking about their trip to Zadar and Split and Sarajevo. Zara listened to Luka talk and her eyes followed his emphatic gestures and sad brown eyes like she was staring at a baby, her baby. Lisa recognized the look. Moreover, she understood the look. Even at a distance she could feel it radiating like a heat lamp. It lit up some extinguished part of her brain, and for a moment she remembered what it was like to look upon her own child and feel calm, exponential love.

They stayed for a few more hours at Grandmother's. They walked into the plum orchard out back and played hide and seek with the kids. There was a lot of rakija. Enough that Lisa tried to turn some away and Luka politely let her know that it was very rude to refuse a drink during a wedding.

"Is this a wedding?" she asked.

"The start time of the wedding celebration is sort of a hazy thing," he said and clinked his glass against hers. She swallowed down the harsh, yellow liquor. It was strong, made by Grandmother out of the plums in her orchard. Grandmother was one of the biggest proponents of drinking it, and despite her age, was able to keep up with everyone—including Luka—without an obvious sign of her intoxication. Lisa on the other hand, found herself singing along to Croatian songs she'd never heard before, shouting the choruses incorrectly and not feeling the slightest bit self-conscious about it. The singers moved out to the orchard and Lisa and Zara talked about the time Zara had visited Chicago. She'd seen a Chicago White Sox game despite wanting to see the Chicago Cubs. She'd mixed up the days and had yet to get over the mistake.

"No one wants to hear about my trip to see the White Sox," Zara lamented. "Even the Cubs. It's all Yankees, Yankees, Yankees."

Lisa had gone to a few Mariner games growing up but wasn't much of a fan of any sports, let alone something as boring as baseball. Still, she liked talking to Zara. The rakija had loosened their tongues and conversation flowed freely. She could see parts of her in Luka. The soft kindness. The gregariousness. She fought the urge to ask about his dad. Seeing one half of his parents, Lisa was able to piece together what Luka's dad must have been like. She saw it in Luka—the fierceness, his bubbling optimism. Lisa wondered what parts of herself Wyatt might one day have. Would he have any? Lisa sometimes liked to think about parts of her she got from her dad but was never able to confirm. When she did something bad when she was younger, her mom would always say, *You're just like your father.* Lisa thought that was just her mom's way of coping but now wondered if it was true. Maybe some parents do give all their negative traits.

They said goodbye and got back in the Audi. Luka drove them back into Slavonski Brod to meet up with Kata and Marko, the bride and groom, and his other cousins and friends. In the car Lisa couldn't stop smiling. Luka drove slowly. They rolled the windows down and let the warm night air flow in. It smelled like fruit and grass. They found the group outside a bar that Luka described as a *motorcycle bar*. Lisa didn't ask him to elaborate. A woman broke apart from the group as they approached and ran up and kissed Luka on the cheek. They spoke briefly in Croatian and then Luka introduced her as Kata, his cousin and the bride to be.

Kata had dark hair and dark eyes like Zara, but she was taller and had a heavy accent. She kissed Lisa on the cheek and squeezed her hand. "Glad you are here."

When they got closer to the group, Luka was surrounded by people who equally hugged him, kissed him, punched and wrestled with him. He emerged from the fray with a very tall man with a thick, heavy jaw and wide build.

"Marko," Luka said. "Meet Lisa."

"Hallo," Marko said. "Pleased to meet you." He shook her hand, more formally than everyone else. Lisa guessed it was because he wasn't family to Luka, at least not yet. They all sat outside at a long table and ordered beers. Lisa was at the end with Luka and Kata. She was pretty drunk, so she sipped her beer slowly. At the end of the table, she felt out of place—like she didn't belong—and wondered if she should've stayed at Grandmother's. Zara had made her feel welcome, like a friend or a mother. Kata tried to talk to Lisa, but her English was very limited. Luka was deep in conversation with someone Lisa hadn't met yet. After a few minutes of labored superficial chatting with Kata about how exciting it must be to be getting married and what a nice boy Luka was, Kata was whisked away by another friend or cousin to the other side of the table, and Lisa was left alone. Unable to shake the outsider feeling, Lisa got up to leave but Luka grabbed her hand.

"Where are you off to? Everything okay?" he asked.

"Fine. I'm feeling a little sick. I think I'll go sit by the river for a minute. For the fresh air."

"You can't just go sit by the river at this time of night. I'll go with you."

"Please." Lisa put her hand between them and pushed Luka back down into his seat. "Please, enjoy yourself."

Lisa walked off quickly. The nausea and stomachache returning. She felt like an imposter. Like it was all a dream and she realized it at the worst possible time, when everything was going well—everything was perfect. The river looked like black bubbling lava in the night. It was colder by the river. Lisa rubbed her shoulders to warm up. She thought about her emergency fund, the money she'd kept to buy her ticket back home. The thought was unintentional. It came from somewhere deep and suppressed. Before it was an impossibility, a forgotten life, but after the messages from home, she couldn't help but think about going back. Watching Luka interact with family here only increased the urge. To watch a functioning, loving family interact over generations was beautiful. She wanted that. She didn't know if it was possible. Her dad had left. Her mom was still a mess in a lot of ways and so was Lisa. They could never have what Luka had. Unless what was Luka's became her own. Unless she and Wyatt became part of this family. The river continued to boil.

Luka sat down next to her, put his arm around her shoulders and exhaled loudly.

"I'm sorry if you are feeling overwhelmed," Luka said. "I know it's a lot. We said we love each other and all of that, but it's still a lot to come meet everyone in my family in a few hours."

Lisa leaned into Luka and put her head between his neck and shoulder. "If I'm overwhelmed, I'm overwhelmed with goodness. It's really good here. I'm happy, but somehow, I've found a way to feel bad about it. Like, I don't deserve it, or I'm worried it will be snatched from me at any moment."

Silence moved between them.

"I wish I wasn't like this. I don't know what to say. Your family is lovely."

"They like you. I can tell. I mean, you wouldn't be able to tell if they didn't, but they do. Trust me. Especially Mom," Luka said.

"I like them too," Lisa said.

"But tomorrow will be a lot worse for you. You will be meeting family that I don't even know about. There's too many to keep track of. Someone's brother's cousin or some shit."

Lisa laughed. They sat watching the river. Lisa had a nice, numbing buzz from the alcohol and from being in Luka's arms. It seemed to get darker to the point where the river was just black moving against black and they could hear it more than see it. Behind them Kata and Marko were singing with their friends and family. It was all perfect, except Lisa couldn't help but feel like she'd stumbled into a tragedy. But she ignored the feeling. She ignored her thundering heart. She turned and kissed the inside of Luka's neck and he turned, his lips meeting hers to kiss more. The sound of raging water filled their ears.

A short time later, Luka and Lisa rejoined the wedding party. Everyone got back in their cars, and they formed a train of vehicles and headed out into the wilderness. Lisa was half awake and Luka was drunk. She would probably have been more nervous if they'd been in the States, or if she was more awake, but they drove slowly. Once they were surrounded by trees, Lisa felt peaceful and safe and drifted off to sleep. She woke up in Luka's arms as he carried her into a large house in the middle of thick, black woods. They had a small room. The house was like a hotel inside, with little rooms, each with their own bathroom connected by a long hallway. Lisa could only remember bits and pieces in the morning. She'd seen things as she was carried to bed but was never really awake.

croatia: twelve

Lisa noticed daylight spilling into the room in what felt like mere minutes after she'd fallen asleep. She heard music outside. A mix of guitar and loud singing. A mariachi band singing in Croatian was the first thing that came to mind. She sat up and was pulled back down by Luka. Their bodies connected beneath the sheets—warm skin, Luka's strong hands on her breasts and lower back. She rolled on top, letting her hips press against his.

Afterwards, they got dressed and headed downstairs. The other young people from the bar—Kata and Marko's friends, cousins, and siblings—were either already out and about or emerging simultaneously with Luka and Lisa. Downstairs the doors were flung open and out on the grass were tables arranged with breakfast, drinks, and the band. Lisa and Luka sat down together at the edge of the woods and ate breakfast and drank mimosas. The sun was warm, but in the shade of the fir trees, the temperature was perfect. Lisa held Luka's hand and drank her mimosa with the other. It was hard to believe how good life was at that moment.

The morning's festivities went on. Lisa and Luka already had a nice buzz from the mimosas. Some people were dancing, others were singing with the band. Lisa couldn't believe their endurance. They'd already been playing for hours, and Luka informed her that there would be other bands over the course of the wedding, so they'd get a chance to rest. Cars started arriving and Lisa saw Zara across the grass. She waved and headed over to Lisa.

"Lisa, you look gorgeous," Zara said. "Don't let Kata see you. You don't want to steal all the looks meant for the bride."

Lisa's cheeks ran hot—part mimosa, part embarrassment. She returned the compliment and hugged Zara. The hug felt genuine. It felt like, if Lisa wanted to hold on to Zara for hours, Zara wouldn't mind. She had a calm, tender aura about her. She was the kind of mother Lisa would've liked to have been. Her thoughts drifted back to Wyatt. She found herself daydreaming of herself like Zara. Wyatt grown up and introducing her to his girlfriend. Zara hugged Luka and held on for a long time. Lisa squeezed an invisible hand tight enough to feel the blood run out of her fingers. It was the closest she'd felt to Wyatt in months.

The first band took a break and enjoyed beers in the sun with the rest of the wedding guests. A second, larger band arrived full of guitar and violin players and singers. Guests continued to arrive. Lisa still wasn't sure when the wedding started but there must've been almost a hundred people at the wedding now. She worried about her ability to keep her wits about her in the midst of so much alcohol. She couldn't afford to get sloppy and embarrass Luka in front of his family. Then again, Luka and some of his friends and cousins were already pretty drunk. It must've been around noon, and they were singing and dancing with the band. Lisa found herself alone in the crowd and decided to take the opportunity to walk in the forest for a bit—escape—before the party got too crazy.

Lisa walked along a worn, dirt trail. It didn't take long for the forest to swallow up the sounds of the wedding, and after a few minutes, she was in a dark and quiet section of trees. It was much different than the woods back in Oregon but also the same. The foreign but familiar feeling was how she'd felt every day since she'd left home. Everything here was the same but different. Like two lives reflected on different sides of the mirror. The background pieces shifted and morphed but Lisa stayed the same. Or did she? She thought she'd changed since being here, and in some ways she had. She felt more mature, more confident in who she was. She also felt like the yearning she'd felt back in Oregon—yearning for freedom, for a future, for youth—was mostly gone. She doubted it was due to satisfaction. She didn't feel saturated. Her soul was still soluble for adventure. There would always be a yearning to escape, to start over, to be free from responsibility, but something had settled her—centered her. It was love. It was Luka's love. It had healed her in such a short time in more ways than she was able to understand. It made her feel whole again, or at least something close to whole.

His love was redemptive, divine in some sense. The shame and guilt she carried was washed away when she thought about being deserving of love from someone as amazing as Luka. What Lisa had realized—what kept bringing the nausea and pains back—was that as much as she loved Luka, and she loved him deeply, she would never love herself. Not like this. Not here. Not with what she'd done. Luka's love had healed her enough to allow her heart to open up to Wyatt, completely, finally. She felt it across the ocean. Across thousands of miles. The yearning for freedom, the worry that her presence was poison, was replaced by a yearning to love Wyatt, to care for him, to keep him safe, and maybe if her love was powerful enough, she might be able to heal him the same way Luka had healed her.

Lisa stopped. She realized she'd been walking in circles and crying. The forest had transported her. She'd straddled the two worlds and now was back.

"Lisa?" someone asked.

Lisa wiped her face and tried to catch her breath.

"Lisa?"

"Over here," Lisa said, her voice cracking.

Zara stepped lightly off the trail and over the ferns and shrubs toward Lisa. Her high heels slipped, and she almost fell, catching herself on the trunk of an evergreen tree.

"Are you doing drugs back here?" Zara asked.

"Am I—" Lisa laughed. "I'm not doing drugs."

"This is just a long way into the woods. I didn't know if you were smoking something. I was just going to tell you that you don't need to go so far away. No one will mind," Zara said. She had a glass of white wine in her hand. She sat down on a fallen log covered in moss.

"I don't want to keep you," Lisa said. "We can head back. I was just walking and got a little lost."

Zara waved her hand dismissively. "Things are getting pretty wild already. We aren't missing much. You know these

Slavonian weddings go until about six, seven in the morning, right? Did Luka tell you that? I don't imagine that weddings are like that in America, but then again, what do I know?"

"They don't," Lisa said. "At least not that I know of."

Zara sipped her wine. "We have lots of time. Will you sit with me?"

Lisa nodded and sat down.

"I hate to be so blunt, Lisa, but that is just who I am. You seem troubled. Beautiful, and good for Luka, but troubled," Zara said.

"Oh, I'm not—no. See, the thing is," Lisa said.

"It's fine. I think I get it. I was checking to see if you were a drug addict, but now that I see that it is not a drug addiction that makes you troubled, I have an idea of what troubles you."

Lisa paused before saying something rude. She collected herself and smiled. "If we're being blunt, I don't think you have any idea what troubles me."

"Fair enough," Zara said and lit up a cigarette. She offered it to Lisa who declined. "Has Luka told you about the storks?"

"The storks?" Lisa asked.

"The storks. Yes. Obviously not. Good. There are these storks here in Slavonski Brod. They are celebrities. International celebrities now. Malena and Klepetan. There are storks that live here, and they fly to somewhere in Africa in the winter. This was the case for Malena and Klepetan until Malena was shot by a poacher. She couldn't fly all the way to Africa any longer and it gets cold here. Winter was coming and Klepetan had to decide if he was going to try and survive the winter here or fly to Africa. Well, he left. Poor Malena lived in a chimney all winter long by herself. But Klepetan, he had to go. The pull, the draw, was too strong for him. He needed to travel, live his life and migrate to Africa. But then, you know, Klepetan came back. He came back and spent all summer with Malena again. I imagine him flying for days, weeks even, and all he can think about is Malena. All he can think is he has to get back to Malena. And when he got home, nothing was different for them. Nothing had changed, despite the months and the kilometers. And this has been happening for decades now. Their love is strong. It draws Klepetan back every year. Year after year."

Lisa looked like she might start crying again and Zara offered her a drink of her wine. Lisa obliged. The cold tart wine calmed her. "Anyway, they're famous. Probably the only reason anyone will hear about this city," Zara said.

"It's a nice story," Lisa said.

"It's not a story. It's a truth. The heart will lead if it is allowed."

Lisa stared up at the canopy of green and the blue sky further above. "I'm ready to head back," she said.

"Of course."

"Zara?"

"Hmmm?"

"Is it really that obvious?"

"Only to a mother's eye," Zara said. She reached out and squeezed Lisa's shoulder.

When Zara and Lisa returned to the wedding, everyone was gathering for the ceremony. Lisa saw Kata peek out of the house, looking radiant in a silky white dress. Lisa found Luka. He was bursting with happiness and inebriation. He kissed her. His tongue had the oaky tartness of chardonnay. Marko stood at the end of the aisle. He looked handsome in his suit. His eyes were watery, and his lip trembled slightly. Lisa was surprised to see him looking so vulnerable. She'd gotten the impression that Croatian men didn't show weakness too often, but perhaps weddings were an exception.

The ceremony itself was brief and beautiful, framed in rich green forest and bolstered by the energetic and white-wine-emboldened wedding party. When Marko and Kata kissed, Luka wiped a tear away quickly, but Lisa saw it. Lisa was less moved by the ceremony. She was still thinking about her interaction with Zara. The pull from Oregon was more obvious than she thought. Did Luka see it too? Luka kissed Lisa and dipped her like they were in an old movie. They slipped slightly in the wet grass and almost toppled to the ground. He laughed as he caught himself and swept Lisa up. They followed the rest of the wedding party, in tow of Kata and Marko, heading toward the band and drinks set out on a table. That sealed it for Lisa. Even if Luka did suspect that she was feeling torn, he wasn't letting on and likely wouldn't. It wasn't who he was. He was content with living from moment to moment. She wondered if he didn't care if she was going to leave, or rather, didn't worry about it, because she was here now and now was what mattered.

The band started playing and people wasted no time getting their drinks, singing along and dancing. The sun ducked behind the splintered tree tips and soft yellow bulbs lit up the reception. Lisa found herself unable to reject every shot of rakija that came her way and soon was on the verge of tipping over the edge into inebriated darkness, and as much as she wanted to—to forget everything and let her emotions be her mind—pangs of nausea kept her from drinking any more. Luka brought her another shot and she poured it onto the grass when no one was looking. Lisa sat down to drink some water and try and eat something to keep the stomach gnawing at bay. Luka danced with Zara. Both of them were sweaty, manically happy, and dancing very well. It was obvious he'd gotten his skill from her. The song ended, and as another started, many of the guests began clapping and moving excitedly to the dance floor. Lisa stayed put, feeling satisfied and happy but also ready to vomit at a moment's notice. Grandmother hobbled out to join Luka and Zara, and soon, Kata and Marko joined as well. They linked hands and began dancing in a circle that perpetually grew as more and more people joined hands and spun. The music was drowned out by the singing. It was all in Croatian and Lisa had no idea what it was about, but regardless, she felt the energy from it, and was moved. The song seemed sad but defiant. Lisa watched Grandmother, Luka, Zara, Marko, Kata and the others laugh and sing. Their sweaty, happy faces illuminated by the hanging lights glowing in the darkening night. They were a family. A family, marked by tragedy, but steeled by it. Lisa couldn't help but reflect on her own family. Her dad leaving and dying before they could ever reconnect, Mom losing years to pills, and now, Wyatt, without a mom or a dad, dealing with a mind he couldn't control, emotions he could not reign. They were never going to be like Luka's family. Lisa felt guilty that she'd never given them the chance. She knew Bryan was never going to reconnect with Wyatt and with her leaving, what chance did Wyatt have to create relationships like this? In a way it didn't matter. Seeing Luka's family so full of love and happiness, connected over decades and generations took the nausea away. She had to go back. She loved Luka, but she had to go back. If she stayed, her decision could echo through untold generations, or it could cause their lineage to stop at Wyatt. That wasn't something Lisa had thought about—was concerned about—until now, but watching the circle move faster and faster, it seemed vital. Like her single decision might ruin more lives than just Wyatt's and her own. Like her love had the innate ability to fix it all. It was overwhelming to think about. She looked at the way Zara and Luka looked at Grandmother. Their eyes showed more than just endearing love, they showed infinite gratitude. Their families had made them who they were. Lisa's potential to save herself and Wyatt was stronger than her potential to love Luka. At least it seemed so in the moment. She remembered the last time she felt so convinced about a difficult decision and she'd thrown her cellphone away and boarded a plane here, to Croatia, and now she was ready to take it all back.

She worried that her brain was rotting. Thoughts seeped into her neurons until they shifted and everything wrong seemed right. Committing to Bryan. Wanting to hurt Wyatt. Loving Wyatt. Leaving Wyatt. Leaving home. Loving Luka. Leaving Luka. Her heart ached thinking about the last two. Something so good couldn't have been a mistake, could it?

The song ended and Luka came over to Lisa with a bottle of wine in his hand. He'd forgone the glass at this point. His shirt was so far unbuttoned it was a wonder it was still on. Sweat sheened his face. His hair was mopped with it. His kiss on her cheek that moved to her neck was sloppy and sexy. She took the bottle from him and drank. The wine was still cold.

"Dance with me?" Luka asked, holding out his hand.

Lisa stood up and walked onto the dance floor. The song was slow, but the crowd refused to change their feverish pace. In the center—dancing with the most ferocity—was Kata with a bottle of rakija in her hand, and Marko with his shirt completely unbuttoned and his thick, black, and wiry chest hair bursting out. It took almost no time at all before Lisa herself was covered in sweat like the rest of them. She drank from the bottle of wine and when it was empty, she drank from Kata's bottle of rakija. She danced with Luka. She danced with Marko. With

Kata. With a stranger. At some point the band was replaced by another band complete with electric guitar, platinum drum set, and a goth-looking lead singer. The music erupted from the speakers. Lisa didn't know any of the songs but felt like she did. Even if they'd been in English and familiar, it likely wouldn't have made a difference. She jumped and sang along with everyone else, her voice lost in the chorus of Croatians, belting out their classics into the dead silence of the woods.

The party kept going. Lisa was half expecting to see the sun erupt in the distance and have everyone continue dancing and drinking until night fell again. In the ecstasy of the party, Lisa wondered if perhaps it was all a fever dream and when the party ended, she would wake up in Oregon. She thought more about the moment in the forest when everything had become so clear. She'd stepped back into her world in Oregon, and now felt trapped between the two places, two lives, like she was imprisoned between the two spots—a spiritual purgatory.

Luka was pure, raw, joyous energy. He'd lost his shirt and sense of balance. He'd been stripped down to his primitive functioning and his primitive functioning was laughing, hugging, kissing, and telling Lisa that he loved her. Lisa worried what her primitive functioning might reveal, but knew she was close to it. She wanted to take Luka into the woods and make wild, intoxicated love to him, but knew they were too drunk for it to be good, or appropriate. She fantasized in her head, and in the moment, that was enough.

Luka pulled her into a spinning dance. The world became a Tilt-A-Whirl of colors, faces and black evergreens against an even blacker night. They fell over in a pile and erupted into uncontrollable laughter. Luka tried to help Lisa up but ended up falling again. Everyone else was too lost in the music or too drunk to notice. Lisa got up and pulled Luka to his feet. He kept his eyes closed even though he was standing. She threw his arm around her shoulder and walked him like that, like a wounded soldier, over to the grass at the edge of the woods.

She sat and Luka lay with his head in her lap, while she stroked his sweat-soaked hair. In the distance, the party looked like lanterns, ready to float up into the sky and disappear into the night. She closed her eyes and could already feel everything leaving.

Luka was passed out. She continued to stroke his hair.

"I want you to know that in the morning I won't be here anymore," Lisa whispered but the words still felt loud and heavy enough to break both their hearts. "And you have to know that it's for the best."

The symmetry of the situation felt surreal. As if Luka were Wyatt and Wyatt were Luka. She was both Lisa and Zara and neither at all.

"In the morning, I'll be gone."

croatia: final

Lisa walked the few miles back into Slavonski Brod in the dead of night. Most of it was through forest roads. She could barely see except for the faintly reflected white stripes in the center of the road. She'd grabbed her bag from inside the house and left before anyone had any time to realize. She'd helped Luka back into bed and kissed him on the forehead before leaving a note that simply said *I love you* by the door. In the silence of the woods, Lisa's mind went wild with guilt and anticipation. The fatigue helped keep it clear. That and the planning she was doing to try and figure out how to get back home.

She got into Slavonski Brod around five in the morning, found the only place open—a coffee shop that also sold magazine and newspapers—and asked for the best way to get back to Zagreb. They directed her to the bus station and within a few hours she was on her way toward the airport. She slept on the bus and awoke at Zagreb International Airport. She was able to purchase a ticket so easily with her emergency funds that Lisa started questioning if things were actually happening. In some ways, it felt like everything was a carefully orchestrated illusion and she'd soon find out that it was all fake. Lisa felt like running off to the edges of the world to test its boundaries and see if it was real, and in a way, she was. At least she thought she was. Then again, she wasn't sure what was real or important anymore. She just knew she had to go home.

Reality struck as she waited for a flight and a horrific hangover set in. She vomited in the bathroom—a loud, acidic-smelling belch that led to unexpected vomiting, choking, and coughing. She was grateful in a way. It grounded her. Things were real again. Pain, discomfort, anxiety, and guilt. She figured Luka would be waking up just about now and finding she was gone. Lisa vomited into the toilet again.

At the bar, she ordered a vodka sunrise and choked it down with a few sinister burps she worried might lead to a sprint back to the bathroom, but they didn't, and the alcohol kept the migraine at bay. She could only imagine the hangover Luka must be experiencing at this moment. She shuffled to her gate, walked onto the jetway, found her seat, and collapsed from exhaustion.

She woke up mid-flight. She'd slept through the takeoff. Something she previously thought was impossible. She stared out the window. The sky was an impossible blue with ethereal white clouds thousands of feet below, and at times, within arm's reach. She started to cry. Luka really was gone.

She cried because she missed him. She cried because she'd hurt him. She cried because he was the best thing that had ever happened to her and she'd ruined it. She closed her eyes and put her head back into the seat, pressing it against the hard cushion and imagining the thirty thousand feet of open air beneath her. It made her palms sweat but also kept her mind off the flood of questions that came at her from every angle. About Wyatt. About her mom. About herself. She desperately wanted a cocktail but wondered if she needed to put that part of herself behind her as well. The stewardess walked by, and Lisa flagged her down for a double vodka and 7UP. She hadn't landed yet. She wasn't that person yet. There was still time before her transformation. Before she had to be a mom. Stop drinking. Start exercising. Eating healthy. Get a job. Still time.

She downed the cocktail quickly and tried to focus on the slowly passing clouds. She clawed at her chest, trying to dig out a pain that struck suddenly and sharply. She wondered if her heart might give out. She'd heard about something called broken heart syndrome once. On a late-night TV show, or in a book she was assigned for school, or maybe someone's grandma had died from it. It was when something heartbreaking happened and your heart literally stopped. She knew it wouldn't happen to her. She was healing a large portion of her heart by going back home. Still, in a way, she was trading one wound for another. She wondered if one day she might see Luka again.

She thought about their time in Sarajevo and drinking from the Sebilj and Luka saying they'd be back. She hoped it was true. Maybe in a year. Maybe in fifty. To Luka, it might not matter. A hundred years might pass but he'd still be living one day at a time. She knew it wasn't true. If he was living in the present, then he was hurting as much as she was.

In a way, Lisa wished she could forget. She wished there was a way to start anew without her painful memories and experiences. She could close her eyes and be born new into the blossoming moment. She could finally be free from the burden of memory. She could experience the present for the gift that it was. Lisa closed her eyes and opened them. She wanted it to be this moment, in the air, straddling two worlds, two lives, no decision final, no hearts broken, no promise unfulfilled. In a way, it was the best she could be, and she found some peace in the possibility that in that moment, she was good. In that moment, she loved across worlds equally. She wanted to stay inside the looking glass—able to be on both sides and neither—forever.

acknowledgments

This book would not be possible without the help of many people. First off, I'd like to thank my wife, Sara, for giving me the time, support, and encouragement to create this novel. I also want to thank Sara for inviting me in and making me part of the Croatian family. To Rick, Ana, Paolo, Bruno, Hanna and many others, thank you for showing me Croatia and being so welcoming and loving.

I want to thank two friends who were an instrumental part of this book becoming a reality. First is Joe Rogers, who is an amazing teacher, friend, editor, and writer. His guidance and lessons helped my writing become what it is today. The second is Elizabeth Muller, a brilliant writer in her own right, whose encouragement and support kept me believing in this book and my writing.

I'm grateful to the other writers who helped craft this novel in its early stages, including Patrick Yumi Cotrell and Jennifer Deane.

I'm immensely lucky to have worked with many people at Ooligan, including Angela, Abby, Tanner, Robyn, Ági, and others, who believed in this novel and helped it come to fruition.

Thank you to my parents who always encouraged me to read, always had a book on their nightstand, and always believed in me.

about the author

S. R. Schulz lives in Portland, Oregon with his wife, three sons, and two dogs. He's been traveling to visit family in Croatia since 2010. He currently works as a family physician just outside Portland, Oregon, and is a faculty member at Oregon Health & Science University. His writing has been published online and in print, including McSweeney's, HAD, Rejection Letters, Maudlin House, Autofocus, and others. *Supersymmetry* is his first novel.

land acknowledgment

We acknowledge and honor Indigenous communities—past, present, and future—whose land we currently reside on here at Portland State University. This includes the traditional and ancestral homelands of the Multnomah, Wasco, Cowlitz, Kathlamet, Clackamas, Bands of the Chinook, the Tualatin Kalapuya (Atfalati), Molalla, and many other Indigenous nations who made their homes along the Wimahl, Nch'i-Wàna, or swah'netk'qhu (all meaning "Big River or "Great River"), also known by its colonized name, the Columbia River. Descendants of these tribes are primarily members of the Confederated Tribes of Grand Ronde, Confederated Tribes of Siletz Indians, and the Chinook Nation. We acknowledge the current and long-standing oppression faced by Indigenous peoples and recognize that we are here because of the sacrifices forced upon them. We encourage everyone to find ways to support and connect with Indigenous communities and the land itself, and to remain committed to their justice and liberation. We also encourage folks to read the PSU Conflict Resolution department's Land Conflict Acknowledgement for further learning about the history of land conflict in this geographical area.

We attribute the name of our press to native peoples in Oregon. The Ooligan (also spelled Ourigan, Eulachon, or the Saak by the Tlingit peoples) is a Chinook word for a small candlefish that is abundant in the Pacific Northwest. The nutrient-rich oil produced from boiling the fish was traded between coastal and inland First Nations all along the Pacific coast, from California to Alaska, bringing prosperity and health to native communities. These routes were known as grease trails. Gradually, the L in Ooligan was replaced with an R, giving us the sound "ooregon". This usage became the name of a place and assumed its current spelling of Oregon in the course of history. We would like to honor David G. Lewis for his contributions to the press, along with his writings in the co-authored article Ourigan: Wealth of the Northwest Coast, which informed the name of our press in 2001.

We acknowledge the lack of Indigenous and people of color representation throughout the publishing industry, both in professional positions and as authors. Our press strives to publish culturally relevant titles from our local, diverse voices in order to make literature accessible and redefine who has a place within its pages. We commit to actively creating space for and uplifting Indigenous and other diverse authors through our work, including our How To: Publishing workshop and continued community partnerships.

Ooligan Press

Ooligan Press is a student-run publishing house rooted in the rich literary culture of the Pacific Northwest. Founded in 2001 as part of Portland State University's Department of English, Ooligan is dedicated to the art and craft of publishing. Students pursuing master's degrees in book publishing staff the press in an apprenticeship program under the guidance of a core faculty of publishing professionals.

Project Managers
Abby Relph
Julie Holland

Acquisitions
Angela Griffin
Emmily Tomulet
Rin Kane
Becca Moss
Alena Rivas
Jenny Davis

Acquisitions: Pitch Team
Angela Griffin
Alena Rivas
Jenny Davis
Karina Agbisit
Elliot Bailey
Paige Brayton
Maya Karkabi
Savannah Lyda
Jazzminn Morecraft
Abby Relph
Theo Thompson

Editorial
Tanner Croom
Jordan Bernard
Jessica Pelton
Marissa Muraoka

Design
Laura Renckens
Ariana Espinoza
Marielle LeFave

Digital
Cecilia Too
Mara Palmieri
Madelynn Sare
Kari Olson

Marketing and Publicity
Yomari Lobo
Rory Minor

Online Content and DEI
Jules Luck
AJ Adler

Operations
Haley Young
Kara Herrera

Ooligan Press (continued)

Book Production
Rori Anderson
Elliot Bailey
Corwin Benedict
Kaitlyne Bozzone
Dumitru Dobre
Maggie Ellis
Amber Finnegan
Samantha Gallasch
Alice Gatto
Janeth Hernandez
Russ Johnson
Julie Kanta
Pierre Kaptanian
Isabel Kristensen
Lydia Larson
Casper Lesalnieks
Lori Mccloskey
Kayla Mullinax
Trang Nguyen
Julia O'Malley
Rachael Phillips
Tidari Pizana
Brittany Shike
Annaliese Smith
Issac Swindle
Shoshana Weaver